CHAINS OF INIQUITY

A Novel Inspired by a True Story

Coto T. King

CTK Publications

ISBN: 978-1-7361709-0-8 (eBook)
ISBN: 978-1-7361709-1-5 (Paperback)
ISBN: 978-1-7361709-2-2 (Hardcover)
Library of Congress Control Number: 2020922787

Cover Illustration by Russell Smith

Copyright © 2020 CTK Publications
First printing edition: December 11, 2020.

www.CTKPublications.com

I give all the glory of this book to my Lord, Savior, and King, Jesus Christ! May His words speak volumes to your heart! - Amen!

Special Thanks to my Mom for always believing in me, no matter what!

Special Thanks to my best friends Deborah Cruz and Megan Cruz, who continue to support me through the good times and the bad.

Special Thanks to Pastor Don Nordin of the CT Church in Houston for allowing me to print his remarkable sermons.

Special Thanks to the Community of Faith in Hockley, Texas, and Pastor Mark Shook for taking me in, baptizing me, and teaching the Word of God to me.

Special Thanks to KSBJ.org (FM 89.3 in Houston, Texas) for helping me and everyone within listening distance find, believe, and praise the Lord Jesus Christ, no matter where or who they are. - Amen!

Your eyes saw my unformed body; all the days ordained for me were written in your book before one of them came to be.
    Psalm 139:16

The soul who sins shall die. The son shall not suffer for the iniquity of the father, nor the father suffer for the iniquity of the son. The righteousness of the righteous shall be upon himself, and the wickedness of the wicked shall be upon himself.
    Ezekiel 18:20

CONTENTS

PROLOGUE

I was standing in my dining room, Seven and Coke in hand, and looking out my sliding glass door to my backyard, watching the beautiful July sunset go down. It had been another hot and humid evening in Texas. Summertime was just starting, and the steamy temperatures were already hitting 99 degrees during the daytime. Roland and I had just enjoyed a super spicy dinner of beer bratwurst with candy jalapeños on toasted butter bread and a side of seasoned spicy corn on the cob that he roasted on the barbecue pit.

As I watched a red cardinal land on the back fence, I felt a slight pain in my chest, just below my heart and above my stomach, where the two sides of my rib cage meet. It had to be heartburn, I thought to myself, but in the tiny corner of my mind came the thought, "I never get heartburn." I was getting older, and my insides were probably rebelling against the candy jalapeños, or maybe even the spicy corn. It was just mild pain; I thought to myself as I went to the bathroom medicine cabinet looking for Roland's antacids.

Roland and I had been living together for eight years. He was a handyman by trade and a brilliant musician. His whole family was musically talented, from his sister being a Jazz singer in the Army to his father being Maestro for the New York Symphony.

Roland starred in his band called Street Puddle, in which he played lead guitar to his original music in small clubs around Houston. I was attracted to his musicianship, his very long hair, and his lightning-fast funny responses to everything and everyone around him. He had the silver tongue that made everyone listen to him. Everyone wanted to be around him, and I saw him through complete rose-colored glasses.

I stood there looking into the bathroom mirror, thinking, "Maybe it wasn't just heartburn. Maybe the dry heaves I keep getting are a sign of something terrible."

Just last month we went to one of Roland's friend's house for a dinner party. Sam had made stuffed BBQ shrimp and steaks on the grill. The meal was terrific, and of course, there was a never-ending flow of drinks. We had stayed way into the night partying and drinking.

Both Roland and I were highly intoxicated, so Sam was gracious enough to allow us to spend the night. Sometime in the wee hours of the night, I was overtaken with the dry heaves. I had gotten up to find my way into the bathroom.

Bent over the sink, I turned on the cold-water full blast and stuck my right wrist face up under it. This simple action usually helps to calm my anxiety attacks. The ice-cold water beating down on my wrist makes my mind focus on it instead of my stomach heaving.

However, this time it wasn't working. My throat was closing again. I could not breathe very well. I started to gag. My stomach started to convulse. I could not stop retching, and the cold water was not working to calm anything. I used to think the retching was due to anxiety, but now I was not so sure. My stomach and throat started to hurt from hacking up nothing for hours on end, and still, the retching would not stop.

It was getting light outside, and the people in Sam's house were starting to stir. My hacking had subsided enough for me to finish getting dressed and grab my keys. I had to get out of the house before someone heard me getting sick.

I made my way out to the driveway and slid into the driver's seat of my car. I put the keys into the ignition and turned on the AC full blast, pointing the vents' cold air onto my face. It was another trick to fool my mind to think of something else. The ice-cold air blew across my face reminding me that I could breathe. As I sat there trying not to think, I was unaware that all the people had left Sam's house.

I heard a knock on the car window. Roland had come to check on me. "Are you OK? Can we go home now?" I'm so glad he cares so much.

When we got home, I grabbed a blanket and settled into the recliner to watch TV. I was shivering because I was exhausted. "That's all it is," I thought. I was convinced at the time that there was nothing else wrong with me. Life went on, and the parties never stopped.

Snapping back into the present and still feeling the after-effects of Roland's hot and spicy dinner, I walked to my bath-room and stood looking in the mirror. Perhaps it is not heart-burn. Maybe it is something more horrible. As quickly as that thought entered my mind, I pushed it to the back of my brain.

I dug around in the medicine chest, looking for the ant-acid pills. There are no dry heaves associated with this pain. I reasoned that it had to be the spicy food and the extra stress I had been feeling lately. It had been a rough couple of months. My father had died in a Galveston hospital bed in November 2004. Rosco, my dog of fourteen years, had died of old age on my back patio in February 2005. Then Roland's father, a man that treated me as his own, had passed away in his small New York apartment in March 2005, just a few short months ago. So many deaths so near to me, the stress of it all was sometimes unbear-able. It left me very sad.

Grabbing the antacid tablets and another Seven and Coke, Roland and I settled down to watch a movie on TV. About an hour into the film, the pain in my chest was getting stronger. The antacid tablets were not working. I knew there had to be some medicine on the market that was stronger for this pain. After all, antacid tablets were for upset stomachs, not heart-burn, weren't they? I reasoned with myself.

Maybe I could find a home remedy or something more potent at the corner drug store. Under Roland's protests for stopping the movie, I threw on some clothes to at least look presentable to a drug store attendant. I grabbed my purse, hopped into the car, and off I went.

As I searched for the medicine at the store, the pain worsened, and my stomach was getting a little bloated. "I just over-ate! I'll be fine!" I kept reminding myself.

Paying for what I thought might work on my heartburn, I got in the car and read the directions on the package. Take one pill every four hours for heartburn pain. Thinking one would be good, two had to be better - right? Grabbing the water bottle that I kept in the car, I downed two pills and headed back home.

Walking into my house, I found that the TV was off, and Roland was on his computer in the back room. He was no longer interested in watching the rest of the movie since I had interrupted the flow of it all with my leaving for the drug store. No big deal, I can finish watching the movie in our bedroom.

Pouring another Seven and Coke, I noticed the pain was getting worse, and my breathing was getting a little labored. I just ate too much! I kept reminding myself. Lying down in bed should help the medicine work, and I would feel better soon. I was sure of it.

Another hour passed, and it was getting harder and harder to breathe easy. Panic started to creep into every nerve ending in my body. I slowly got out of bed. Slumped over, I painfully walked to the computer room where Roland was doing whatever Roland does on his computer.

"I need an ambulance," I told him, trying not to sound scared.

"Are you sure, Sans?" Sans was his nickname for me. "Ambulance rides are very expensive even with insurance," he said, still facing his computer screen.

I was so glad he was finally thinking about my expenses. "I think I need a doctor. My chest hurts bad," I said, taking a shallow breath, "It's hard to breathe."

With reluctance, he got up, "I need to take a shower first. I don't want to go out in public looking like this."

I laid back in bed and waited until he was ready to drive me to the emergency room. It did not bother me that he chose to shower and that it took priority over my life and well-being.

Somewhere in the tiny corner of my head said that it just did not matter anymore.

After grooming his hair, brushing his teeth, picking out the perfect clothes, and putting on his best smelling cologne, he was finally ready. I, on the other hand, couldn't care less about what I looked like to people. I wore my oldest torn t-shirt and shorts. My hair was a mess, and I did not care to brush it. I grabbed my pillow off the bed to hold over my stomach to help ease the pain during the 15-minute journey in the car ride to the hospital emergency room.

I felt every rock we drove over as the shock waves from it rattled thru my entire body, racking it with excruciating pain. Finally, we arrived at the hospital. To my dismay, preceding patient's cars filled every parking space near the emergency room door, so we had to park about 100 feet away. That was about 99 feet too far for me. I got out of the car and could not straighten up because my insides hurt so much. I had to walk bent over, and even doing that took great effort. Roland walked on ahead of me.

As the doors slid open to the emergency room, I looked around, and the place was packed. I walked over to one of the only chairs still available and sat down. I could not sit straight up, and the pain was getting worse by the minute. I was clutching my stomach as my breath became more labored and shallower.

Roland headed to the nurse's station to check me in. As he approached, that charm of his was on full blast. "Can I help you?" the pretty nurse said.

Roland flipped his ponytail over his shoulder and smiled, "My girlfriend is sick and needs to see a doctor. Her stomach hurts."

I watched him as he flirted with the nurse that was writing down my information. "So, what do you do for a living?" she asked, bating her nine pounds of eyelashes at him.

"I'm the lead guitarist for a band called Street Puddle." He had this monstrous smile on his face, "You should come to see us play at The Snake Pit tomorrow night. It's over on Westheimer."

He was such a pretty boy, with dreamy blue eyes. "Ask for me, and you won't have to pay a cover charge."

"I know exactly where that is!" she swooned.

Still smiling that smile that melts all the hearts of all the women, "We are the headlining act, so we go on at 11:00 p.m."

I couldn't watch him flirt anymore. I had to think of something else. I had to redirect my mind off the increasing pain in my body and the growing pain in my heart.

Time was dragging by as I sat there, watching everyone get admitted before me. Ambulances kept arriving, and the EMT's took their wards straight in to see the doctors. "I knew I should have called for an ambulance," I said to no one in particular. "I would have already gotten help by now."

Another hour went by, and a nurse finally called me into a small room. But to my dismay again, it was only a triage room where she took my vitals and promptly made me go back and sit in the waiting room. It was getting hard to keep my eyes open and to think straight. Time as I knew it was slowing down.

"Sandy Ryan?" I heard a nurse say, and I almost passed out, not from the shock of finally being called, but from the physical pain that was racking my body. An orderly helped me into a wheelchair. Finally, I got to see beyond the double doors that had barred me from help for so long. He wheeled me into the first exam room that was empty and helped me into the bed as the nurse prepared to hook me up to an IV. My only thoughts were *someone is finally going to help me.*

As the IV tried to replace the fluids that I had lost, I waited again for a doctor to come. The pain was getting so bad that my mind was shutting down. I shut my eyes and tried to think of something that did not resemble excruciation.

The door finally opened. It was the Doctor. "Is she allergic to anything?" I could not answer. I was concentrating on just breathing.

"No, Doctor," Roland said as he looked at me, lying there suffering.

"Does she drink?" The Doctor asked.

"Like a fish," Roland told him, which was a true story.

The Doctor ordered X-rays to be taken and left the room. After a few minutes, the nurse appeared. "I'm going to give you morphine for the pain." Finally!

She injected the morphine into the IV. It was only moments before I felt the effects. My eyes closed as the darkness enveloped me. I drifted off into the nether. Time passed unnoticed until I felt hands on me. The morphine was wearing off. The pain was returning in magnified force.

Roland was standing next to me.

"Where am I? What is going on?" I was frightened beyond belief.

"It's OK, Sans," he hesitated, "It's going to be OK. They are just moving you into a hospital room."

That didn't help. I was still terrified. My mind was trying to come out of the dark fog. I tried to concentrate as best I could. I tried to remember what had happened. Why do I hurt so much? Why was I here? Why couldn't I think straight? I told Roland to call my sister Isabella because the only part of my mind that could still comprehend anything told me I was dying.

"Call her, tell her to come." I said between the shortened breaths, "tell her I don't think I'm going to make it." I pleaded and hoped it did not fall on deaf ears.

The nurse injected me with another shot of morphine, and I went back to the sweet darkness where there was no pain, except this nothingness was powerful. It was a total eclipse of my mind that went from light to dark in an instant.

I fell without objection into the giant black hole of the universe. That huge void that living minds struggle to comprehend. It was a vast black hole filled with absolute nothingness.

I could not think.
I could not speak.
I could not hear.
I could not move.
I could not feel.

I was not there.
I did not exist.

There was nothing, and for how long there was nothing, I had no idea. Time and space were no longer a concept, as there was no pain or memories. My being was not there anymore.

There was nothing to fight, nothing to call out to, nothing to feel, nothing to understand. No light. No sound. No smell. No taste.

Absolute nothing.

CHAPTER 1

As my brain went into the numbing darkness, my body went into shutdown mode. My heart stopped pumping the life-giving blood.

"She's flatlining. Bag her!" The Emergency Room doctor yelled at the nurse, who frantically put a mask over my nose and mouth. At the same time, another started making compressions on my chest, trying to resurrect my dying body.

The Doctor reached for the intercom system, "Code Blue, Code Blue to ER Room 3. Code Blue."

I felt nothing as my body lay on that cold, sterile bed dying, but my soul woke up and went on a journey through the past. Oblivious to what was happening. Oblivious to pain.

Mike Jenkins, my real biological father, was a pilot when he fell in love with Janice on a long flight across the country. Janice was a budding young stewardess. After a long courtship, they eventually married and had Isabella, my sister, and then me.

As the years went by, my father was plagued by cataracts. The doctors tried to cut the cataract out with a scalpel. It was the only thing they knew how to do back then. There was no laser surgery, just a razor-sharp knife, and very steady hands.

The procedure was very long and extremely unsuccessful. My father went permanently blind in one eye. The airlines require pilots to have a 20-20 vision, which he did not have anymore. The loss of his beloved job and the loss of his sight lead him to drink heavily.

And then, as if God were playing some cruel joke on him, the chemicals in his brain became unbalanced. No one around him knew that he was bipolar. No one back then really recognized the symptoms. And my father continued to drink. Mike was starting a very long uninterrupted life of being bipolar and very, very angry.

My mother, sister, and I were returning from Sunday School one spring morning just before my Birthday. We walked into the house and found everything made from glass lying on the floor in pieces. Every drinking glass, every plate, and every bowl were in shards. It looked like a tornado had hit the inside of the house.

Everything that was anything stood broken. Nothing survived my father's wrath. Not in the kitchen, and not in any other room of the house. Glass was everywhere. My sister and I were terrified.

Mom packed our bags, and we fled to her best friend's house, Ms. Lindell. She had two sons. John and Billy. There we stayed until the court system ordered my father to vacate our home.

It was a cold March morning, and it was my Birthday, as I watched Mom, my sister, and Ms. Lindell leave to go to the grocery store. That left me all alone with Ms. Lindell's sons. After convincing me they were playing a game, John and Billy dragged me into a closet and proceeded to sexually molest me.

They told me not to tell, or something terrible would happen. I could not tell my Mom. I was too afraid. When Mom came back to surprise me with tickets to the Rodeo for my Birthday, I was in shock. Mom thought it was because of the surprise tickets. She had no clue. To this very day, I have never been back to the Rodeo. It reminds me of the day I was first sexually molested.

I was only six.

"Keep the compression's going," the Doctor yelled over the loud monotone of the heart monitor that indicated my heart was still flatlining... my body was dying.

A couple of years later, my mother broke the news to Isabella and myself that she would marry a traveling salesman named Raymond Davis. Raymond was father to Faith, Madison, and two twin boys Raymond Jr. and Dan. This event threw six kids into a tailspin.

My mother, my sister, and I lived in a four-bedroom house until the other people unceremoniously descended upon us after the marriage. I was to now room with the youngest of Raymond's kids, named Madison. My sister Isabella was to room with Faith, the eldest of the six kids. Raymond, my stepdad, had the fourth room in the house as an office and renovated the garage into another space for the two twin boys, Raymond Jr., and Dan.

Madison and I never really had anything in common, other than the fact that we had to room together. But the other four were all so close in age that they hung out together and had the same friends. Isabella, Raymond Jr., and Dan's ages were only a month apart, and Faith was only a year older than the three of them.

When the four of them entered high school together marked the start of our very dysfunctional family's downfall.

Raymond and Janice were very religious people. They attended Church with all six of us present. They held Church group meetings at their home to worship the Lord and get to know one another socially. Raymond and Janice were climbing up that social ladder. They were blind to the horrible and evil things that were happening to their children. They continued to court their Church friends into believing that all was well in the land of the Davis's. Preaching and preaching to the six of us while projecting the image of a happy family.

They still had no clue.

The cardiac crash cart came bursting into the room.

My stepsister Madison fell in love with my cousin that lived in Galveston. It was hard at first to wrap my head around this. My stepsister falling in love with someone *in the family*?

It was socially unacceptable! But I never really understood what was so wrong with it. Madison was not blood-related to my cousin. And technically, I was not even blood-related to my cousin. His mother was adopted by my Grandparents, which made him family, but not blood-related. Madison and my cousin could have met on the street and lived happily ever after if my mother had not married Raymond. But that was not the case.

The crash cart technician pulled out the defibrillator paddles and hastily poured gel on them as the nurse rammed the endotracheal tube down my throat to force my lungs to start working again.

My mother insisted that Madison see a psychiatrist because surely, as the sun rose, she had to be insane. That scared the hell out of me. I feared for the first time that my mother would send me to a psychiatrist. I feared that she would find out that the Lindell boys molested me. Mother would blame me for it or just not believe me at all. I feared that for a very long time.

I never wanted my Mom and Raymond to find out my horrible secret because I knew they would lock me up and throw away the key.

The technician rubbed the defibrillator paddles together to get the gel to cover each paddle's entire surface. The Doctor yelled over all the activity, "Has someone contacted her family? Get them here now! She's not going to make it much longer."

Janice and Raymond caused such an uproar about Madison and my cousin that Madison eventually called herself a lesbian and fell in love with a young lady named Amelia. This little dark secret was never mentioned at the Church home group gatherings. Such a dirty little secret indeed.

"CLEAR," the technician yelled. Everyone removed their hands from my dead body.

It was around that same time when all six of us started smoking cigarettes since it was the cool thing to do back then. When Janice and Raymond left the house to go shopping or to Church, all six of us made our way to the backyard, lighting up and peeking through the fence pickets to watch for their return. As soon as we heard the wheels of their van pull into the driveway, we would smash out the cigarettes and run inside, not caring that we all reeked of smoke.

Placing the defibrillator paddles on my chest, the technician reached for the button.

My stepbrothers had just rolled a big fat marijuana joint and asked me if I wanted some. Mom and Raymond had just left to go to Church. Raymond Jr. and Dan coaxed and coaxed me until I finally gave in and took a couple of hits off the joint.

The effects of the drug blew my mind! Everything in the world seemed hilarious to me. I was higher than a kite, and I liked it. That is when both of my stepbrothers started sexually molesting me habitually. That is when smoking pot turned into taking Quaalude's and drinking cheap wine. That is when I started sneaking out at night to escape with my best friend, Natalie, who lived around the corner. That is when I fell in love with a guy named Mason.

I was only twelve.

In a desperate attempt, the Doctor grabbed the defibrillator paddles and sent high voltages of electricity to my heart. As the dangerously high voltage made contact with my body, my back arched as my whole body jerked a foot off the hospital bed. And my soul continued its journey through the past.

Mom and Raymond got wind of this love affair I had with Mason they ordered me never to see him again. As my mother stood at the top of the staircase in our house, she screamed down to me, "You do not know how to love. You are too young."

That might be true about the love thing. No one has ever taught me about that. It was always something *dirty*, not something nice like love. Mason showed me affection. He showed me that I did not have to be groped and abused. He cared about me, and this is what they wanted to take away from me? The only person on this planet who cared about me? There was no way I could explain that to Mom and Raymond.

My mother glared down the steps at me. *I do not know how to love? Really?* I shot the bird at her and ran to my room. Raymond saw this and was hot on my heels. I slammed the door to my room and locked it. Seconds later, Raymond was attempting to beat the door down. I watched the door come two inches off the frame as the lock tried to hold it in place. I stared at the door in horror. I knew he would break through it soon.

Unlocking my bedroom window, I climbed out and ran for my life. Running and running. Faster and faster. I knew Raymond would kill me if he ever caught up to me. I ran to the only place where I knew they would not look for me. I ran to their Church.

Still, the monotone of the heart monitor was flatlining. My body was still dead. No heartbeat. No brain waves. Nothing.

It was 1977, and all six of us kids were now in the same High School. Me being the youngest, I was just a freshman. Despite my parent's orders not to see Mason, I still did. Rumors of our escapades together ended up scribbled on the boy's bathroom walls of the high school. I was the whore, and my stepbrothers said nothing. They said nothing to no one but their friends because they were still partaking in the festivities.

I could not tell Mom or Raymond for fear that they would think I was insane and have me locked up in the loony bin. There was no way that their precious baby twin boys could ever commit a crime like that. So, I kept smoking pot, and taking pills, and drinking. It was the only thing that made all of it fade to the background.

"Hit it AGAIN," the Doctor yelled at the technician.

It was not that unusual for any of the six teens to wait for

Janice and Raymond to go to sleep at night so they could sneak out of the house through a window. One night after smoking a rather large joint, my stepbrothers, Raymond Junior and Dan, decided they had the munchies and wanted to go to the Jack in the Box to get some food. It was the same Jack in the Box that employed them.

Before they snuck out of the house, they snuck into my room. After groping me, they asked if I was hungry. I told them I wanted French fries. What kid does not love French fries?

They made their way out of the house and robbed the Jack in the Box of 200 dollars. When they returned home, they gave me a bag of Doritos, not the French fries that I wanted. But I did not care; I was just tired, and I wanted them out of my room.

That same year, my stepbrothers went to work for *The Sunrise News,* a newspaper that circulated hard copies of the news to homes in the Houston area. A guy named Greg usually picked them up in a yellow van that had an upside-down teardrop for a window. He took them to other neighborhoods to sell the newspaper.

Greg was cute. Every time he came by the house to pick up Raymond Jr. and Dan, I made sure I was always on my bike riding around the front of the house so I could talk and flirt with him.

Greg had an apartment. No parents. No siblings. Just him. I wanted that, and I wanted him. Finally, Greg asked me to a party that he was having at his apartment complex. All the cool kids were going to be there. I was so excited.

I told my Mom that I was spending the night with Natalie, which in a way was the truth. Once Natalie's parents were asleep, she and I slipped out the window and made our way over to Greg's apartment and the big party. We got there just as the mushroom tea was ready to drink.

Some of Greg's friends had gone out to the cow pastures just that morning to gather psilocybin mushrooms. They usually found them growing on the dung of cows. Greg took the mushrooms and made them into a tea. We drank the tea for its hallucinogenic effects.

I got so stoned off the tea that I fell into the pool at Greg's apartments and almost drowned because I thought I could walk on water. Just like Jesus.

AGAIN, the technician rubbed the defibrillator paddles together to get the gel to cover each paddle's entire surface.

Many things kept me occupied on the weekends, one of which was to go to the outdoor drive-in movies. Of course, no one watched the film because the whole parking lot turned into one giant drug party for all the teens.

One weekend, I found Mason at the drive-in. We smoked hashish, which is a powerful drug made from the marijuana plant. I remember Debbie Boone singing *You Light Up My Life*, and the whole parking lot looking like the waves in the sea. Mason knew I was way too stoned to go home, so he took me to his friend's house to sleep it off. My Mom thought I was spending the night with Natalie.

After rubbing the defibrillator paddles together, the technician reached for the button again.

In 1978, a boy asked me to the junior prom at high school. I was thrilled that a boy older than me was interested until the boy walked me out to the baseball field and proceeded to unzip his pants and force my head down onto him. I hit him repeatedly, trying to get away until he finally loosened his grip on my head, all the while laughing cruelly down at me.

I ran as fast as I could to my house, tears streaming down my face. I was so ashamed. The unwelcomed sexual advances and abuse were everywhere.

I cried out to God, "This can't be normal. DO something!" But there was no answer. God never heard me. He did not care.

Even He did not want me.

"CLEAR!" The technician yelled.

By the end of 1979, I was a Junior in High School, and I was dating a guy named Luke Ryan. He was a couple of years older than me and did not go to my High School. He had no idea all the hateful things people did to me there. Luke had a job. A real job! And he liked me for me. Not for some sexual plaything.

The defibrillator paddles made contact with my chest as the heart monitor's loud monotone indicated my heart was still flatlining. My body was still dead.

I fell in love with him.

My back arched, and my body jerked upwards off the bed as the electricity's high voltage was delivered thru the paddles.

During that same time, tensions with my Mom and Raymond were escalating. I hated the very ground they walked on and the air that they breathed. They still had no clue but continued to preach to me, from high on their pedestals as they faked their way through Church groups, telling them our family was perfection.

"We are losing her... Hit it AGAIN!" The Doctor yelled.

Luke had an apartment where he lived alone. He asked me if I wanted to move in with him to get away from my parents. I accepted his offer. Luke didn't know about my stepbrother's abuse. I was too ashamed to tell anyone about that.

The next day I skipped school. As both of my parental units were at work, and all the others were at school, I cleaned out my bedroom of everything I owned. I only left the bed and its sheets. I left no note to my Mom or Raymond.

No nothing. Kind of how they left me, abandoned and empty.

I was only seventeen.

As my body jerked upward for the third time, the high voltage electricity finally had done its job. The faint blips on the heart monitor indicated a heart rhythm.

Over the next couple of weeks, my mother pleaded with me

to come back home. I diligently refused. After a few weeks, Luke asked me to marry him. He was the most delightful, sweet, sincerest thing to ever happen to me. Of course, I said yes!

In August of 1980, I started my senior year in high school married to the guy who loved me and saved me. I was off the market to all the sexual predators.

In 1981, the high school mailed me my graduation papers. Without ceremony, fanfare, or hoopla, those papers marked the end of a season of pain, humiliation, and suffering.

"She's back. Thank God!" The Doctor sighed with relief. "I want to put her on pentobarbital. That will keep her in an induced coma, which will allow her to heal."

The good Doctor hesitated a bit too long before adding, "Hopefully."

CHAPTER 2

"Raymond, Get the phone."

"It's late Jan, let the answering machine get it. Go back to sleep."

"No, answer it," Janice insisted.

It was a cold rainy night as my Raymond rolled over to pick up the receiver, "Hello?"

Janice felt the silence as she wondered who could be on the other end of the phone. "Perhaps it is Sandy," Janice thought. "It must have been a huge misunderstanding that had driven her away from us so long ago."

The deafening silence from her youngest daughter had gone from days to weeks. Then from weeks to months. From months to years.

It was now two and a half decades since they had last talked. There were no answers to all the questions that plagued Janice's mind.

Raymond jumped out of bed and stood, "Would you repeat that, please."

The chills gripped Janice and raced down her neck to the bottom of her feet. Every hair on her body was standing at attention as she watched Raymond collapse into a nearby chair.

"We've gotta go now, Jan. We have to go NOW." The urgency in his voice broke Janice out of her reverie. *Go? Go where?*

"That was Logan, a good friend of Sandy's, and he's at the Forest Ranch Hospital. He said he was with Sandy when they brought her in earlier that evening."

Then Logan had told Raymond what no parent ever wants to hear, "Can you come? She's in a lot of pain, and it's critical."

Janice's thoughts ran rampant. He is calling the wrong number! This phone call cannot be real. It must be some form of a cruel joke. She is a healthy young woman. Why? Why?? WHY???

She was soon brought back to reality when she heard Raymond speaking to her, "Come on, Honey, I think I know where the Hospital is. Let's go!"

That is all it took. Tears streaming down their face, Raymond and Janice tried to gather their things for the trip to the other side of town. They had no idea what to expect when they arrived. They held each other close and prayed. Janice and Raymond were Christians, and their faith in the Lord Jesus Christ was strong.

Houston is a big town, ranked the 4th largest city in the United States. Raymond and Janice lived on the southern edge of Houston, close to Clear Lake City and NASA. The Hospital where I laid fighting for my life was 65 miles away, on the northwestern edge, just outside the great city's limits.

"Oh, why don't we have GPS? Even at this time of the night, it would take us almost two hours to get there, Ray."

"Let's pray that God will be merciful to her and keep her alive until we get there Honey."

Janice couldn't help to think, *would I be able to wrap my arms around her and tell her how much I loved her? Hurry Ray! Hurry!*

There were only a few cars on the road as the city slumbered. Raymond punched down on the accelerator, making the trip a fast one. Finally, the Hospital was in sight. The Hospital's florescent sign *Forest Ranch Medical Center Emergency Room* glowed in the darkness.

"Turn here, Ray," Janice pointed. Raymond turned into the emergency room parking lot. They got out of the car, dreading what they might find.

Raymond walked up to the reception desk. "My daughter was brought here about two hours ago."

"What's her name?"

"Sandy Ryan."

"Aww, yes, they moved her to ICU. Go down the hall to the

elevators and up to the 4th floor."

"Can you tell me what happened?"

"The nurses there should be able to fill you in."

"Thank you."

Raymond and Janice made their way to the elevators, still not knowing what to expect as they made their way to the Hospitals' ICU floor. They exited off the elevator, and the cold, harsh, sterile environment hit them in the face.

The nurse attending the receptionist's desk was staring at them sympathetically. "Can I help you?"

"We are here to see our daughter, Sandy Ryan."

"She is in room 4B11 just around the corner. I will send the Doctor in a few minutes to speak with you."

"Thank you," Raymond said as they turned to walk the short length to the room that was sustaining the life of their youngest daughter.

They stood before the door and bowed their heads. Their strength to open the door came only from the Lord. Slowly Raymond turned the door handle. They heard the beeping of the biorhythm machines and the low noise of the lung machine making compressions on my lungs.

Wires and tubes were running out of every exposed piece of flesh I had. Bags and bags of the fluids that helped sustain my life were positioned on both sides of the hospital bed. Tears were running down their faces as the horrible scene was presented to them.

Janice longed to put her arms around her youngest daughter, but the web of tubes and wires prevented her from it. All they could do was stand in the room and bow their heads as they put their trust in the Lord.

They reached for my tube infested hand just to touch me and know that I was still alive. Janice squeezed my fingers, but there was no reflex. No response. My hand was as limp as my body.

"Mr. and Ms. Davis?" The Doctor said as he entered the Intensive Care room.

"Yes, Doctor."

"She has been diagnosed with sclerosis of the liver, and it is so bad that her liver is beginning to shut down. We ran many more tests and found that the rest of her major organs appeared to be systematically shutting down, also."

Then he said what no parent ever wants to hear. "Her body is shutting down. I will give her about a 10% chance of living through the night. I am so sorry. We are doing all we can to save her."

My body laid there, fighting for my life. My soul continued its journey through the darkness of my past.

In 1983, I had lost track of my best friend, Natalie. After searching for her and the answers to why she just disappeared, I came across evidence that indicated that she had been forced into Human Trafficking. There was no way for me to help her. It broke my heart that my only friend was lost, never to be found again.

In 1987, still married to Luke, I found myself pregnant. Battling in my mind whether to keep the child or abort the fetus, I finally decided that I could not live with myself if I killed another human life.

In December of 1987, lying on a cold, sterile hospital table, the doctors cut my belly open and pulled from me, my only child. A daughter I named Renee after my Aunt Renee, who died from cancer, and who I adored.

No one in the operating room said good job. No one said I am so proud of you. No one said your little girl is perfect. No one said I was radiant and lovely.

The nurses said that I had to be a bad mother since the child was so small. That I did not care about my baby because I had smoked cigarettes during the pregnancy. How could I do that? What a horrible person I am. I did not deserve to have a child.

The nurses did not let me hold her. They immediately whisked her away, as the Doctor pumped more morphine into my body so he could sew my stomach up.

One month later, Dan, my stepbrother, and his wife Maria, who is Amelia's sister, the lady of whom my now lesbian step-sister Madison was shacked up with, gave birth to their only son Malcolm.

In 1988, I could not stand my life. I was a bad mother and a bad wife. Nothing was right in my life until I met a man who convinced me that I was a decent person and that I should leave my husband of eight years.

It was supposed to be a separation, not a divorce, until the divorce papers were served at the apartment where I was staying. The courts gave custody of my only child, Renee, to Luke. I was to pay child support.

One month after my divorce was final, Dan and his wife Maria got divorced. Three months after that, Luke married Maria. I was amazed at the speed at which that happened. Was Luke in love with Maria all this time? Was that why Luke served me the divorce papers during the separation? Was he planning this all along, and I only opened the door for it to happen?

None of it mattered anymore. What was done was done. Malcolm and Renee were no longer cousins. They were brothers and sisters.

In 1990, while I was still working for Shell Oil, the oil market crashed in response to Kuwait's Iraqi invasion. I was given a severance package and let go. But I was not worried since I was close to breaking into the Entertainment Business with a sound engineering degree.

Shortly after being let go, I went to work for an amusement park and learned theatrical lighting and pyrotechnics. That job barely paid the bills. Because I was making so little money, I fell behind in my child support payments. Letters came to my house about how they would throw me in jail if I did not pay up.

I knew I had to do something to keep me out of jail. I broke down and called the only person I thought might help me. I called my Mom, but Raymond got on the phone first. After he listened to my plight, he told me, "You can just rot in jail." He did not put my Mom on the phone to talk to me. Raymond was the *Man of the House*, and my Mom flawlessly obeyed him. If he did not want my Mom talking to me, she wouldn't.

Raymond's words burned into my memory and scarred my soul forever. I was heartbroken again. *I am finished with these people!* This time I never wanted to be near them, hear of them or speak to these horrible people that are supposed to be my parents. These people with their holier than thou attitude. Never again, and I wrote them out of my life for good.

In 1991, I started dabbling in paganism and witchcraft. Why not? God had turned his back on me all my life. He let all the horrible things happen to me. God allowed the perpetrators and rapists to go unpunished. God had made it very clear that even He did not want me.

As I practiced witchcraft daily, I justified it in my mind by saying how Christianity is littered with paganistic rituals, and flawed humans wrote the Bible. Humans make all kinds of mistakes. Humans are not perfect. The whole book is based on human interpretations, not something that came straight from the horse's mouth.

I continued to sit in on pagan rituals that would call real spirits from the other side into this plane of existence. I played with Ouija boards daily. Wearing a pentagram around my neck, I said spells and believed that things would change. I told myself it was white magic, not dark magic. *Do no harm, do as ye will* is straight out of the Wiccan Rede. I called upon the spirits and the Mother God to do my will.

And further and further, I chased the rabbit down the hole. I became fascinated with the Illuminati and the Grand Mason's. These secret societies. The forbidden. The unwanted. The elite.

My Grandfather was a high Grand Mason, and my Grandmother was a part of Eastern Star, the Grand Mason's female version. To join Eastern Star, you had to be married to or be the descendant of a Grand Mason. Yep, that was me, alright. I came close to joining but never took that final step. Something in the back of my mind always stopped me.

In 1993, I got my big break. I stuck my foot in the door to the *International Alliance of Theatrical and Stage Employees.* IATSE. I was in the big times now, baby!

People that were a part of this Union worked for the Symphony, the Opera, the Ballet, and Broadway. All the big production companies in the world. This Union's headquarters are in New York, New York. The Union was a place where sex, drugs, and rock 'n' roll were very prevalent. This Union became my playground.

In 1996, I met Roland. A long blonde-haired, witty, sexy, blue-eyed, silver-tongued, Rock Star. Now he was my Rock Star. A year later, he was moving in with me. For the eight years that he lived with me, I never noticed how degrading he was to me. How bad he treated me. I suppose all the abuse I received growing up had a part in dictating my tolerance for that. Or maybe that is how I believed the world to be.

The fights Roland and I got into were terrible. We both had horrible tempers. One night before a recording session in his studio, we got into a nasty fight. He shoved me so hard that he knocked my shoulder out of the socket. I never went to the hospital because I could not afford to. I told myself the pain was not that bad. It took weeks and weeks before I was able to use my arm again.

On another night, our fight was so bad that he broke everything in the house. It reminded me of my birth father, who did the same thing to my mother. I convinced myself that this kind of behavior was just my lot in life. It was the new normal. See no evil. Hear no evil. Speak no evil.

Until now, as I lay in my hospital bed, unable to move, the words screamed in my head, "My so-called family did this to me."

As the words formed in my mind, they burned in my heart. *I hate. I hate them. I hate ALL of them and what they represent. My own family. They raped me. I HATE THEM. Take, take, TAKE... never give.* They robbed me of my childhood. They robbed me of my teen years. They forced me to be an adult way before I was supposed to be. They raped my life. Yes, it was them. I had no choice.

There is no God.

A real God would not allow this to happen.

Into the dark abyss, I fell. There was no bottom. In my mind, the screams got louder and louder, but they did not wake me up. My gut-wrenching screams pierced my ears. But no one heard. No one cared.

I was alone in the darkness.

Janice and Raymond embraced each other as tears ran freely down their faces. Their hearts and minds screamed out, "NO! Satan, you cannot have her. She belongs to Jesus!"

The Doctor continued, "because of her severe pain, I put her in a medically induced coma. With her liver failing rapidly, it would surely take her life if I did not do this."

He wrote down the vitals that were blipping on the screen beside my bed, turned, and left as abruptly as he came in.

My parents did not know that I drank hard liquor every day to escape the abuse and overbearing actions over the eight years I was with Roland. I learned over the years of abuse to just live with it, and to live with it meant self-medication, whether that be alcohol or drugs. It did not matter anymore because that was my lot in life.

It was way easier to drown myself in a bottle than to argue and fight with Roland. He was the Rock Star. He and his beloved band Street Puddle. He deserved all the attention. His friends worshiped the ground that he walked on, and he was as charming as a rattlesnake.

I remained the nothing. I was the person that paid all the bills. The person that gave him a roof over his head. The person that loved him unconditionally. The person that was dating the

Rock Star, and I drank to forget all that it was and mourned all that it was not.

The head nurse came into the room just as the Doctor left. "Mr. and Ms. Davis? We will be doing an MRI every hour to check the progression of her organs or lack there-of."

Janice and Raymond stood there trembling. Everything seemed to be happening so fast. They had no idea what they could or should be doing to help. It seemed the more they talked to the Doctor and the nurses, the more questions they had. *Does she even know we are here?*

Then amid their questioning everything, the Doctor came back and interrupted their thoughts. "You both need to go home and get some rest." He paused a little bit too long, "There is nothing you can do here now."

Janice and Raymond stared at the Doctor as thoughts of concern swirled in their heads. How could he tell us that? Doesn't he have children? How could he be so insensitive? What if our daughter needed us during the night? If we went home, who would hold her tight and tell her how much she is loved?

The nurses finally convinced them, and they reluctantly left the Hospital. Exhausted from the whole ordeal and the long ride home, they called their church prayer hotline. They explained the urgency of the prayer request.

The prayer team assured them that they would be praying and believing that God would hear them from his throne in heaven. They prayed that He would be merciful and compassionate. The team prayed for peace to flood their hearts, and to trust, and believe.

Raymond and Janice's faith were strong. They did believe that God was in complete control and was holding me by the hand.

They believed His promises.

As I laid there in that cold, sterile hospital bed hooked to every lifesaving machine that was ever invented, I felt no pain. But somehow. Some way. I made it through the night, and that 10 percent chance of survival was turning into 40 percent, then 60 percent.

As the days and weeks rolled by, Raymond and Janice could see small improvements each time they visited. But I was still in a coma and breathing with a ventilator.

For five and a half weeks, I was out cold. Machines were breathing for me, tubes were feeding me, as my soul continued its lonesome journey.

Five and a half weeks. That is 39 days or 936 hours. It is 56,160 minutes of complete oblivion.

Dark oblivion.

For five and a half weeks, I was not on earth. All I once had, all I once was, did not exist in this darkened plane of oblivion until my soul went unceremoniously, slamming back onto this broken body that laid on that cold, sterile table.

No fanfare. No angels. No gates. No nothing. I was back, and the pain was real. Every muscle and every bone in this body screamed of pain.

And my mind blacked out yet again.

CHAPTER 3

As the mist cleared, I saw Jesse, one of the lead singers in Street Puddle, sitting with Roland through the bar's window on the main street of Galveston. They were waving and laughing at me as I stood outside, looking in at them.

They kept pointing at me and laughing. I could not figure out why they were doing this. Why am I always the outsider?

The cold rain pounded my body and made me shiver. It was coming down even harder now. I was drenched to the bone. I looked up and down the street, silently watching the rain sheet down in the light of the streetlamps. It was late at night, and the streets were deserted. I could hear the waves on the beach crash into the shore just a few blocks away.

The waves sounded strange in the downpour. They were beckoning me. Slowly I walked towards the seawall. My feet never touched the ground. I could smell the sea salt air and hear the sea's waves crashing into the wall. I could see the long jetties made from granite protruding into the sea like long jagged monoliths.

Shaking the rain out of my eyes, in the cold, wet darkness, I watched the full moon rise over the jetties as the dark, ominous clouds rolled over it, threatening to shut out the light it emitted completely.

And then I saw it. A tiny light was fluttering in the distance. It was floating just at the sea's edge of the jetty, and then it was gone in a blink of an eye.

Was it my imagination? It had to be! Could it have been someone in danger? Someone slipping into the sea?

It was so dark now that the clouds were fully covering the light of the full moon. I started towards the end of the jetty. My shoes never really grasped the granite rocks that I walked on. The waves were lashing at me and threatening to pull me under as the cold rain continued to hammer my body.

I saw it again.

Blink

and then, as quickly as it came, it was gone.

I tried to hurry. I tried to run. My feet still not touching the granite. The faster my legs moved, the slower I got to the tiny light. The clouds were rushing across the moon. Rain pelted my face continuously. I wanted to run faster, but my legs never got the message.

The Jetty was long, and the granite boulders were jagged. The wide, deep dark crevasses between the granite rocks threatened to grab me and pull me under the water. And then I froze in amazement as I watched the tiny light blink on and proceed to slowly strengthen in its illumination.

I looked up to see the clouds across the full moon disappearing rapidly, as I brushed the long rain-soaked locks of hair out of my eyes so I could see it better.

It was a black wall that shined in the light of the clear full moon. A very black... cold... dark... unforgiving wall.

The tiny light was growing with each step I took towards it. Inch by inch that my body drew closer, each hair on the back of my neck stood at attention. I shivered as the rain continued to streak down my face and pound my body.

I stopped dead in my tracks as I inhaled a deep breath. I recognized what it was.

NO! No. It couldn't be.

Shining in the full illumination of the moon was a pyramid. Was it the Eye of God? I brushed the wet hair from my eyes to get a better look at it.

Shivering uncontrollably now, I saw that it was a very dark, black pyramid. It was drawing me to it. I saw the sea waves lashing all around it viciously. I had to get there, but the path to it was so treacherous.

I ran full stead towards the pyramid. My feet were floating above the granite rocks. Finally, I came to a pass. It had to be at least twelve *feet in span. There was only the sea between me and the pyramid now.*

I took a deep breath... tried to run from where I stood... and I jumped... and fell—never reaching the pyramid.

I fell into the cold hard water that surrounded it. The waves were pushing me down. Coughing, my lungs were exploding in my chest. I tried to breathe as the rain was falling harder. I was drowning... gasping.

It hurt. It hurt bad. I went under gasping. My body was freezing, and then it went black.

Back I went into the nothingness... again.

"She's starting to move a little," Sara, the night nurse, said to the Doctor as he held my left eye open and flashed a penlight across it to gauge my eye movement.

Janice and Raymond stood nearby, watching and praying for my reactions.

"The opiates are keeping her brain in a deeply unconscious state," he opened my right eye and flashed the penlight across it, "it's allowing her to heal without pain." He reached for the bronchoscopy tube and ran it down my mouth, "You just saw reflexes, that's all. She doesn't feel pain right now. She has no idea what is going on here." The Doctor ran a tiny brush through the tube inserted down my throat to scrape my lungs and retrieve samples of my lungs lining.

"I'll increase the opiates. That should decrease her movement considerably." The Doctor placed the sampled lung tissue in a vile. "I'm going to send these samples to the lab. If they come back with positive results, we can then take her off the ventilator."

The Doctor reached for the med drip on the IV attached to my neck, started the flow of more pain killers, and then left the room. It would be several more hours before the lab returned the results.

Janice and Raymond waited patiently.

Two hours later, the Doctor came back into the ICU room. "The lab results are positive. It's time to take the breathing tube out and see if she can breathe on her own."

Mixed emotions ran through Janice's mind. Her faith in the Lord was strong, and she knew she had to trust the Lord and trust that He would not let her daughter down. Janice prayed, "Breathe the breath of life into Sandy, Lord, make her breathe freely."

She watched as the Doctor started to remove the long tube from my throat. Janice and Raymond held their breath in anticipation. Slowly the Doctor pulled on the tube until he reached the end.

Even the Doctor held his breath until they all saw the slow rhythm of my chest going up and down. Although I was still sleeping in a coma, I was breathing on my own.

Janice shouted, "Praise the Lord!"

"Let's give her a few more days to breathe on her own, and then we can take her out of the coma. You guys go home now and get some rest. We will call you if there are any changes."

Raymond sat in his favorite recliner, watching the news as he waited for Janice to get ready to go. The weatherman was warning about an impending storm that was brewing near Florida.

"The tropical depression that hit the Bahamas yesterday has now produced Tropical Storm Katrina. It is headed directly for the Florida coast. All storm projections show that there is no chance that this storm could turn and head to Galveston with the current wind patterns."

The weatherman droned on. "The storm should strengthen as it moves over the warm waters of the Atlantic and is expected to reach hurricane status before making landfall on the coast of Florida tomorrow morning. This storm should not produce a lot of rain for the Houston Area..." and the forecast continued.

"Come on, Jan, let's go. They are going to wake her up today.

Let's not miss it!"

"I'm coming, Ray," Janice yelled down from the top of the stairs.

And my coma dreams kept coming. There were dreams about my car falling off a 13-story building. Dreams about sneakers and washing machines. Dreams about hiding from drug dealers. Dreams of my father and dreams of my grandmother. Dreams of ships that I could not disembark from, and dreams about trying to fly a plane out of an oasis to get help. But the last one went like this...

I was on a gurney being wheeled down a very long hallway. The nurse had just laid my favorite blanket across my legs. It was the quilt my Grandmother made me.

The nurse was laughing at me, "We will get there when we get there! Now be still and enjoy the ride!"

"But you have to hurry!" I screamed in joy, laughing as she hurled me down the hallway, "I can smell it from here! Hurry!"

Faster and faster, the nurse went and finally burst through the double glass doors. I could smell the hamburgers and oh my... the French fries! I adore French fries! I was so hungry!

"I see eye movement. She's coming around!" The Doctor stood by the bed as he watched the drug-induced haze wearing off me. Raymond and Janice were watching, too, as I slowly opened my eyes.

They had wheeled me into another part of ICU where I could be watched from the nurse's station. I was no longer in my own room but in an extremely large room that held many more ICU patients. The nurses at the nurse station cheered as the Doctor proclaimed me awake, just as the double doors to the large ICU room opened and the orderly came in carrying a bag from McDonald's. The smell of hamburgers and fries went wafting through the air behind him.

I opened my eyes and saw my mother standing over me at the foot of my bed. She screamed, "Praise God! Jesus saved your life!" She was pointing at me. "You should bow down and thank Him!"

My Mom and stepdad were ecstatic. I, on the other hand, could not speak and could barely move. The long weeks of lying in a hospital bed, not moving, had taken my speech along with my muscles. All I could do was stare at them, horrified.

"Welcome back!" The Doctor stood next to my bedside, holding my wrist in his hand. Why are they in my room? Why is she screaming at me? Didn't they know how hard I fought to get here? Didn't they know it was my own will to survive the darkness that saved my life? Jesus? HA!

He never came.

He never cared.

He was not there.

Nope, it was me! All alone, I fought to save my life! I fell back to sleep, exhausted but no longer in a coma.

During the next few weeks, I remembered small segments of things that happened in the hospital as I drifted from being conscious to unconscious.

I remember the night I tried not to breathe as they wheeled out the dead person in the quarantine room that was five feet from the hospital bed where I was lying. I remember ducking under the covers so I would not catch what killed him.

I remember the cleanup crew in space suits going into the room to remove the remains of their efforts to save the person. I remember them taking the body out of the quarantine room as I held my breath. The people in space suits pushed the dead body within feet of my hospital bed.

I remember being scared out of my mind.

I remember the horrible pain. Why did I come back? The pain was unbearable. Pain sucks pond scum. Every muscle and every bone in my body hurt from not moving for so long. My muscles had wasted away.

I remember the nurses screaming at me in the middle of the night to "breathe, Sandy, you have to breathe."

The doctors had hooked me up to a different ventilator to help me breathe, as my brain had stopped wanting to send that command to my lungs. I did not breathe in or breathe out in normal rhythms. Each time I stopped the normal rhythm, an alarm went off, and the nurses would yell at me to breathe.

The nurses kept asking me if I remember anything about how I got there. What happened to get me here? Did I know how long I was in the hospital? Did I know what year it was? Did I know my name?

And my mind drifted back to the day when I almost died thirteen years ago trying to break into the Entertainment Business.

In 1992, I was doing gigs with a small company that consisted of setting up and tearing down band gear. My boss stored the band's gear in his warehouse on the southeast side of town. We transported the band gear to and from the gigs in a small box truck that had a compartment over the cab.

On a Friday evening, I had been dispatched to a small club in Beaumont were a band we kept gear for was playing. The band's equipment consisted of a drum kit, keyboard kit, microphones, sound system, small lighting system, and a PA. I had stuffed the small box truck to the brim. Every nook and cranny of the truck was crammed with something. Even the small compartment over the cab of the truck was stuffed with road cases. The door to the back of the truck barely closed as I put the padlock onto it. Hopping into the driver's seat, I set out for the Houston warehouse to deposit the band's equipment.

It was a typical day with no rain. The roads were dry. It was approaching the rush hour in Houston on a six-lane highway called I-59. I was heading east as I reached the top of the overpass. Looking into the driver's side mirror, I saw a low rider car coming directly at me. He was drunkenly swerving from lane to lane. I knew he was going to sideswipe the truck if I did not do something fast.

I reacted by steering quickly to the right to get the truck out of the way. The top-heavy truck could not handle the steering wheel's swift move and started to teeter-totter very close to the overpass's railing, which was 30 feet off the ground.

If I did not sway the steering wheel back to the left, the truck would go over the rail, and I would crash down off the overpass. In hopes of stopping the top-heavy truck from teetering closer to the railing, I swerved the steering wheel back to the left, but this just sent the small box truck into a tailspin in Houston's rush hour traffic.

Everything in the cab of the truck went flying as it spun round and round. The truck finally came to a stop in the middle of the 6-lane freeway facing the oncoming traffic.

I watched in slow-motion horror as the 18-wheeler that was recently trailing behind me was now facing me. It was rushing towards me at an alarming speed. I smelled the burning rubber as the 18-wheeler's tires were locking up to slow the massive vehicle.

It was 50 feet away from me as I watched the tires of the 18-wheeler start to smoke in an effort to stop.

Twenty feet away, my heart started to race uncontrollably. There was no way that I could get out of the box truck. The cars on my left and the cars on my right still rushed by on the highway.

Ten feet away, my mind said he's not going to stop. I was in a head-on collision in the worst way. I was going to die.

Five feet... four feet... it's slowing down!

Three feet, two feet... Oh, my God!

He is stopping! My heart was racing!

One foot and the 18-wheeler was slowing to a stop. His bumper just kissed mine. There was no collision.

I could not move. I just sat there with a death grip on the steering wheel. My knuckles were white. The driver was able to stop the 18-wheeler from killing me. I sat shaking from head to toe in a cold sweat. "Thank you, Thank You, Thank You, God!"

It was no small miracle. I knew God had a hand in this. Perhaps He cared after all! I am not a very religious person. I do not go to Church, but I believe that there is one God.

My early childhood experiences with the Church was not very good. I guess I just never *got it.* Church to me was like school and tests. It was like English classes and dissecting sentences into nouns, adjectives, adverbs, and verbs. You did it, but it never really helped you. It was like asking, "Why do I need to learn History? I'll never use it in real life!"

My Mom had my best interests at heart when she forced me to go to the Lutheran Catechism. It was a course given by the Lutheran Church to prepare converts to Baptism. It taught and tested you on the Ten Commandments, The Apostles' Creed, The Lord's Prayer, The Sacrament of Baptism, Confession and Absolution, The Sacrament of the Alter, Morning Prayers and Evening Prayers, and finally Grace at the Table.

It was enough to turn me off to the Church forever. They all spoke in a different language. Church people used the formal words of Thee and Thou, and Thou shalt not.

I did not want this, and I did not ask for it. I did not understand it. I went because Mom told me to. It was important to her. I wanted to just get it over with as quickly as possible.

The nurse rolled a wheelchair over to my bed, which popped me out of my daydream. I was happy to see her because she was going to bring me down to the showers today. I was going to have a real shower finally! I still could not walk very well, but physical therapy every day was helping with that.

I longed to go home. I could not stand this sterile environment much more. But a warm shower! A real shower! With soap! And hair shampoo! Now that would be heaven!

The nurse helped me to sit on a bench in the showers and turned on the warm water. All the dirt from the long dusty road I walked on for the last five and half weeks was washing away. Oh my, it felt so good!

I asked her to wash my hair because my arms were not strong enough. I have very long hair. As she poured the shampoo on my head and tried to massage it in, she said, "I'm sorry, Sandy, that is the best I can do for now."

"What do you mean? What's wrong?" I asked, visibly shaken.

"I'm sorry, Sans, but your hair has a very tight knot at the back of your head."

So that's why my head hurt all the time. I had been sleeping on this massive knot for weeks. "Can't you get it out?"

"You might want to soak it in oils like avocado or coconut when you get home. It might loosen up then. But if not, it will probably have to be cut out."

I broke down and cried. The tears did not stop running down my face. The nurse saw my distress and offered, "Your family put your hair up in a bun to try to get it out of your face while you were in a coma. You rolled around on it for five weeks, which made it into an impossibly tight knot."

She watched the tears roll down my face and continued sympathetically, "You were in a coma, and we didn't want to do anything until you woke up. I'm sorry, but we couldn't tell them not to do it."

She lifted my hand to feel it. I was sickened. My beautiful long hair. How could they? Nothing has changed with these people. They still have their high and mighty attitudes and their selfish ways. They still preached down to people.

It was their way or no way. I could not walk yet, and now I would be bald for a year because of my family's selfishness. They always did what they wanted. I could just hear my mother now, "Let's put her hair in a bun. It will be so cute."

Did they stop to think that I would roll around on it for the entire time that I was in a coma? Did they think that it would make me feel good? Did they stop to think that it might hurt to roll around on this rock that was now attached to the back of my head?

No. They did as they pleased. They could care less about what I wanted. So typical. I fought for my life, and they gave me no credit. They said Jesus saved me. I never saw Jesus. I was the one that fought to survive. I was the one that brought myself back to this hell hole, and for what? To lose all of my hair? To be ridiculed by others because now I was going to be bald because of their stupidity?

This last escapade was the absolute last straw. How could they talk down to me? The insensitivity of it all! How could they? I never want to be around these people. Nothing has changed. These self-centered, egotistical, selfish, high, and mighty people were my so-called family.

Never again. I am done with all of them.

AGAIN.

Forever.

That is what started my motivation to get out of this godforsaken, sterile, white-walled hell hole and go home. People die here every minute, and I needed out of this disease-ridden jail. Now!

I had made a pack with the Doctors that when I could walk down the hall and back by myself that they would release me to go home.

I sat in my hospital bed, listening to the rain pelting the window. It sounded like it was getting harder and harder. The nurse came by and turned on the news for me. The Channel 13 newscast was just starting, "Welcome to Saturday's mornings broadcast, it's August 27th, 2005."

My gaze fixed on the TV screen above my hospital bed. It still amazes me to know that I lost over a month's time. It was time passing that felt to me like only five minutes, not five and a half weeks. I had no idea what was going on in the world.

The newscast continued, "Hurricane Katrina made landfall yesterday near Keating Beach with 80 mph winds, just two miles south of the Fort Lauderdale International Airport in Florida. The storm's eye spent close to six hours on land before plowing into the Gulf of Mexico's warm waters. Today, officials expect the storm to reach a category three intensity. Hurricane Katrina is now 66 miles southeast of New Orleans. Governor Blanco has declared a state of emergency. He has activated the state of Louisiana's emergency response and recovery program under the command of the Director of the State of Homeland Security, Emergency Preparedness, and FEMA."

Hurricanes are bad, especially if you are on the dirty side of the rain bands. "Well, at least it's not coming down Houston's throat," I thought to myself as the day nurse was rolling the infamous wheelchair towards my bed.

"It's time for your therapy session."

I was ready. I was more than ready to ramp up my exercises and flee from this godforsaken place.

On Sunday, August 28, 2005, Hurricane Katrina slammed into Louisiana's coast as a category five hurricane with maximum sustained winds of 175 mph and gusts up to 190 mph. New Orleans was ground zero. But the massive hurricane was not finished with its path of destruction.

On Monday, the hurricane made its second landfall as a category three hurricane at Bay St. Louis, Mississippi, with sustained winds of more than 125 mph, and a final third landfall in St. Bernard parish and St. Tammany parish as a category three hurricane. And then it got even worse.

The levee was breached at the Industrial Canal in Louisiana. This left the parishes entirely underwater. The National Weather Service advised people to flee to higher ground. As the water rose, the hospitals in Louisiana reached out to Houston's Medical Center and all the hospitals in Houston and the surrounding areas for bed space. The hospital I was in had to start releasing patients who were well enough to go home.

That was music to my ears! They had just given me the Golden Ticket! I would be homeward bound the very next day!

As I was waiting for the nurse's aide to bring me my release papers, my mother came to my bedside. "I'm so very proud of you!"

All I could do was stare at her. Fuming.

"I love you very much. I am so glad you're going home today."

I still couldn't bring myself to say anything. I knew I only had words of hate for her and her high and mighty family.

"Is there anything I can do for you? Do you need me to come with you to your house?"

That hit a nerve. "You've done enough. Don't call me. I'll call you!"

Fighting tears, my mother left my room. Outside the hospital, she cried out to the Lord, "Lord, wrap your arms around her while I can't. Send your angels of mercy and peace to cover her when she sleeps. Lord, I trust you completely. Heal Sandy's body, mind, and soul. I pray this in the name of Jesus. Amen."

For our struggle is not against flesh and blood but against the rulers, against the authorities, against the powers of this dark world, and against the spiritual forces of evil in the heavenly realms. (Ephesians 6:12)

CHAPTER 4

I had tried soaking the knot on my head in every different type of oil on the market. Roland painstakingly picked at it for hours, trying to save what used to be my beautiful long brown hair. But to no avail. No matter what I tried, it would not break free.

I cried on the way to the hairstylist, who spent two hours trying to save my hair only to fail miserably. The only thing left to do was to cut the knot from my head. Once removed, it would leave just two inches of hair on the entire backside of my head.

My heart sank. There was no way I would cut what was left of my hair off to match the backside. That would leave me almost bald. For days and days, I cried. The emotional distress is horrible. I can now empathize with chemotherapy patients and how traumatic and devastating losing one's hair is. How losing one's hair diminishes your confidence. How it makes you just want to crawl in a cave and hide from the world because you look like a freak.

I am one of five women that work in the entertainment industry dominated by men. Women in the industry must work harder, be smarter, and stay ten steps above everyone else. There is no way that I could walk into my job with a bald head and still maintain the respect that I have been given over the ten years that I have worked on and around theatrical stages.

I had one advantage working for me. Because I was a stagehand by trade, I could wear jeans, t-shirts, and ball caps without questions from others. No one would ever question my appearance.

Taking a needle and thread, I sewed into two ball caps fake

hair that matched my own. These ball caps would serve me until the back of my hair catches up to the rest of the hair on my head.

Every day that I had to put that ball cap on, it reminded me of those that put me in this situation. Those selfish people who put my hair in a bun only to let it become a rock. A rock that could not be untangled. A rock that had to be cut from my head.

And every day that I had to wear that ball cap, my anger for them grew.

Eight long months later, in 2006, the bills from my stay at the hospital were piling up. Working as a stagehand meant I was working for myself. There was no health insurance unless I purchased it, which translates to I have no health insurance.

The five and a half weeks' stay in the hospital tied to every lifesaving machine possible led to insurmountable bills. There was no way I could pay them in this lifetime. My only option was to claim Chapter 13 Bankruptcy. It would be five long years before my credit would resemble anything like an average person.

The stress of the lawyers, judges, and the court system threw me into a new kind of hell. The lawyers picked through my financial life with a fine-toothed comb. It was like being raped all over again. I hated it, but there was nothing I could do. The very roof over my head was in jeopardy.

And then there was Roland. I could not stand to be in the same room with him anymore.

"Sans, why are you so distant all the time?" Roland moaned. "I have been there for you throughout all of this. I visited you every day while you were in the hospital. I held your hand. I talked to you. I looked after your house. I paid all of your bills." He droned on and on, "Why are you treating me like this?"

I like to think that I am a very smart woman. Roland's power over me came on very slowly at first. Until I started brushing off my friends, and my circle of people got smaller. Then I stopped talking to them all together, which left me with only Roland.

I didn't believe in myself anymore. It was all about Roland, the rock star. I was always the wrong one, while Roland was brilliant, charming, and persuasive. The good outweighed the bad. Until it did not anymore.

Something came over me when I was in that coma. My eyes saw things from afar. My eyes saw things from a new angle. My eyes and my heart saw the truth.

When I came home from the hospital, I could not stand for Roland to touch me. I had banished him from my sleeping quarters, and he was now living in the spare bedroom. I could not listen to his lies anymore as I now saw him as the overbearing demon spawn he truly was. The only thing I could not see was how to get him out of my life and out of my house forever.

"I'm going to move back in with my mother. It's the only way to work this out," he said, as the tears started to stream down my face. "Don't cry, San's. We'll work this out, but we need to be apart right now."

I couldn't stop crying, but what he didn't know was they were tears of joy, as I felt this great burden being lifted off my shoulders. All I could do was stare at him as he left the room to pack up his things. And the tears kept coming, as my heart knew I would never see him again.

I was done with men. Every man that had ever entered my life physically and mentally abused me in one way, shape, or form. No more. I would rather live with dogs than let another man hurt me again.

With that planted firmly in my mind, I started to rebuild my life and live my life for just me. To hell with my so-called family, and to hell with men. I am prepared to drudge thru the rest of this life alone.

Five years later, in 2011, I sat at my laptop, thinking about how things change. I now spend my days working exceptionally long hours and playing a massive multiplayer online game called World of Warcraft.

World of Warcraft was where I could lose myself in the online world of myth, magic, raiding, and war. It was a place I could ride Dragons and fight my enemies. It was a place where you could repeatedly die, only to be resurrected by magic.

I spent hours and hours a day playing this game. I made friends with many people everywhere in America and even abroad. World of Warcraft was my obsession. My friends in the game became my new family.

We would spend hours speaking through headsets to each other. It was how we coordinated raids on the enemy. It was how we won wars. But it was not always about the game. It was about friendships too.

On one particular night, while I was patiently waiting for a raid to start, I looked up from the game, and my eyes went directly to the digital radio clock that sits on my end table. It showed 11:11 p.m. It's getting late, I thought, but I didn't care. The raid was more important to me.

Finally, I saw the count down on the screen start. 5... 4... 3... 2... 1. The gates to the enemy's dungeon flew open, and we were off to do battle and search for valuable loot.

After about two hours in the dungeon, our raid team finally came to the boss's room. It took us fifteen minutes to kill him, which rewarded us with honor points and valuable gear. I was thrilled and exhausted all at once. As I took my headset off, my eye wandered back to my radio clock. 01:11 a.m.

It is late. Heading off to bed, I was not thinking about the numbers my brain just saw. It only registered when I started seeing it everywhere. On license plates, on billboards, on TV. In emails, on my phone, on eBay, and on digital clocks. Everywhere I looked, I saw it.

"LOOK NOW! " Something in my head told my eyes to look just at the precise moment.

Eleven Eleven. Such a simple number. One, One, One, One.

11:11. I was obsessed with the number. Was I the only person on this planet that saw Eleven Eleven everywhere?

My iPhone was filled to the brim with pictures of 11:11 in some form or fashion. There were pictures of cars with license plates that read 1111. Photos of my lock screen on my iPhone just when the clock read 11:11 or 01:11. Tons and tons of images depicting 1111. I had to document it. No one would believe me that I saw it everywhere.

I was watching an auction on eBay on my iPhone. When the auction ended, I had to take a picture of it. The date and time stamp of the auction was 11-11-11 at 01:11:11. I kid you not.

Just today, I sent out an email. After I clicked on the send button, I looked at the time stamp on the email. "11:11 a.m. (11 minutes ago)"

11:11 was everywhere, and my eyes saw it every time. I turned to the World Wide Web and Googled "eleven eleven" only to find that I was not alone in this strange phenomenon. There are a lot of people that see this number all the time. It was not that random at all.

Google listed everything you ever wanted to know about the number eleven. From biblical prophecy to a synchronistic portal, to angels, and a way for them to communicate with us. I found that the number eleven could be a sign from the Spirit and Angel realms. It is also a number that is associated with dreams and wishes coming true. Some folks even believe that it is the link between the mortal and the immortal. Whatever the true meaning is, I continue to see it everywhere and on everything.

I was becoming increasingly obsessed with this weird occurrence. So much so that I enlisted the help and guidance of the famous psychic Chris Browning. I wanted to ask Chris precisely why I saw Eleven Eleven all the time. If this was something coming from the spirit world, I wanted to know. I wanted to know now.

I made the appointment to speak to Chris personally through his website and patiently waited for the appointed date to come.

"Hello, you are on the phone with psychic Chris Browning. How are you today?"

"Hi, Chris! I am OK!!"

"What is your question, Sandy?"

I started with the obvious questions that everyone wanted to know the answers to. Things like "Will I be rich?" and "Will I be successful at my job?" But before I asked him the momentous number eleven question, I wanted to know about my Grandmother who passed in the year 2000, ...eleven years ago.

My Grandmother was a full-blooded German who lived in Fredericksburg, a small town in the Texas Hill Country. She was two months away from her 100th birthday as she lay in a hospital bed dying. My mother and my sister Isabella sat near Grandmother's bed. They watched as Grandmother appeared to be fighting some sort of battle. Mom and Izzy felt their hair stand on end as goosebumps ran down their arms and up their backs.

They knew there was a battle raging in the room. A battle between good and evil. A battle not of this earth but a war in the spirit realm.

The nurses felt it too and would not come into the room. Everyone felt it as they passed by the window to Grandmother's room. Everyone shuttered. Everyone looked away.

Mom was crying as she watched her mother, my grandmother, violently push her arms down her body, trying to ward off what was attacking her. "Please, Momma, just call his name. He will help you. Please, Momma, say his name. Say the name of Jesus. Call your Lord Jesus."

Grandmother was fighting the evil that everyone felt present in and outside of the room. She thrashed back and forth, moaning and crying.

"Jesus. Just call him Momma. Say his name now. Say, Jesus. Please, Momma, call him." My mother begged relentlessly.

Finally, my Grandmother forms the one word that would save her for eternity. "Jesus!"

As that one word passed from her breath, The Lord took her to the other side.

"Tell me what happened with you that same night Sandy." Chris prodded.

"I was sitting alone at my desk in the computer room in my house. It was a very calm, quiet night in my neighborhood. The winds outside were not blowing. Nothing stirred, not in my home or my neighborhood. I sat in the silence of the room playing a game on my computer. My dogs were fast asleep at my feet.

"Just before midnight, I sensed this force coming straight at me, and before I could react, I felt this force go right through my chest. It made every hair on my body stand at attention. My whole body tingled with the sensation.

"Just as I exhaled, as this force left my body, the sound of a thousand June bugs was banging on the window of the room. My dogs woke and growled. I knew they heard it too.

Tap... Tap... tap... TAP... tap... Tap...

"The tapping lasted for what seemed like five minutes. Five very long minutes. My heart was pounding in my chest as my mind raced with the possibilities of what was fixing to come through the window, which was positioned right next to the front door to my house.

"I crept into the living room and peeked out the front door's peephole. The porch light was on, and I could see through the hole that there was nothing there. My dogs, Bear and Rosco, sensed my fear and took a stance to protect me as I grabbed the wooden bat that I kept close to the door. Slowly I turned the lock to the open position and inched the door open. I raised the bat above my head, ready to strike whatever was there. Fear and curiosity moved me on.

"As I opened the door about a foot wide, I expected to see a thousand dead bugs on the porch. I expected to see bugs flying in the air around the yellow bug light on the porch. But there was nothing. No dead bugs. No evidence of anything hitting the window. There was nothing on the ground surrounding the window. The wind was not blowing. The huge oak tree in my front yard was still. I knew it wasn't my imagination Chris."

There was a slight pause before Chris answered. "Sometimes, when our loved ones cross over, they like to tell us that they are OK. They try to touch us, to grab our attention, to let us know they are OK. That was your Grandmother, letting you know she's free and in Heaven." Chris explained. "Do you have any more questions, Sandy?"

Oh boy, here we go, "Can you tell me why I see Eleven Eleven everywhere?"

"That's not so uncommon as you think, Sandy. It is your higher self. It is telling you that you are on the right track. It is something that your higher self has left for you to find. It is a sort of a bookmarker or a road marker."

"OK! Thank You very much, Chris! It was a pleasure to speak with you."

"And you as well, Sandy! Have a blessed day!"

I hung up the phone. OK! I see Eleven Eleven because my higher self is telling me all is okay, but I didn't really believe in a higher self. I believe in a supreme being. I believe in God. But a higher self? I wasn't so sure about that.

I continued to search for the answers. The worldwide web is a magnificent place for information. Seek, and you shall find. I was led to many different websites, from the self-help gurus to the paranormal phenomenon. I searched and searched until I came across a book called *The Secrets of the Universe* by Linda Bernstein and a theory called *The Law of Attraction*.

Secret? What secret? I want to know the secret! Why haven't I been told about this before?

The web told me that the Law of Attraction is a new age philosophy that states that positive thoughts bring positive things and negative thoughts bring about negative things. It was explained as being like karma and the full circle of things. Do wrong to someone, do bad things, and bad things will happen to you down the road.

Do good things, and good things will come to you. Positive thoughts bring positive things, and negative thoughts bring negative things. *The Secrets of the Universe* not only preached the Law of Attraction but backed it up with scientific theory. It went as far as saying that you are God, Spirit in Flesh, the Eternal Life.

That hit a nerve. I knew this is what Chris was trying to explain to me. My higher self. God in a physical body. Spirit in the flesh. Eleven Eleven.

I kept reading and soaking in what this theory stood for and meant. I pondered that thoughts are things, and desirable outcomes such as better health, abundant wealth, and abundant happiness can be attracted simply by changing one's thoughts and feelings.

I think I can...

The Secrets of the Universe even quotes The New Testament from the Bible. You know... That book written by humans for humans. It says that we are the heir to *THE Kingdom*, that it is our birthright.

The more I read, the more it all made sense to me. The kingdom is my birthright! I was convinced that this all was the truth, and I couldn't get enough of it.

Now, I am not one that seeks out the advice of self-help books or people at seminars that preach about how to make your life better and how to succeed, but this was something different. *The Secret of the Universe* was built on and around proven scientific principles. Scientific principles that have been around for ages. By God, it was science and the Universe. It was quantum physics. This book pulls references from the Bible. God's Word. It must be true. It wasn't snake juice sold on the side of the road.

And it sucked me in from head to toe.

Hook, Line, and Sinker.

I had to read more. I had to change my life for the better. I had to build and think it now to make my future better. I can do this.

I can. I can. I think I can.

Ask, Believe, Receive!

The enemy comes only to steal and kill and destroy. (John 10:10)

CHAPTER 5

Eleven Eleven.
One, One, One, One.
It's such a simple harmless number.

"House lights to half... Go," the stage manager called over the headset. Another show was starting. We had spent the last two weeks in technical rehearsals for the 5-hour premiere opera, and now it was finally opening night—opening night to the final opera of the 2011 season.

I kept the control room completely dark, so I could see the stage through the smoke colored glass that separated me from the audience. The seven touch screens of the lighting console were the only thing that was glowing in the darkness. It looked like NASA's Mission Control. This is power!

I was contracted with one of the largest Opera Companies in the world to run lighting for their live performances. I knew this lighting console like the back of my hand. I spoke its language fluently. This console is what kept everything alive on stage and off stage. It turned the lights on just at the precise moment, as it plunged other parts of the stage into total darkness. It was dramatical. It was powerful, and it was just the way I liked it.

I reached for the fader on the console that controlled the audience house lights and took it halfway down. "House is half," I called over the headset. Taking the house lights down usually settled the audience members and alerted them that the show was starting.

The stage manager took another two minutes as I patiently waited for the next "G-word." It was the single simple word that starts everything. It was *the* command. We never spoke the G-word out loud unless we actually meant for something to happen on stage.

"House lights Out... GO!" There it is... the G-word! GO! I slowly plunged the audience into complete darkness.

"Main Curtain out... GO!" Up went the main curtain, and the show started. We were off and running!

A five-hour opera. That's a long time. You could watch two movies in five hours. You probably could get through most of a novel in five hours. You could play a lot of games in five hours, which is precisely what I did.

I turned to my gaming laptop that sat next to my lighting console and logged in to Warcraft. Yes, five hours is a long time, and playing Warcraft with my friends online is how I liked to spend it.

Fifteen years in a control room working for a prominent theatrical Opera company was the only life I knew. I had no friends other than my Warcraft family. I had no contact with people, and I didn't watch or read the news by choice. The Law of Attraction has taught me that watching the news is bad. The news pounds into your mind all the negativity of the world.

Negativity brings about negativity. Think negative and get negative. Who got shot. Who got robbed. Who got raped. Who died. Multiple car pile-ups on freeways, people dying, tsunamis that kill thousands of people somewhere on the other side of the world, terroristic attacks, all the hate, all the death and destruction everywhere you turned, everywhere you looked. All that negativity was not good. I vowed that I wouldn't allow myself to see, hear, read, or think about it.

The Law of Attraction says to not think about the people around the world and their destruction. That all that mass thinking about them and that mass praying for them would only bring about more mass destruction.

I don't want the things of destruction getting bigger. I won't think about them. I won't listen to people that talk about them. I won't!

Negative thoughts equal negative reactions. Newton's physics law states that "For every action, there is an equal and opposite reaction." Negativity brings about negativity. That concept was plain and simple to me.

Don't do it. Don't think about it. Negative thoughts bring about negative things. I do not want negativity in my life. I want abundance. Shut out the negativity! I screamed this in my head repeatedly!

Don't watch! Don't Listen! Think positive, think abundance. Ask for abundance. Believe in abundance. Receive abundance. I believe. I will receive.

How do people allow themselves to be brainwashed day in and day out with so much negativity? I do not let myself watch commercials, news, or live TV at home or work. I will not allow myself to be exposed to the negativity of the outside world. I don't listen to the radio, for the constant barrage of commercials that drilled into your mind about poor health issues. Negativity!

I didn't want my mind to think about poor health because I did not want poor health, so I turned it off. I shut it out, by choice, all the negativity of the world. Think only positive thoughts. Positive thoughts bring positive things.

I think I can. I think I can. Think positive! I can make it better!

I spent the summer brainwashing myself with mind tapes. My mind soaked up everything I could get my hands on about the Law of Attraction. I read in a Law of Attraction Magazine about this man who started to leave dollar bills in places where people would find them. He would imagine the exact moment that they would find the dollar bill. He imagined their happiness and smiles. He felt himself being happy seeing this.

This simple action eventually brought him hundreds of dollars because he put out into the universe that money was no object. That it brought happiness, and that is what he wanted the universe to bring back to him. He stated the fact that this worked.

What the heck! I'll give it a try. What's a couple of bucks if the universe would return much more than that?

I started putting dollar bills in places people would find them. I would imagine them happy and excited when they found it. Give money and receive money. If I gave, I would receive. Linda Bernstein said so. She did it. In the *Secrets of the Universe,* she said she gave everything away. It was her last hope, and the universe gave it back and so much more. She even said that feeling gratitude for the money you've paid out guarantees you will receive more.

The Law of Attraction and Warcraft. It's what made my world go round, and a five-hour opera gave me the perfect opportunity to practice them both.

I looked up from the battle I was playing on Warcraft to see the fat lady singing. Seriously! The last Opera of the season had finally ended. The Opera singers were taking their final bows to a standing ovation from the audience.

They don't call it the *GRAND* Opera for nothing. The sets are huge and magnificent. The world-class singers came from every part of the Earth. The designers are Tony Award winners. And it all showed here in the final bows as the audience stood to applaud the excellent production.

Finally! The opera season was over, and it was time to spend the next three months relaxing until it all started again with the following season. It was finally summer vacation!

Linda Bernstein's book says to count your blessings, and things will get better and be thankful for everything you have because the flipside is that the negative things would increase. I sure don't want anything canceling out the blessings that I should receive.

All summer long, I practiced and practiced. I never argued. I blessed everything and everyone. I praised the people around me. I banished terrible thoughts from my head. If I heard people complaining and arguing, I would walk the other way. I didn't want the negativity to rub off on me. I smiled and imagined myself in a better life.

The people who have practiced the Law of Attraction

claimed to have gotten excellent results using a vision board, which is just a poster board with pictures of the things you want in life. On the vision board were images that depicted stacks of money, yachts, trips to exotic places, and 25,000 square foot houses on acres and acres of land. If it worked for them, what was the harm in trying?

"I can do that! I can do that pretty easily! I can start a vision board!" I thought to myself.

Being the technical geek that I am, I took the vision board one step further. I found a digital picture frame that could constantly display all the pictures that I could cram on to a flash drive. Instead of a vision board, it was my vision picture frame.

I love Newton and science! *For every action, there is an equal and opposite reaction.* If I feel happy and grateful that I have lots of money means that I will have lots of money. Throwing that thought out into the Universe means that the Universe had to throw it back at me.

For every action, there is an equal and opposite reaction. My vision frame contained pictures of 25 million dollar houses. Houses that I would imagine myself walking through each of the myriad of rooms and at the same time making myself and my brain feel grateful that it was mine.

I would walk through the home theater and imagine sitting on the luxurious theater chair, eating popcorn, watching the latest film releases, and strolling through the work out room and the wine cellar. And finally, dipping my toe into the indoor-outdoor endless pool that had a jacuzzi fit for fifteen people.

My vision frame had pictures of yachts and jet skis, expensive cars, private planes, and stacks and stacks of 500 dollar bills. As my brain processed each image, I felt and imagined it was all mine. All the abundance that I deserved.

I imagined a day in this life. I imagined walking down the pathway from my 25 million dollar house, though my patio to the lake below, which had a dock for my yacht's and jet skis. When I mowed my front lawn to my 120,000 dollar house, I would imagine that I was mowing the lawn of my 25 million dollar house.

Every chance I got, I watched these pictures. I became so obsessed with it that I started playing them over and over on my iPhone. I was brainwashing myself into believing this is what I have now, at this moment, in this hour. Right now!

As the summer had ended, it was time to move back into the theater and time for the 2012-2013 opera season. Operas are not small productions. At the very minimum, it took eight 53 foot 18-wheeler trucks to load in just the set pieces. That doesn't include all the lighting gear, carpentry gear, props, and wardrobe. It took weeks and weeks to get a show open and running.

The opera company employed hundreds of people, all on union rates, and could not afford to spare a single minute for mistakes or slowdowns when trying to get a show open for the public. Production companies spend millions on advertising alone. The dates for the shows are engraved in stone. They could not be changed for mere production errors.

And that's when it happened. The mistake that cost the opera company eight hours of re-work just for the lighting crew. One miscalculated error that cost a small fortune to correct. A simple, critical, mathematical error that set the opera company back an entire days' worth of time.

It was a miscalculated digital lighting assignment error. And that's when it hit me in between the eyes. I saw dollar signs. I could fix this error, this critical mistake, to where it would never happen again. I could save production companies all over the world thousands and thousands of dollars and time. It was a simple fix to a simple mistake. It was mathematical. It was logical.

I can build a software program that would error check the math behind the lighting. This digital lighting assignment error would never happen again if production companies used my software. It was the start of DMXWare LLC and *The DMX Chart*.

For the entire 2012-2013 opera season, I didn't play Warcraft. I spent my time coding *The DMX Chart*. Hours and hours of programming to perfect the code, test the code, and build hype about it on social media. When it was finally close to being done, I felt I could start selling the product soon.

People were excited to try it. I was ready to quit the long hours and mentally draining job I had as a lighting programmer for the prominent opera company. I pulled out my pension, which I calculated should sustain me until my company, DMX-Ware LLC, would take over and financially support me.

I saw this in my head. I saw my company succeed. I saw myself making millions. I saw myself in that 25,000 square foot house. I saw myself driving that yacht. I saw myself driving the jet skis and the cars. It was within my reach.

The Universe was giving back to me. It was all true. The Law of Attraction was real! And I took that giant leap off the entrepreneurial cliff.

Now the serpent was craftier than any of the wild animals the Lord God had made. (Genesis 3:1)

He has great power and intelligence, and a host of demons who assist him in his attacks against God's people (Ephesians 6:11)

He is a serpent who can bite us when we least expect it. He is a destroyer. (Revelation 12:11)

Your adversary, the devil, prowls around like a roaring lion, seeking someone to devour. (1 Peter 5:8)

CHAPTER 6

"Now boarding flight 475. Houston to LAX". The announcement knocked Isabella out of her troubled thoughts.

Her background as a psychiatric nurse had started five years ago with the well-known Riverside Advanced Behavioral Health Hospital in League City, Texas. She had been trained to treat individuals with a wide range of emotional, behavioral, developmental, and psychiatric disorders.

She had excellent work ethics and spent the last five years with the psychiatric patients at Riverside analyzing, observing, and writing reports for the Therapists and Psychiatrists to use in their patient treatments.

It wasn't until March of 2014, a mere six months ago, that she took a job at The Rock Nursing Home in Texas City, Texas. They had offered Isabella a bump in pay, so she took the job. Five months after she accepted the position, they fired her.

In raging fits, Isabella called The Rock Nursing Home, repeatedly harassing them and even threatening them to the point that The Rock Nursing Home filed a restraining order against her and got the Webster Police department to put out a warrant for her arrest. Isabella was going to jail if the police ever caught up to her.

In the midst of all that, Isabella applied for unemployment against The Rock Nursing Home and was denied. Isabella couldn't accept that, so with the last little bit of money she had in her bank account, she bought a ticket to California to visit her stepsister Faith.

The trip would do her good to be so close to the ocean. Besides, her nephew was to be married there in the next few days, and she didn't want to miss the happy occasion.

"Last Call for Flight 475, Houston to LAX". Isabella boarded the flight and settled down in her chair for three hour trip to the San Jose Airport in California.

My sister Isabella and I were never really close. She had gone her way in life, and I had gone mine. I was surprised to hear my sister's voice at the other end of the phone line one late evening in September of 2014.

"Hey, sis!"

"Izzy!"

"I need your help, little sister. I am in California going to see Faith, and someone stole my purse at the airport. It had everything in it. My money, my ID. Everything. Can you help me?"

I hadn't heard from my only blood sister in a very long time. Of course, I would do anything to help her. "Tell me what you need. Money? How much? $100, $200? $1000?" Money was not a problem since I got the check from my pension. $1000 was just a drop in the bucket.

"$500 should get me a hotel and a car. Can you wire it to me?"

"Of course, I can! Tell me where to send it."

She gave me the address of a Walgreens near the hotel she wanted to stay. I looked it up online and wired her $500. Once that was done, I called her back. "Ok, you should have it. Just give them this code to pick up the cash. It's 9754387. What else do you need?"

"Food would be nice. There's a Papa John's Pizza near here. Could you order me a pizza and coke and have them send it to this hotel room?"

"Of course, I can!" I laughed. "You must be starving! I'll call you back once it's on the way."

Thank God I am a computer nerd, as I looked up the nearest Papa John's near the hotel's address and placed an order with them. One large pepperoni pizza with extra cheese and a large coke. It was to be delivered within the hour.

Satisfied that she would have food soon, I called Izzy back and told her it was on the way. "What else can I do for you?"

"I was looking at this brochure of a dolphin boat tour that's three hours long. I would love to see the dolphins!"

My sister was always into the sea and dolphins. If she had not studied to become a nurse, I believe she would have been an oceanographer. "So, is this boat tour near where you are at?"

"Oh, yes! There's a tour that leaves at 9:00 a.m. Can you book me a seat on it?"

Now, this was getting weird! My sister that just got mugged, wanted to go on a boat tour to see dolphins. Apparently, she did not want to get to Faith's house anytime soon. "It's probably a stress reliever!" I thought to myself—no big deal. But the more I thought about it, that red flag was slowly running up the flagpole.

Shaking the negative thoughts from my head, I asked her the boat tour's address and looked it up on my computer. "I'll book you a seat for 9:00 a.m., just don't be late because it says on their website that the ticket is nonrefundable."

"Thanks, Sans"

"It's the least I can do. I am glad you are ok. Call me after your boat ride, and please don't be late, or they will leave without you."

"Ok, thanks, Sis! G'Night!"

I woke up the next morning to dis-jointed text messages from Izzy. They looked like she was drunk when she wrote them. Or maybe she didn't know how to text very well. Not everyone is tech-savvy like me. But some text made absolutely no sense at all, and they were from all hours into the night. She apparently did not sleep either. I called the hotel and talked to the manager.

"She left early this morning in a cab. She didn't seem like she was coming back."

"What makes you say that?"

"She left with some guy she met at the bar last night."

"She went to a bar?"

"Yep, met some guys there and came back here to pick up some things and left again."

That red flag that was slowly running up that flagpole? It just hit the top and kept going. This was not good news. "You have my credit card number. Just put her bill on it. Let me know if she comes back, and Thank You for all you did for her."

"Your welcome and I'm sorry for the bad news."

"It's not your fault, but thanks again." I hung up the phone.

A knot was growing in the pit of my stomach. Izzy wasn't acting normal. She never made it to the boat tour. She left with strangers to God only knows where. All I could do was wait to hear from her again.

Two days go by, and I get a voice mail from Izzy. "I made it to Faith's, and the whole freaking family pissed me off, so I left. I'm on my way up north now to see my best friend, Sharon. Love you!"

Isabella's words and actions started to sound all too familiar to me. Many years ago, my blood father swept me up into his bipolar reality. He had grandiose schemes about how he could become a millionaire. He spent every waking hour believing that he had the money to execute them.

God had blessed him with the silver tongue. My father could talk hell into buying ice cubes, and they would profusely thank him for it, never knowing what hit them. Isabella also had this gift.

No, this was not good. Isabella was starting to act just like my real father, who was bipolar. She had all the same symptoms that he did. Sleeplessness, weird off the wall ideas, plots to make millions, and a silver tongue to back it all up.

No, this was not good at all. All I could do was wait for whatever the universe was going to throw back at me.

Isabella sat in the airplane coach section. She was flying back to Houston with a layover in Austin, Texas.

"Where are you headed?" The businessman seated next to Isabella asked.

"I'm going to Houston to start my new business. It will be right on the water in Clear Lake City. I'm going to call it The Hanger, which will employ all Veteran personnel. I'm building it in honor of my Father, Mike Jenkins. He was an airplane pilot in the Air Force."

"That sounds fascinating and very honorable!" The businessman replied.

"Yes, my father was a Veteran. I want The Hanger to be a unique center with dance floors, lights, and a DJ sound system. It will have a place for arts and crafts shows, yoga, bake sales, fundraiser events, car washes, and everything under the sun. I already have the bank's funding, and the perfect spot picked out for it."

"Well, congratulations, and I know it will prosper!"

Isabella peered out the window, "But I think when this plane lands in Austin, I'll just rent a car and drive back to Houston. It's such a beautiful day."

The plane was on its final descent into the Austin-Bergstrom International Airport as Isabella was left scheming on how to make her plans for The Hanger a reality.

"Thank you for flying Continental, and enjoy your stay in Austin." The captain's voice came over the PA, startling Isabella out of her visions for the future.

She was determined more than ever to make her plans work. "But first things first, I need to rent a car!" She thought to herself as she made her way to the car rental counter and pulled out her cell phone to call one of her best friends that went to high school with her. "Rachel! What's going on, Chica? It's Isabella!"

"Izzy! How's it going?"

"Hey, I'm in Austin, and my car was just stolen along with my purse. I didn't know who else to call."

"Oh, my heavens! Are you ok?"

"Yes, I had gone into a convenience store just for a second, and I turned around, and my car was gone. I have no money or any way to get back to Houston."

"Oh, Isabella, I am so sorry. What can I do to help you?"

"Can you rent me a car? I'll pay you back when I get back to Houston."

"Sure! That's not a big deal." Rachel owned a wrecker driver service in Houston and knew what it was like to be without wheels.

"Cool, I'm sitting at the car place now. Do you mind giving them your info?"

"Not at all. Hand the phone over to them."

"Oh, thank you, Rachel! Thank you! You're a lifesaver!"

Isabella hopped into the newly rented red Chevrolet Impala, rolled down the windows, and turned the radio to her favorite country music station. She was high on life, and the day was gorgeous! She punched the gas pedal to the floorboard and sped 120 mph towards Houston singing, hootin' and hollerin' as only a Texan can do.

It was late at night, just 32 miles outside of North West Houston, when Isabella realizes that the car was running on fumes. Her gas gage was sitting on empty. "You've got to be kidding me." She screamed, banging her hands on the steering wheel, "this is just perfect."

She notices the sign on the side of the road for Gas - Food - Lodging and Love's Truck Stop. It's was just a quarter-mile down the road. Slowly she exited the freeway, pulled into the Love's Truck Stop parking lot, and made her way to the nearest gas pump and parked.

Grabbing her purse off the rental car's front seat, she made her way into the Love's Truck Stop sundry shop. As she browsed the jewelry, T-shirts, and various Texas paraphernalia they had for sale, she spied the coffee shop just off to her left. "That's exactly what I need right now," she said to the coffee shop waitress as she approached the entrance.

"Well, here's a menu, my friend, let me show you to a table! Just follow me!"

Isabella followed the waitress to a quaint little table for two. The table sat next to a window that overlooked a well-lit pasture of horses. "This is perfect! You know I'm in the market to buy a couple of horses for my new club I am building. Those horses over there would fit right in! Do you know if they are for sale?"

"No, darlin', I wouldn't know nothin' about that. Can I get you a cup of coffee?"

"Yes'm. Black with a little sugar."

"Comin right up, Darlin'."

Isabella sat there staring out the window admiring the horses, sipping her coffee, and writing in her journal. *I can't believe that The Rock fired me... Really?* She underlined the word "really" six times and circled it. *That's insane. Who do they think they are? I'm the best psych nurse on this planet!* She underlined the word best three times and drew a smiley face next to it just as the waitress came back to refill her coffee cup.

"Can I get you something to eat?"

"That would be awesome. I'll have a steak with eggs on the side, biscuits with gravy, and hash browns."

"How would you like that steak cooked?"

"Medium well!"

"It'll be right out."

"Thank you! I appreciate that!"

After Isabella ate her meal, the waitress returned to refilled her coffee cup. She placed the bill face down on the table. "I'll be back in a little bit to pick that up."

"Thank you," Isabella said as she picked up the bill and looked at the $25.76 that she owed to the coffee shop. She knew she didn't have any cash on her. She didn't have any money to her name. Not in her bank accounts, not in her purse, not in her rental car. All her credit cards were maxed out. Isabella was broke.

Somewhere inside her brain, she knew this, but her bipolar brain would not register that fact. So, Isabella just sat there writing in her journal about her new business, The Hanger, smoking cigarettes, drinking more coffee, and visiting with whoever would sit next to her that would listen to her wild dreams.

After about an hour, the waitress came back and asked Isabella to pay her bill. Isabella pretended to rummage thru her purse. "I must have left my wallet back at the rental place. If you don't mind waiting a few hours until the bank opens, I can get your money then."

"Sure, no problem." She poured Isabella another cup of coffee, turned on her heel, and proceeded directly to the night manager's office.

"Hey Brandon," She knocked on the manager's door. Seeing that he wasn't busy, she proceeded to walk in. "There is this woman that ordered and ate dinner. She has been sitting there ever since sipping coffee for over two hours. I asked if there was a problem and could she please pay her bill. She claims she left her wallet at the car rental place back in Austin, and she has to wait until the banks open at 6:00 a.m. to get money to pay her bill."

"I'll take care of it," Brandon said as he got up and started walking in Isabella's direction. "Hi. My name is Brandon. I am the night manager here at Love's Truck Stop. Is there a problem?"

Izzy looked at him and smiled sweetly, "I was trying to explain that to your waitress. See, I am going thru a divorce, and I have to wait for the bank to open, or I have to wait for my attorney to answer my call because my accounts were frozen due to the divorce."

"I understand, miss. Please let me know when you get ahold of your bank or your lawyer and can pay your bill."

Isabella smiled brightly, "Can do!"

Brandon made his way back to his office and dialed the po-

74

lice. Ten minutes later, the Waller County Sheriff's Department pulled into the Truck Stop.

"She's over there." Brandon pointed to Isabella, who still sat sipping coffee and chatting with whoever would listen to her.

The Sargent made his way to her. "Can you come with me, Miss?"

"Why, I haven't done anything wrong."

"Please don't make a scene and leave with me peacefully," he said, grabbing Isabella's forearm and proceeded to lead her out to the backseat of his police car. "Do you have any ID?"

Isabella dug in her purse and handed her Texas Driver's License over to the Sargent. He shut the door with her seated in the backseat and called her driver's license number into dispatch.

Dispatch ran a search on Isabella's license, "She has a warrant out for her arrest in Texas City," the dispatch officer told the Sargent. "Looks like it's a harassment charge."

The Sargent opened the back door of the police car, "Step out of the car, turn around and put your hands behind your back."

Isabella got out of the car and tried to plead her case with the Sargent. "Really, officer, this isn't necessary I can pay for the damned dinner. I explained that to the stupid waitress. I am just waiting for the banks to open."

He repeated the command. "Turn around and put your hands behind your back. NOW!"

As Isabella made no motions to comply with his command, the officer grabbed her left arm and spun her around, slapping on the handcuffs. "You're under arrest."

"What the hell for?"

"There is an open warrant in Texas City for your arrest." He not so gently put her cuffed body back into the backseat of the police car and locked the door.

"Oh My God, you have got to be kidding me." She wailed at the top of her lungs over and over. She finally stopped when she was deposited at the jail cell that awaited her in Waller County, Texas.

She was immediately processed and sent before the 506th District Court's Magistrate on Oct. 10, 2014. The Magistrate informed her that she had out of county charges specifically in Galveston County for harassment. That means Galveston County has first dibs on her if any police force picked her up.

The court Magistrate looked at Isabella and stated, "You have the right to remain silent, the right to have an attorney present during any interview with peace officers or attorneys representing the state, and the right to terminate the interview at any time. You are not required to make a statement. Any statement made by you may be used against you in court. You have the right to retain an attorney. If you are unable to employ an attorney, you have the right to request the appointment of an attorney by completing an assessment form. Bond is set at the amount of $500 surety or cash." The Magistrate proceeded to slam down the gavel. "Court dismissed."

Isabella sat in her cell in the Waller County Jail. The only way she was allowed to communicate to the guards was through an Inmate Request Form that would eventually be given to the jailer's guards. In turn, the guards would read the request and act or not act on what was requested. Either way, the Inmate Request Form was sent back to the inmate with or without the guard's response.

Isabella sat in her jail cell, staring at the cement walls and cast iron bars that were her new home. As the jailer on duty passed by her cell, Isabella called out to her, "Please officer, may I use the phone? Please?"

"You've read the rules missy, any request you make needs to be written on the Inmate Request Form."

"But your right here, and I am asking now. Please may I use the phone?"

"No, fill out an Inmate Request Form." and with that, the guard went on her way.

Isabella finally got ahold of the sacred Inmate Request Form from the jailer and wrote, "Need to use the phone. Please may I use the phone at the officer's desk? I've been given the phone numbers to a few Galveston County Bail Bondsman. I have monies in my property. Thank you, I have a $500 Surety case/bond for a misdemeanor."

That should get their attention! All she had to do now was wait.

Lieutenant Rochen sat at the Guards Desk, bored to tears. She had five more hours on her shift at the Waller County Jail for Women and not much else to do there to keep her awake. "Hey Lindsey, did the jailer bring the Inmate Request Forms back from her rounds yet?" Lieutenant Rochen knew that those forms were a sure-fire source of entertainment.

"Yep! She just dropped them off. Wanna look at them, Lieutenant?"

Lieutenant Rochen had a massive grin on her face. Like it was finally time to open all the Christmas presents. "It's what I live for, Lindsey! Reading all those requests from those who have no rights." And with that, she burst out in laughter as Lindsey handed her the stack of Inmate Request Forms.

After reading half of them, she came across Isabella's, "Hey, look at this one from cell block #54! This poor woman thinks she's in some kind of fancy hotel! She wants to use our phone to call her lawyer. She says she has money. Do you think she's trying to bribe us?" The lieutenant handed the piece of paper to Lindsey to read.

"That's always the case with the new ones. They think they are all high and mighty when they get here. Wantin' to boss us around like we are their maids. It's downright comical! They either get it or they don't until we have to put them in their place."

"Give that back to me, Lindsey," the lieutenant took out her pen and began to write. *No. You were given your free phone call when you were booked in here. You contacted your spouse. You can either use the phones in the tank to contact a bondsman, or your family can contact a bondsman. OR wait to be transported to the Galveston County Jail.*

That should shut her up for a while!

It was hours before Isabella saw the jailer making her rounds again. "Officer! Officer!" She yelled and waved her hands outside the bars to get her attention. "Over here!"

Slowly the jailer made her way over to Izzy's cell and handed her the Inmate Request Form she had filled out. "Here ya go, missy! Enjoy!"

Isabella opened the folded piece of paper and read their response, "I don't get it," she said aloud, not caring who heard her, "they have a phone sitting right there on their desk. A phone they hardly use. What's it gonna hurt if I made one little phone call. Huh?"

Several days later, Isabella flagged down the jailer to get another Inmate Request Form. Izzy writes. *As suggested by Lt. Rochen, I should contact my family to meet me in Galveston. I need you to activate the phone in this tank. Please! Or allow me to use yours.*

The jailer made her way back to the Guards Desk and handed the stack of forms over to the Lieutenant. "Hey, Lindsey! Guess who wrote us another love letter." She handed the paper to Lindsay.

"Let me guess.... cellblock #54!"

"You are correct, ma'am! She still wants to use our phone." Just as the lieutenant finished that sentence, the intercom came to life.

It was Isabella on the other end, "Ummm, excuse me, peoples. Is anyone there? Hello? Hey, I need to use the phone. Could you please turn the damn thing on? Hello?"

Lieutenant Rochen had steam coming out her ears, "I can't believe the nerve of this woman. Hand me back the form.

The lieutenant furiously wrote back. *The phones are off due to Court. They will stay off until Court and Transports are over. Using the intercoms for NO Emergency are reasons for disciplinary actions. You got a copy of the Inmate rules and regulations. I know you got one because I was the one who booked you in, and I have signed papers that say you got it. If you have failed to read it, that is your problem, but that will not stop me from running disciplinary actions on you. I have sent another copy for you to read.*

Isabella sat in her cell, wondering where her court-appointed attorney was. She had asked for one yesterday, but no one answered her back. Isabella was bored and anxious all at the same time. She wished she could smoke a cigarette and have a nice cup of hot coffee. But everyone was so rude around here. She knew they wouldn't bring her anything. Perhaps if she were friendlier to the Guards, she could get them to bring her these things.

She grabbed her last Inmate Request Form and wrote; *please consider my offering of a solution and not a problem. Please allow me one, maybe two outside calls to my attorney cousin that lives in Galveston. Everybody will benefit. There will be less time for Waller Staff interventions. There will be no need to wash my filthy clothes. It will take less money that the state spends to house and transfer a FIRST-TIME offense, which is a misdemeanor, and which by the way was in the form of a text message, and the text message was considered harassment in Texas City, Texas (Galveston County).*

Hours and hours passed before she got her response back. *We can't do anything for you because these are not Waller County charges.*

Izzy has always been a God-fearing woman. Unlike me, she prays and goes to Church pretty regular, so when Waller County finally picked Izzy up to transfer her to Galveston County Jail, Isabella writes in her journal a note to her friends in the Waller County cell block as she is being transferred to the Galveston County Jail system.

    Ladies of cell block #54,
    It has been my exclusive pleasure to have spent time with each of you! (smile) God loves you - He knows your loves. He hears your

cries. He feels your pain. He will restore your losses tenfold!! He will make way for you. Love Him, trust Him in all your ways, and he will direct your paths!

After a two-and-a-half-hour road trip to the Galveston County Jail, she was deposited into her new home. With no more Inmate Request Forms to keep her entertained, Isabella sat down and wrote a letter to God.

Oh my God, what has happened to me? I am broken, but not apart from you. I have been hurt deeply, but I do not mourn the many losses. I have a family who has shunned and persecuted me. I do not care. I've made so many new friends and acquaintances. Each and in their own way are a blessing to me. What do you want, Lord? I give you my own life and my child. What did I not do? What? Tell me! I will do it! Lord, Oh Lord, PLEASE show me what I cannot see, feel, or hear. Please, I beg you. I loved my Dad. I looked up to him. I trusted him. Why! Why! WHY! HOW has he managed to single-handedly run off my family? Why did you allow this to happen? What, if anything, can I DO to stop this? Please, Lord! Help me. I cannot do this anymore ALONE.

"Inmate #373379," the guard yelled down the cellblock and stopped in front of Isabella's cell. The shouting startled Izzy out of her reverie. "Please stand and place your hands behind your back, then walking backward, place your hands through the food slot."

"Oh my God, what the freaking hell is this now?" Isabella yelled at the guard.

"Just do it now or face additional time on your pending sentence."

"Where are we going?" Isabella pleads as she does what the guard ordered her to do. She placed her hands behind her back and then pushed them through the food slot.

"You're ordered to appear before the Court Magistrate." The guard snapped the cuffs on Isabella's wrists. "Now, take four steps into your cell so I can unlock the door."

Isabella took four steps forward. The loud clanking of the heavy metal lock being moved jarred Isabella into reality. She started shaking uncontrollably. The guard grabbed her upper right arm to lead her to the Court Magistrate.

Isabella was led to sit in a pew that was positioned in front of the Magistrates bench. The only other person in the courtroom besides the Magistrate was the bailiff who barked, "Inmate #373379 approach the bench."

Isabella stood from her seat in the courtroom as the guard took hold of her right arm and led her to the front of the Magistrates' seat. Her court-appointed attorney stood next to her side, as the Court Magistrate monotonically states, "This court by the authority of the State of Texas does believe that one Isabella Jenkins, hereinafter styled the Defendant, heretofore, on or about the 4th day of October 2014, in the county of Galveston and in the State of Texas did then and there harass, annoy, alarm, abuse, torment or embarrass The Rock Nursing Home and cause the telephone of The Rock Nursing Home to ring repeatedly against the peace and dignity of the State of Texas. How do you plead?"

Isabella's court-appointed attorney pleads with the Magistrate, "Your Honor, I respectfully ask that the court determine the mental state of the defendant, Isabella Jenkins Schmidt, before making a sentencing judgment."

The Magistrate shuffles through all the paperwork presented in the case against Isabella, "After careful examination of the evidence and the complaint, this court orders the inmate, Isabella Jenkins Schmidt, to comply with a mental assessment. Upon completion of the assessment, this court will make a judgment on the pending sentence. Isabella is to be released on her own recognizance, with the promise to appear at all future court dates. Failure to appear will result in an immediate arrest." The Magistrate slams down the gavel, "Court dismissed."

The guard took hold of Isabella's arm, "I am taking you back to your cell to await your discharge papers. Once the discharge desk receives the papers, you will be processed out."

"How long does that take?"

"24 to 48 hours, depending on the discharge desk. The discharge coordinator will conduct a brief assessment. Then you will be free to go."

After fourteen hours of pacing in her cell, the guard finally escorted Isabella to the discharge desk. The attending Sargent looks at Isabella and states, "Inmate #373379, let me see your wrist band."

All inmates are tagged with a wrist band that has their vital information on it and their inmate SPN number, or System Person Number. That number will follow them for the rest of their lives. Isabella presented her left wrist to the Sargent so she could scan the information it contained and verify that Isabella was who the court was releasing.

"OK, Ms. Schmidt, this first page states that you must go to Horizon General Hospital on October 15, 2014, for your mental health assessment. Failure to do so will result in a warrant for your immediate arrest. Sign here."

Isabella signed her name at the place indicated by the Sargent.

"This states that you promise to appear before the court Magistrate on November 6th, 2014, for sentencing. Sign here."

Again, Isabella signed her name, acknowledging her understanding.

"These are the belongings you had when you were arrested. Please make sure all of your things are in this bag. If they are, sign here."

The Sargent handed Isabella a large clear plastic bag that contained all her clothes, jewelry, and papers. Isabella looked through the bag, then signed her name to the acknowledgment.

"You are free to go. Exit through that door." The Sargent points to the exit door.

Isabella resisted the urge to break out in a flat run as she went through it.

On October 15, 2014, as ordered by the court, Horizon General Hospital starts assessing Isabella's mental health. The hospital's Mental Health Mental Retardation Authority (MHMRA) psychologist orders an MMPI, the Minnesota Multiphasic Personality Inventory. The MMPI is a psychological test that assesses personality traits and psychopathology. This test is primarily intended to test people who are suspected of having mental health and bipolar issues.

When the doctors completed the test with Isabella, they found that she was indeed bipolar. The attending MHMRA doctor set up Isabella's next psychiatric appointment for October 24, 2014, and ordered her to take the prescription medication called Abilify for her Bipolar episodes. Then the doctors petitioned the court.

To the Honorable Judge of said Court:

I.   *Doctors at MHMRA petition the court pursuant to Texas Health & Safety Code Section 574.104 that seeks an order to authorize the administration of psychoactive medication to Isabella Jenkins Schmidt, the "patient," and they respectfully show that*

II. *The patient Isabella Jenkins Schmidt has been diagnosed with the following conditions: "Bipolar due to psychotic features."*

III. *Petitioner has determined that administration of the following class(es) of psychoactive medication marked below is the proper course of treatment for and in the best interest of the Patient: "antipsychotics."*

IV. *Petitioner believes the patient lacks the capacity to decide regarding psychoactive medication administration for the following reasons: "Severely psychotic delusions regarding her son and parents."*

V.   *Petitioner believes that if the patient is not treated with the class(es) of psychoactive medications specified in paragraph III above, the patient's progno-*

sis is: "poor."

VI.   *Petitioner believes that if the patient is not administered the class(es) of psychoactive medication specified in paragraph III above, the consequences will be: "severely poor continued delusions in functionality."*

VII.   *Petitioner has considered the following alternatives to psychoactive medications to treatment of Patient: "counseling."*

VIII.   *Petitioner has determined that the alternatives listed in paragraph VII will not be as effective as the administration of psychoactive medication for the following reasons: " Severely psychotic agitated functionality."*

Isabella never made her next court-appointed date on November 6, 2014, as ordered by the Magistrate. Galveston County put out a warrant for her arrest.

CHAPTER 7

After her release from jail, Isabella stayed with a friend named Keith in the Kensington Place Apartments in Houston when she received the report from her mental assessment that she had taken at MHMRA back on October 15, 2014. In the report, the psychologist from MHMRA demanded that Isabella be medicated for being bipolar. He suggested Prozac, or possibly Abilify.

She had read it over and over again. Each time she read the report, more and more steam came out of her ears. She had read it so much that she started scribbling in the margins to justify why she did not believe that the report was correct. She had full intentions of sending her rebuttal to Horizon General Hospital's Patient Advocates, condemning the psychologist who worked under MHMRA. Izzy decides to write the Patient Advocates a letter.

I do not believe I need an injectable dose of Abilify. I have willingly taken Abilify and Ativan routine doses. I have taken Buspar in the past under Dr. Blankar's care (psych) and did quite well. I have taken Lithium 300 after I had my baby in 1995 for Post Paternal Depression. PPD was not covered on my insurance plan, but BIPOLAR was. So, Dr. Lisa Clarke labeled me bipolar to keep me in house to be treated for postpartum depression (1995).

I was diagnosed with PTSD in 1990. My then alcoholic husband had a blackout and destroyed our home, then beat on me. It triggered memories of my natural father, Mike Jenkins chasing my mother with a butcher knife and breaking out windows during my 4 to 12-year-old stage of life.

I have taken the MMPI - the Minnesota Multiphasic Personality Inventory. I am not bipolar. I am more like clinically depressed with situational stress. I missed my appointment with the Psychologist at MHMRA on 10-24-14. I rescheduled it to 11-3-14. I understand my insurance will not cover Abilify and Out of Patient costs of $2200.00. I will take a large dose of Boletus if necessary to satisfy the doctors at MHMRA and the courts, but I don't have $2200.00 - or - the doctors could call my family members who desperately believe I need the medication and have them pay for it.

Isabella couldn't take much more of this. Upon impulse, she decided that all her clothes, money, food, and everything else she needed were at Mom and Raymond's house. She hopped in her Jeep and headed to the Southwest side of Houston.

Parking in front of the house, she walked up to the front door and rang the doorbell. Minutes passed, and no one came to the door, so she rang the bell repeatedly. Giving up, she started banging on the door and the window next to it. "Heyyyyyy! Let me in! Preston? Mom? Raymond?" With her fists, she pounded harder and harder on the front door. Finally, screaming at the top of her lungs, "Someone answer the door!"

Preston, her son, was inside watching and listening to her antics. He had no intention of letting his mother into the house, especially since Janice and Raymond, his Grandparents, were not home. Faith had called them when Isabella was in California and told them of her insane escapades and all the horrible criminal things she did when she was in California. Preston knew from experience that his mother was on a manic depressant bipolar rampage again.

"Preston! I see you peeking through the window. OPEN THE DOOR!" Preston didn't answer. "Come on Preston, all my credit cards, cash, clothes, and medications, are in there. I need them, son! Please, Preston, open the door."

Preston still refused and didn't answer.

"Damnit, Preston, I will break this door down. OPEN IT NOW!"

Preston did not want to hurt his Mom, but he knew it was the bipolar disease that made her this way, and he might not have a choice. When he couldn't take anymore, he went outside with his loaded handgun and pointed it at Isabella's forehead. "You need to leave NOW!"

Isabella started to back away with her eyes fixed on the boy. She walked slowly backwards to her Jeep that was parked in the street. The passenger's side door was unlocked, and Isabella got in. Her hands were shaking as she called the police from her cell phone.

Minutes later, she watched as a Houston Police Department cruiser came speeding down the street towards her. They pulled into the driveway, and two officers got out. Preston, still standing in the driveway, was there to meet them.

"What's the problem here, son?" The First Officer asked Preston.

"That lunatic wanted in the house," he pointed to Isabella in the Jeep. "I don't know who she is anymore. I asked her to leave, and she wouldn't. So, I pointed my gun at her to make her leave."

The second officer walked to the Jeep parked in the street and asked Isabella the same question, "What's going on here, Ma'am?"

"This is my house. I have been living here for the last six months. That is my son." She said, pointing to Preston, "He pointed a gun to my head and won't let me in the house to get my stuff."

"Can you prove you have been living here and this is your house? Do you have a driver's license?"

"My purse was stolen in California along with all my things. I barely made it back to Houston. You can call my Mom. She will verify that I live here."

Isabella gave the Officer Mom's cell phone number. When he called it, Raymond answered, "No, Sir, Officer, Isabella Jenkins is not welcome in our house."

The officer turned and faced Isabella, "Your stepdad said you are not welcome here."

"What do you mean not welcome here? I have been living here since early April due to my divorce situation."

"I'm sorry, Ma'am, but you will have to leave."

"But all my things are inside that house."

"I'm sorry, Ma'am, you will have to leave now."

With reluctance, Isabella started the Jeep and took off down the street. "I need a place to think," she thought to herself as she drove to the IHop restaurant.

The front door greeter took her to a table in the far corner and handed her a menu. "What can I get you to start with?"

"Just black coffee for now. Thanks." Isabella knew that it always helped her to see things more clearly when she wrote something down. She took out her notebook and wrote:

Charges for Raymond Davis (my stepdad):

1) No notice to evacuate after living there for five months, which was "welcomed" by him.

2) Emotional pain and humiliation by the Houston Police Department Officers.

3) Damages incurred: Unable to attain monies, credit cards, keys, clothing, RX Meds from home.

The more she wrote, the madder she got.

Unable to pay upgrade with T-Mobile. I had to reschedule the appointment with the court-ordered Doctor. I will have to pay extra now. I had to pawn items for food, gas, and a trip to Biloxi Casinos in Louisiana, costing me $500. Unable to pay the storage bill. Son put a gun to my head.

She paused and looked at what she had just written in the notebook. Preston. My Son. My Son pointed a gun to my head. My Son tried to kill me. My own Son.

She was furious at this. In a rage, she slammed down some change on the table and left. Isabella drove as fast as the Jeep would take her down the residential neighborhood where her parents lived. Her wheels squealed as she turned the corner onto their street.

She eyed her son's car that was parked in her parent's driveway. The front of his car was facing the street. Her foot slammed the gas pedal down to the floorboard. As her tires squealed in protest, she turned the Jeep into the driveway and rammed her son's car, head-on, at full speed. "That will teach the little fart blossom to point a gun to my head." She laughed out loud. She backed out of the driveway with the bumper of her car hanging on by a thread and headed to her friend Keith's house at the Kensington Place Apartments.

Preston was sitting in his room playing Call of Duty on his Xbox when he heard the crash. He ran out of the house just in time to see his mother's Jeep turning the corner with her bumper flopping in the wind. His car was almost totaled. He called 911, who in turn sent out a police officer to investigate.

"You said your mother did this?" The officer questioned Preston.

"Yes, her name is Isabella Jenkins Schmidt, and she is bipolar and on a manic rampage."

"Did you see her actually do this?"

"Not really. I was inside playing on my Xbox and heard the crash. I ran outside and looked down the street just in time to see her Jeep turning the corner. Her bumper was really damaged."

"OK, Son, we'll keep an eye out for her. The best we can charge her with is criminal mischief."

"As long as she goes to jail and stays there, that's all that matters."

Later that evening, Preston got a call from the Police, "Preston, we picked your Mom up, and we are charging her with criminal mischief. She will go before the judge tomorrow."

"Thank you for telling me this."

"You're welcome, Son. I wish there were more we could do for you."

Isabella was released the next night on her own recognizance as she promised to appear before the judge at a later date in time to plead her case. Weary from the whole ordeal, Izzy made her way to The Ruby Legacy Inn near Walnut Street in Webster, Texas.

She strolled into the lobby and approached the front desk. "Yes, Ma'am, Can I help you?"

"I would like a room, please."

"No problem," the clerk said as he started looking through the reservation reports to find her a room, "Will a single room with a queen-size bed be sufficient for you?"

"I think that will be just fine, sir!"

"And how would you like to pay for the room?"

"Well, I have points that I have acquired from a stay in Rockport, Texas, back in August of 2014. My husband and I were vacationing there."

"Yes, Ma'am, would you like to use the points now?"

"Yes, sir."

"And what name would these points be under?"

"Schmidt! "

The clerk looked up the name on his computer, "Thomas Schmidt?"

"That would be him!"

"Yes, Ma'am," he pulled the printout of her room fees, and the points applied deducted from it. He hands the paper and a pen to Isabella, "Please sign at the bottom while I get the keys to your room."

Isabella picked up the pen, and hastily signed the paper. Grabbing the keys to her room, she turned on her heel, telling the clerk, "Have a nice day!" as she exits the lobby to go and find her hotel room.

In the meantime, the company that facilitated the hotel points program sent an email message to the rightful owner of the points Isabella just used. Thomas Schmidt, Isabella's x-husband.

Thomas read the email and was furious. He called the cops and reported Isabella for identity theft since she used his name and stole his points without his permission.

Isabella had just filed the bathtub and was fixing to slip into the warm bubbles when the Galveston County Constables beat down her hotel door. "Ma'am, this is Galveston County Constables. We need to speak to you about Thomas Schmidt. Open the door, please."

Isabella hurriedly slipped on some clothes and opened the door. She was wondering what might have happened to her x-husband to make the cops come searching for her. Did he die? Was he in trouble? What is going on here?

"Are you Isabella Jenkins Schmidt?"

"Yes, what do you want?"

"Turn around and put your hands behind your back."

"Why? I haven't done anything wrong."

The officer grabbed her left wrist and spun her around, and slapped on the handcuffs. "Ma'am, you are under arrest for using your ex-husband's points without his permission. He has filed identity theft on you."

"Oh, My God! You have got to be kidding me. Those are my points too."

"Tell it to the judge. Let's go."

The officers read her the Miranda Rights, put her in the police cruiser's back seat, and took her to the Galveston County Jail.

It's strange how the Texas court systems work. People who do wrong get released back into the public on only their promise to return and be judged for the wrong that they did. Do you think they will return? Does the court system take into consideration the long list of charges against the wrongdoer before releasing them back into the public?

The short answer is NO. Isabella was released from jail the next night on her own recognizance with the promise to return for her appointed court date. Her rap sheet was growing longer and longer with each and every day.

Over the next week, Isabella's deranged rampage continued to escalate. She set out to terrorize her parents and her son with phone messages all hours of the day and night. Sometimes she would just call at two in the morning. When someone picked up, she would say nothing until they hung up.

She redialed Mom and Raymond's number, and the answering machine picked up. Isabella was in a mood. "Well, good Christian people, it is now 4:00 a.m., and I have to get up at 5:00 a.m. to go to work. But guess what! I don't have a car. I don't have a car because you wouldn't open your door to let me in, so they took me to jail and towed my car away. I hope you had nothing to say to the police that came to your door when I left." Beep.

The next night Isabella, enraged with hate, wrote vulgar, nasty things in shoe polish on Janice and Raymond's cars. She threw raw eggs at their vehicles. Nothing was beneath her. She even asked a neighbor, who lived across the street from Mom and Raymond, for some chalk. The neighbor thought she meant well, so he gave her their child's basket full of sidewalk chalk. Isabella proceeded to write *Raymond is a pedophile* up and down the street and on the sidewalks of where Janice and Raymond lived in attempts to shame them. Nothing was sacred to her.

The same night she called them again at 2:00 a.m. The answering machine picked up. "Hey, Ray, Baby! I'm just curious. What did you tell your neighbors when I wrote rapist all over your driveway and your car? Did you tell them that I am bipolar? Well, it's going to be funny when I file a police report. I know it's been over thirty years, but if it humiliates you the way you have freaking humiliated me... so be it." Beep.

And again, that same morning at 4:00 a.m. "You know? The more I think about it, stepdaddy, I really don't want to humiliate my sister any more than you have already humiliated her. You need to meet me at the courthouse at ten o'clock in the morning. And you're going to give me five thousand dollars. And if you don't, Raymond, I swear to God, I will put your freaking ass in jail. Do you hear me? I'm serious." Beep.

And again, thirty minutes later. "You better get yourself blessed, and you better get you some peace because I'm coming after you with everything that I have, Raymond. EVERYTHING that I have, Raymond. I will own your home. I will own your cars, and your ass will be in jail." Beep.

And again, fifteen minutes later. "And another thing Ray Baby. I'm calling John Schafton too. You know the family lawyer. Wouldn't he like to know you raped your daughter! Yeah. John Schafton. You call his ass. You're gonna need him because you're going down, Raymond. I am sick of you. You can't touch me because your weak, and you're going down. And the second I can get my mother from underneath your claws, I will. You tell her that. You make me sick. You lay one hand on her, and I will personally strangle you." Beep.

And that afternoon. "I'm finally attending Texas A&M, and I will get my Ph.D. in Hospital Management in three short years. Oh, and by the way, I just bought an airplane, and I am taking flying lessons." Beep.

Janice sat there listening to her daughter's messages as the tears streamed down her face in waves.

On November 18th, 2014, Isabella pulled into the parking lot of The Rock Nursing Home. She was still upset about them firing her and then denying her unemployment benefits. Isabella got out of her Jeep with full intentions of confronting them with it. The receptionist at The Rock Nursing Home recognized Isabella as soon as she stepped through the front entrance. She called the police.

Within minutes the Texas City Police Department had Isabella in handcuffs and took her to jail for criminal trespassing on The Rock Nursing Home's property.

"Isabella Jenkins Schmidt?" The bailiff said to the defendants that filled the room awaiting arraignment. Isabella stood up, and the bailiff grabbed her right arm, escorting her to the front of the judge's bench.

"Isabella Jenkins Schmidt, you are charged with criminal trespassing on The Rock Nursing Home's property. What do you have to say for yourself?"

Isabella stood before the Judge and attempted to explain her side of the story. "Your Honor, I was on the way to see Nanette in Texas City, Texas. Nanette lives behind The Medical Center and The Rock Nursing Home. I ran out of gas between the Medical Center and The Rock. I was closer to The Rock than the hospital, and it was cold and raining, so I entered The Rock and went to the front desk to use the phone and call Nanette or a wrecker service. Tonya recognized me and called the police, stating that I was trespassing on their property. I had no intentions of any type of harm."

The Judge glared at Isabella, "The Rock Nursing Home has a standing restraining order on you. You were to stay away from The Rock Nursing Home's property. If you came within 500 feet of their property, you would be arrested for criminal trespassing. Which you did, and you were. This case will be rescheduled for November 21, 2014, three days from today."

SLAM went the gavel, and the police officers hauled her off to jail.

Isabella was thrown into a holding cell for the next three days, where she sat stewing on her hatred and anger for The Rock and the blasted court system. On the third day, she was brought before the Magistrate of Texas City.

"Isabella Jenkins Schmidt, you are charged with criminal trespassing, how do you plead?'" Isabella looked at her court-appointed attorney, and he mouthed *Not Guilty* to prompt her. "Isabella Jenkins Schmidt, I ask you again, how do you plead?"

"Not Guilty, your Honor."

"Mr. District Attorney, state your case."

The DA for the state stood, "By the authority of the State of Texas, we do believe that one Isabella Jenkins Schmidt, hereinafter styled the Defendant, heretofore, on or about the 18th of November, 2014, in the county of Galveston and in the State of Texas did then and there intentionally or knowingly enter a building of another, namely, The Rock Nursing Home without the effective consent of the said The Rock Nursing Home and the said Defendant had notice that the entry was forbidden against the peace and dignity of the State."

The Magistrate glared at Isabella, "Bail is set at $500 with the promise to appear for the court date hearing on December 17, 2014. Bailiff remove the defendant." Slam went the gavel. "Court dismissed."

Isabella was sent to the out-processing room, where she signed her life away with the promise to appear on the appointed date to plead her case further.

Janice and Raymond couldn't take much more of Isabella's manic rampages. They had to find a way to help her. They had to find a way to get her to take the medication that would return her brain waves back to normal.

"Look, Jan, we need a way to get her to take her bipolar medication. Without it, her episodes will only get worse."

"I know that, Raymond, but how?"

"We can petition the State to have the Court order her into a mental facility." Raymond sighed, "It's the only way. She's been in jail so many times now, and the court keeps resetting her cases. She's becoming a flight risk. We all know she will not show up for any of her court dates, even if she remembers she has them."

He searched Jan's face for some kind of support, then continued, "Look, Jan, all we have to do is fill out this paperwork that I already downloaded from the Court System." Janice looked mortified as Raymond continued, "If the psychologist at the mental facility does not find sufficient probable cause, she will be released pending a final hearing. But we know that won't happen. They will definitely find that she is bipolar. We both know that to be true."

Janice's tears flowed freely now as she watched Raymond write in the petition to the Court all of the terrible things Isabella had done to them and others.

"I stated in the petition that if Isabella becomes agitated that her criminal mischief increases exponentially." Raymond passed the papers to Janice, "You have to sign them too."

Janice reluctantly signed the papers that would commit her oldest daughter to a mental facility and handed them back to Raymond.

"I'm going to give these to the judge today personally. Are you coming with me?"

Janice couldn't think of anything else to defend her daughter with, "Of course, Raymond, let me get my things, and we'll go."

Neither spoke as they drove the 25 miles to the Harris County Criminal Courthouse in downtown Houston. After Raymond submitted the paperwork to the clerk, they only had to wait a few hours for the Judge's decision.

"Mr. And Mrs. Davis?" The Bailiff inquired.

"Yes, we are here."

"The Judge will see you now."

Raymond and Janice stood before the Judge in the criminal court building. The Judge declared to them, "Mr. and Mrs. Davis, I am so sorry for everything you have had to deal with regarding Isabella. It is ordered by this court that Isabella Jenkins Schmidt is to be held in immediate protective custody and to be immediately transported to the Harris County Psychiatric Center. The Patient Mental Health Facility shall detain her pending further orders from this Court."

The Judge slammed down the gavel so hard that it made Janice jump. The warrant for Isabella's arrest was issued. It was now up to law enforcement to find her and transport her to the mental facility.

Isabella showed up a few nights later at Janice and Raymond's house, wanting to speak to her son Preston.

"Call the police now, Janice," Raymond said.

As Janice dialed 911, Raymond went outside to try and stall her, "Izzy! What's going on?"

"I want to speak to my son. I know he's in there."

"Izzy, he doesn't want to talk to you. Not after you totaled his car."

"He had that coming. How does your own son point a gun to your head and threaten to kill you anyway?"

"Look, Izzy, I know it probably wasn't the best thing in the world for him to do at the time."

"You got that right, Pops."

"You just scare him a lot with all of your escapades."

Izzy was yelling at the top of her lungs now just as the Houston Police Department cruiser was pulling into the driveway unannounced, "I am his mother. I have the right to do as I wish with my son."

She stopped yelling just for a second. The sound of a car door opening and shutting made her spin around only to see the two HPD Officers heading in her direction. She turned back to Raymond, "How could you? Did you call the cops? On what charge? You are the one they should be coming to take to jail, you sorry son of a ..."

"Isabella Jenkins Schmidt?" The peace officer that looked like a linebacker interrupted Isabella's speech.

"Who wants to know?" Izzy hissed.

"This is Isabella, officer." Raymond pointed to Izzy.

Izzy wanted to run, but before she could process that thought, the officer had already grabbed her right arm, spun her around, and slapped on the handcuffs. "Isabella Jenkins Schmidt, you are court-ordered to be brought to the Harris County Psychiatric Center for evaluation."

"You did this to me, Raymond. I will hunt you down for this. You will not get away with anything! If it's the last thing I do." She screamed and screamed her vengeance as the officer not so gently shoved her into the backseat of the cruiser that would take her to the mental facility.

Tears were running down Janice's face, "Raymond, I hope we are right on doing this to her."

"It's her only chance Jan. Let's pray it works."

The entrance to the Harris County Psychiatric Center and the Patient Mental Health Facility was a plain red-bricked building. No one would have guessed that it held people with a mental health condition. The officers escorted Isabella to the admissions desk and waited until she was admitted before they left.

CHAPTER 8

"Isabella, the doctor will see you now. Please come with me." The nurse said as she reached for Isabella's wrist to read the bracelet that had Izzy's vitals on it. The nurse wanted to make sure it was Izzy before grabbing her right arm to escort her to the doctor's office.

Izzy made her way to the only chair in the office and sat there fuming. Does this jerk think I am insane? Doesn't he know who I am? Doesn't he know that I am a psychiatric nurse? Does he really think I'm going to answer him truthfully?

"Isabella, I am going to start you on a drug called Risperidone. It should prevent the probable potential of *THIS* from ever happening again in the future. "

"You're kidding me. There is absolutely nothing wrong with me. My parents were mistaken to even think about putting me in a psych ward. Please just release me now, and I will not bring charges against you in the future."

"Now, Isabella, you know we can't do that. It is ordered by the Court that you are to be evaluated here."

Shifting restlessly in the chair, Izzy tried to change the doctor's mind, "Just don't put me on Risperidone. I have taken Prozac in the past with good results. I will take that drug instead." She hesitated for a second, "I will try Abilify 5G as suggested by my doctors before."

"Alright, Isabella, we shall try Abilify first." He paged for the nurse to come and get Izzy and take her back to her room.

Now that's better! He sees it my way! This might not be so bad, after all. "God, I hate that stupid psychologist. He absolutely has no clue," Isabella said as the nurse was leading her back to her room.

"Isabella, really now, we are all here to help you get through this. Please just work with us."

"None of you have a clue as to what you're doing, so just shut up and leave me alone."

The nurse left Isabella alone in her room to brood over the events that took place over the last couple of hours when she heard a phone ringing somewhere near the nurse's station. A man and a woman were laughing very loud, which broke Isabella out of her reverie.

My tongue is tingly, and my throat is parched. Isabella grabbed her left wrist and felt her pulse as she sat down on her bunk bed. My pulse is in the '70s. *I am not going to be alarmed... yet.* Isabella's eyelids fluttered and then finally shut as she drifted off into a light sleep. It was the drugs that got her this time.

Several hours later, the sound of someone shuffling near her door awoke her. She tried not to let whoever it was figure out that she was awake. But she had to see who was there. Barely opening her eyelids to just a sliver of a crack, Isabella watched as a young black female in a multicolored sweater stood watching her in the doorway. She was carrying a clipboard in her right hand and a pen in her left.

She just stood there, not saying a word and not writing anything down. Finally, after what seemed like hours, the woman flipped a page on the clipboard and moved on out of the doorway to wherever she was going next.

"How sad," Isabella thought as she rolled over and went back to sleep only to be woken by another loud voice.

"Line up! Line up now! It's dinner time." Arthur, the patient advocate, was knocking on every door.

Dinner was finally being served. Unfortunately, the nurse had to pass out the nightly medications to everyone before anyone could eat. "Here you go, Isabella," the nurse said, holding out a cup with water and a smaller one that held Isabella's meds.

Isabella took the water and meds from the nurse and didn't attempt to ingest them. "Isabella, you know I can't leave, and you can't eat dinner until I watch you swallow those meds. Now get on with it."

Izzy's stomach was growling, and she could smell the fried chicken wafting in from the cafeteria. She let out a heavy sigh and downed the meds. Her hunger had won that round.

Dinner was pretty good, considering the hospital cooked it. Fried chicken, French-style green beans, a nice fruit salad, and a big dinner roll was on the menu. At least she wasn't going to starve to death in this place.

Dinner was followed by an hour in the courtyard where the trees were big, and the birds were singing. All the flower beds were in bloom with vibrant colors of blue, pink, and red. It was a peaceful place just to sit and relax. That is until Arthur came into the courtyard, "Alright folks, I know it's a beautiful evening, but it's time for everyone to head back to their rooms for the evening."

Isabella didn't care. She felt drained and would be glad to lay her head down on a pillow for a while. Back in her room, she propped her pillow up in a corner against the wall and tried to fall asleep since the meds she had taken earlier made her feel like she was choking every time she laid her head down.

Just as she was about to drift off, Isabella heard something, or someone, push the door to her room open and step in. The lights were out in the room, and Isabella tried not to breathe, thinking that that would give her away as to where in the room she was. Just before Isabella was about to exhale, the person turned and left the room. Maybe it was the medication she was taking that was playing tricks on her mind.

Either way, it kept Isabella up the rest of the night. "Take a deep breath," She kept telling herself. Her throat was dry, and her tongue felt thick. Her fingers were tingly, and her legs felt very heavy. She tried not to panic, but no one has checked in on her in a while. She ran her fingers through her hair, pausing just as she reached the ends, "Great, now my hair is all tingly," she said out loud.

She was glad she only took half the medication the stupid

nurse gave her before dinner. What's that? Now my ears are ringing, and I have a metal taste in my mouth. She reached for her left wrist and felt her pulse. It was racing. My head is dizzy! I'm going to faint but wait... I hear male voices off into the distance. They are laughing. They are laughing at me!

Isabella screamed, "I have the right to be presumed mentally competent unless a court has ruled otherwise. I decide not you!" Over and over, she screamed this in her darkened room until she finally passed out.

After 48 hours of observation and psychiatric evaluations, on December 3, 2014, a Certificate of Medical Examination was released to the court with the psychiatric findings:

I, Dr. Shwartzke, examined Isabella Jenkins Schmidt (hereinafter referred to as Patient). The patient has been under my care for less than 24 hours. I am of the opinion that the patient is mentally ill and is likely to cause serious harm to others. The patient is suffering severe and abnormal mental, emotional, or physical distress; is experiencing substantial mental deterioration of her ability to function independently, except for indigence reasons. The patient cannot provide for the proposed basic needs; including food, clothing, health, or safety; and cannot make a rational and informed decision about submitting to treatment.

Furthermore, the detailed factual basis of such opinion is as follows: The patient has bizarre and grandiose statements and behavior. I am of the opinion that the patient, because of her mental illness, presents a substantial risk of serious harm to self or others if not immediately restrained. The detailed basis for such is as follows: The patient has consistently harassed and damaged the patient's family's property.

Emergency detention is the least restrictive means by which the necessary restraint may be affected. The facts that form the basis for my medical opinion regarding the Patient's imminent risk of harm unless immediately restrained are great.

Despite the psychiatric doctor's expert opinion, on December 10, 2014, The State of Texas could no longer legally hold Isabella in the psychiatric treatment facility. With this in mind, Izzy checked herself out of the Psych Ward with no medication or prescription. She vowed to herself that she would never take medications for her supposedly mental stability again.

She knew she was not bipolar. This was all just one big nightmare. She knew that the farther she can get away from the psych ward and their stupid nurses, the better.

Isabella was a psych nurse, which meant she knew the answers to every question the psychologist would ask her to determine the state of her mental health. This problem became the largest problem the family faced.

Izzy knew the answers that would bring about a good and positive diagnosis of mental health. Even if it were a new doctor that she was forced to see, that silver tongue of hers could speak the psychiatrist lingo that would eventually get them to believe she was in perfect mental health. Unfortunately, the longer her manic episodes lasted, the worse they got. It was getting harder and harder for anyone, doctor or not, to believe that she was mentally healthy.

She went back to Keith's house after her detainment. It was her only friend left she could trust. She sat next to him on the couch in the living room, staring at the fire in the fireplace. She was stewing in her juices about being locked up in a mental ward. "Really, Keith, they had the nerve to have me locked up for nothing. Those idiot parents of mine."

"I'm sure it was all a misunderstanding, Izzy. No real harm came of it. You're out now. Just try to relax."

"No harm? Really? The drugs they made me take did no harm? The insufferable psych doctor did no harm? The degrading things the nurses made me do did no harm?" The more she voiced her feeling about the whole incident, the angrier she got. "I am going to complain about that idiot formally. Maybe they will fire him for being so incompetent."

On December 13, 2014, Isabella registered a complaint against the psychologist assigned to her in the Psych Ward, but nothing ever came of it. This was her statement:

I was wrongfully accused of "shoplifting" by my mother. It was stated that I was "incapable of making decisions regarding my home." I was detained for nine days by the Harris County Mental Health Department. The doctor demanded I take Risperdal for schizophrenia, yet, had no test or diagnosis of any kind. I agreed to re-start Prozac, yet the doctor denied the request. He started me on Abilify 10 mg. I weigh 100 pounds. 10 mg is too much for one that weighs 100 pounds. I took 5 mg and had a reaction. He still diagnosed me with Abilify 10 mg and accused me of adjusting the medication. The doctor was arrogant, rude, forgetful, passive-aggressive, and medically inept.

By December 17, 2014, Isabella's problems with the law were mounting. She did not show up for her Galveston County Court Date for the criminal trespassing charge that The Rock Nursing Home filed against her. The judge had no choice but to issue a warrant for her arrest.

Isabella sat on the couch, wrapped in a blanket. She remembered that Christmas would soon be upon them. She decided to write to her family a letter.

Season's Greetings, my dear family!
Since Sept of 2014, I have been fired for caring about our seniors' wellbeing and had my employment blackballed. I have had the pleasure of visiting family in California and watched my Godson wed his soul mate. I have been wrongly accused of stealing a Texas A&M plastic watch from Love's Truckstop in Waller County and jailed for about fourteen days.
I was accused of criminal trespassing when I called for a wrecker in a downpour from The Rock Nursing Home and was jailed for

eight days in Galveston County. Then, after I was almost killed when my two front tires blew out on Dec. 1st, my dear demented Mother was concerned that I shoplifted her sweater and could not make decisions about my home. She had two constables remove me from my house at 10:30 a.m. on Dec. 2, 2014, and placed in Harris County Psych Ward for nine days.

Oh, I forgot... before the Harris County Psych Ward, my dear husband accused me of "Identity Theft" while I stayed at The Ruby Legacy Inn in Galveston. Two more Sheriffs beat on my door while I lay naked in the bath. But, through all of this, I know God hid me under His wing, and I am stronger for it. Sometimes you have to lose your life to find it. May God Bless each of you through the new year.

She put the letter in an envelope, stamped it, and put it out for the postal carrier to deliver.

He was a murderer from the beginning and has nothing to do with the truth because there is no truth in him. When he lies, he speaks out of his own character, for he is a liar and the father of lies. (John 8:44)

CHAPTER 9

Months had gone by and I had lost track of Isabella. In the middle of January 2015, I started getting disturbing texts from a phone number I didn't recognize. I knew it had to be my crazy sister. She was mass texting at least nine different phone numbers. This new rampage was escalating fast.

Isabella picked up the phone and dialed Janice and Raymond's house. Raymond recognized the phone number on the Caller Id and let it go to voice mail. "Raymond, you are an arrogant, self-centered, narcissistic, controlling pedophile that should not be breathing my air." She paused as she took another angry breath, "If you ever hurt my mother, make no mistake about it. I will hurt you. Go back to hell where you came from, or better yet, I will send you there myself. I bought a 9MM colt that has your sorry ass name written all over it." Beep.

Her voice mails and her texts were vulgar as she continued to threaten to kill both Janice and Raymond. The group texts she sent to me and nine other people were so horrible and repulsive that it was hard to read them, but I had to keep up with her.

I just wanted to knock her out of this bipolar stupor and bring her back to reality. All hours of the night, the angry texts kept coming, and anyone who responded to her would bring on a renewed barrage of anger. I could not take or hear any more about Izzy and her rampage.

After a very long night of reading the hateful text messages, I fought back by spamming her phone with text messages that read "I am bipolar" and "Please help me get to a hospital." Over and over, I copied these text messages and texted her with them. Her phone would receive close to 5000 text messages over two minutes.

I knew her phone would be receiving the texts so fast that it would not let her respond to them until she received the very last one. I knew it would lock her phone up for a very long time and perhaps even lock it to where she couldn't do anything else with it. My sister was not very tech-savvy. There was no way she could stop it.

I hoped that any bystander or cop who came in contact with her would look at her phone and see the messages. They would see her plea for help and maybe get her to a hospital. It was also my revenge.

This is so negative. I have to get this crap out of my life. How could she do this to me? I did not need her insanity interrupting my new business. I did not need this black mark lurking to poke its head out and possibly destroy the reputation of my very young company. "This was not something I need in my life," I thought as I drifted off to a night of very deep sleep.

BANG bang Bang BANG

The noise jarred me out of a dead sleep. It was two in the morning. It sounded as if someone was in the process of breaking down the front door. I flew out of bed, grabbing my phone and dialing 911 in the process. I knew it had to be Izzy beating down my door. She had come to hurt me. I knew that in her bipolar rampage that she had come to kill me.

Long ago, my bipolar father, Mike Jenkins, was driven by rage and had threatened to drive by my house and shoot to kill me through the three front windows of my living room that faced the street. Years after his death, I was finally able to sit comfortably in my front living room. And now it was happening again, but this time it was my sister that was coming to make good on every threat she has made. I knew she wanted to hurt me, and that thought made my skin crawl.

"911, what is your emergency?"

"Someone is beating down my door. I need the police here now. I'm scared."

"Hold on a moment, Ma'am."

I waited for a short moment, which seemed like years. I heard my heart beating in my chest. My hair stood on end, and my hands were shaking from the adrenaline. The operator came back on the line, "Ma'am, open your door. It's the Sheriff's Department."

Wow! That was fast! "Are you sure? I just called you."

"Yes, Ma'am, they identified themselves as police officers. I'll stay on the phone. Just go look."

I peeped out my digital peephole and saw nothing. Whoever banged on my door was gone now. "Are you sure? I see no one thru the peephole."

"Yes, Ma'am, they are still there. I have them on the phone. They are parked in your driveway. I'll stay on the phone, just please go look."

You're kidding me, right? It all seemed very strange. How did they get here so fast? They were already here? What the... "Are you still there?" I said between heavy breaths. "Stay on the phone with me. I am opening my door. Just don't hang up. I'm going to walk out the door."

I slowly turned the doorknob and inched the door open. I still saw nothing. The driveway to my house would not be in view until I walked the 40 feet of the sidewalk leading to it. My whole body was shaking with adrenaline. "Don't hang up... I am walking down the sidewalk to my driveway."

I heard nothing. The wind wasn't even rustling the leaves in the trees. The hair on my neck was standing at attention. Peering around the bushes that surrounded my driveway, I saw two Harris County Sheriffs' cars parked at the very end of the driveway. I slowly exhaled the breath I was holding out of fear.

"Ma'am, are you alright?" They immediately started walking towards me. I looked at them with confusion written all over my face. Why had they come if they were not answering my 911 call? "Ma'am, we received an anonymous call that you or someone in this house was suicidal and on the verge of death. We needed to intervene immediately."

And then it hit me like a ton of bricks. Izzy's rampage and hateful trickery. She had called the cops anonymously and told them I was suicidal. She told them I was attempting to kill myself. She is the only one twisted enough to come up with that scenario. My sick sister. The ex-nurse. The ex-psych nurse. The bipolar ex-psych nurse.

I explained this to the cops and showed them her text messages. The young officer turned to me with sympathy in his eyes, "Do you mind if we come in and look around?"

"Of course not, follow me." As I opened the door, Rio, my six-month-old fearless protector, my tiny Chocolate Labrador puppy, immediately rolled over and let the officers pet his belly.

They took a look around and noticed nothing out of the ordinary. At four in the morning, the officers left satisfied that it was just a prank call.

"I can't take any more of this insanity." I sighed to myself. I logged into my iPhone account at Verizon. Clicking on the button that would allow you to change your phone number instantly, I was presented with a list of new phone numbers. Randomly I picked one and clicked on the button to confirm the change. It took effect immediately.

Goodbye Isabella. I never wanted to hear from my twisted sick sister again. I needed to divorce myself from the situation. I could not have this type of negativity in my life, and I didn't need her harming my new business. I wanted nothing more to do with her.

Period.

If only changing your phone number could actually do that. At least it was a step in the right direction.

As the days went by, I hired a programmer to put the finishing touches on my software while I increased the audience on all the social media channels. Months and a lot of money went into building a buzz for the new software that should transform the lighting industry and take it by storm.

To pass the time I took Rio, my Chocolate Lab, to the local dog park to play. There I met my dear friend Deborah, her daughter Megan, and their baby German Sheppard named Balthazar. We hit it off right from the beginning.

Deborah and Meghan started their own food truck business that catered to the 18-wheel trucking industry, which Deborah had been a dispatcher for. The mother and daughter team had purchased a food truck with their savings and loans from a bank.

Their food truck was currently being equipped with all the necessities to keep their food business alive on the streets. As they waited for their finished food truck to come out of the shop, we traded horror stories of playing the waiting game for our businesses to take off.

Tossing tennis balls to Rio and Balthazar, we talked about being independent and owning our own businesses. We talked about the hardships, the expense, the sacrifices, and the thrill of it all. Our identical hopes and dreams for our futures brought the three humans and two dogs closer together.

There wasn't a cloud in the sky as I met my new friends yet again for another romp in the dog park. It was nearing the holiday season, and neither of us had any good news about our businesses. Chunking the tennis ball as far as I could, the dogs raced after it, and I turned to Deborah, "Have you heard anything yet?"

"They are waiting on a part for the oven now. It's always one thing or another. I feel like the world is against us right now. I have no idea why this is taking so long," Deborah sighed. "We're running out of money playing this waiting game."

I listened to her empathetically, but I had no words of comfort or wisdom for my new friend, as my own business was starting to show signs of the same type of stress. I shook that thought from my head. Negative thoughts equal negative things. I will not allow myself to produce anything negative about my business.

I looked at my new friends, and all I could do was hug them both as we ended the day in the dog park. If I continue to think positively and think about everyone using my software, my business will succeed. The Law of Attraction said so. Even if the Law of Attraction didn't already predict my success, I knew I had a great product. I knew it was only a matter of time before it caught on with every production company out there.

I know in my heart that this company... my company... will be a success! It was only a matter of time. And with those positive thoughts swirling around in my head, I pushed myself even harder to drum up the business on the web. I still had cash in the bank, so life was still good.

Rio sat at my feet as I worked on my couch with my laptop. His sad puppy dog eyes were willing me to toss the tennis ball to him. "No, Rio, I have to work on this. I can't play with you every hour of every day. That would be in the perfect world, my darling baby boy!"

Rio continued to stare and poke me with his nose. I tried to get him to lay down, but he wasn't having any of it. I turned my attention back to my laptop and the internet to dig deeper and deeper into finding ways to advertise my software. My perfect baby labrador put his paw on my leg, begging me to play with him.

Ok, I get the message! "You know what, Rio?" He cocked his head at me with a look of anticipation. His tail was wagging 90 miles an hour. "You need a playmate!"

His tail started wagging so fast I thought he might take flight at any moment. "I'm going to find you a brother! I'm sure there is a puppy out there in need of a roof over his head." Laughing, I tossed the tennis ball down the hall and watched him run happily after it.

I started looking for free puppies on Craigslist and came across a cute long-haired pup that looked like Tramp from My Three Sons. Now that was a puppy! "Free to a good home," the ad said. "OK, Rio, I'll call them!" He sat at my feet, tennis ball in his mouth, wagging his tail.

"Hello?"

"Hi! Do you still have the puppy?"

"Yes, we do!"

"How about we meet in a dog park, and if my Lab and the pup play well together, I'll take him home with me."

"That sounds great! We are close to the Gene Green Dog Park in Northeast Houston. We can meet you there today around 2:00 p.m. if that's ok with you?"

"Sure thing! I'll see you there around 2:00 p.m." And off I went to pack up my pooch and head to the other side of town to meet Rio's potential brother.

The dog park was nestled way back in a very wooded, vast human park. It was a pretty good-sized fenced-in area equipped with lots and lots of mud puddles. A doggie's dream world! That is when I saw him.

The cutest little long-haired white and grey dog you ever saw, with a healthy coat of mud all over him. He had two little schnauzer's chasing after him as they were running from mud puddle to mud puddle.

"Rio, go play!" I said as I unhooked his leash and started to walk in the direction of the long-haired English Sheepdog and their owners.

"Hi, I'm Sandy! I called you about the puppy. That Chocolate Lab over there is Rio!"

"Well, Hi! So good to meet you!" We shook hands. "We call him Shaggy. It just seems fitting to him. Look, they are playing together already!"

"Cool, nothing can keep Rio away from a good mud puddle! I see Shaggy likes them too! Can you tell me a little about him? How did he come to be rescued?"

"My wife had gone to the rescue center in search of a kitten when she saw Shaggy. They were about to euthanize him. He had gotten to the point where he wouldn't eat or even stand up on his own. They said it was depression. See, Shaggy came to the rescue center with his Mom. The rescue center placed his Mom with a forever home, which left Shaggy there by himself. He never got over losing his Mom. My wife saw Shaggy and told the shelter that she would find a good home for him. So, she brought him home and placed the ad."

"Oh, that poor thing! Thank God for your wife!"

"Look! Shaggy and Rio seem to be having fun together!"

"How about I take him home with me for a week, and if they still like to play together, I will keep him!"

"Sounds good!"

We exchanged phone numbers and information as I packed the two puppies up into the backseat of my car. There they were... The boys! Rio and Shagz! I looked at Rio, "See, now you have a playmate, and I can get back to working on my software!" All was right with the world again!

Over a couple of months, I watched my friends Deborah and Meg go down the financially broken road. I watched from close by, as I saw the same symptoms of their failing business pop up in my own.

It was a scorching hot summer day as I packed up Rio and Shaggy and headed to the dog park. Deborah, Megan, and Balthazar were already there. "So, what are you going to do?" I asked my best friend and tossed the tennis ball to Rio.

"The landlord is going to evict us by the end of the week. We're having a garage sale to get rid of most of our stuff and keep the lights on for a little bit. We are waiting on a friend's trucking company to start up. I could probably dispatch for him from home. That would at least give us enough money for a roof over our heads."

"So, when would you know about the job?"

"A couple of weeks, I suppose."

"That's a long time. What about the food truck?"

"We are going to try to sell it back to the guy that made it for us, then dissolve the company."

"Wow, I am so sorry!" I hugged my best friend, "let me know how I can help."

"Pray for Meghan and me! Do you believe in God?"

That kind of threw me. "I believe in God. I believe that he is the God of the Universe."

"Well, that's ok then, just pray for us if you want to."

"Sure, thing, my friend!" I had no words left to say about that and promptly put it out of my mind.

Turning my thoughts and efforts to my own failing business, I figured that if I am going down, then I am going down fighting. You can find anything and everything on the Internet. The World Wide Web. The Net. The Superhighway. Cyberspace. Yep, this is where I will plead my case and start to rally people around the globe to my cause and my business.

Crowdsourcing websites are a place where you can put a project of any size and subject in front of people who could financially invest in your project. If I wanted my business to succeed, I needed investors. I navigated to the Kickstarter website, one of the first and most significant Crowdsourcing websites that hit the Net.

For the next two weeks, I created a video that made my business sound promising and rock solid. I pleaded my case as to why I started it, who I was, and my entertainment business background. I spoke to an audience I could not see or hear and told them how my software would help save millions of dollars for the production companies that were touring the world. I told them they could not live without this software.

I didn't stop at just Kickstarter. I begged for help on every Crowdsourcing website I could find. I asked entrepreneurs for mentors and small business startup help. I had to admit that I had no clue what to do to help my company anymore.

Another week went by, as the knot in my stomach grew from fear of the worst. Not one person even nibbled on the hooks that I planted all over the Net. I knew I had to turn to my family. It was my last option. I had nothing else and nowhere else to turn.

I had to ask Mom and Raymond for any kind of help they could give me.

Perhaps my aunts or uncles could help. It was a long shot, and I was getting desperate. I knew I had to shelf my anger from my childhood. I told myself fifteen years was a long time. Things had probably changed. I had to find a way to bridge the years of non-communication.

I only knew I had to try.

I woke up and rechecked my bank balance. Only $900 left in my checking account and no cash coming in. No job. No money. I kept imagining that my business was taking off. It had to. I saw it in my head. I meditated on it. I watched my vision frame. I tried every technique that I could find through the Law of Attraction.

Nothing. The Universe had denied me. I knew I had a great product; it was just a matter of getting it out to the public, but I was broke. It takes money to make money, and there was nothing more I could do for my dead company.

Like Deb and Meg, it was time to start selling everything just to keep the lights and water running. My dogs and I needed food. The pantry was running bare. I knew that I had six months before the mortgage company would start foreclosure proceedings on my house—six months to find some kind of income.

Six months period. That is all I had, or I would be on the streets. My company was dead. I had jumped off the cliff in 2014 and burned every bridge I had. A year had gone by, and I not only hit rock bottom hard, but I tunneled miles and miles underneath rock bottom, heading straight for the pits of hell. I was in serious trouble.

Hundred plus degree weather and high humidity are typical summertime weather in Houston, making an air conditioner in your home mandatory for survival. I sat at my kitchen table, staring at my laptop, which was displaying my current bank balance—$534.23.

I still can't believe I got myself into such dire circumstances. How can I be so stupid? What in the hell was I thinking? Start my own business, sure thing. I know what I am doing... NOT!

As I sat there chastising myself, I started to smell a tiny whiff of smoke. Thoughts of my house catching on fire went racing through my head, and running a fast second was how I stopped paying homeowners insurance since I couldn't afford it anymore.

There's nothing plugged in anywhere in this house because I can't afford high electricity bills, so that smell came from where I wondered? I ran from room to room and found nothing out of the ordinary. Then this horrible thought popped into my head. You know you always smell something burning when your fixing to have a heart attack. Maybe that's what is happening? But wait! Is it a heart attack? Or is it a brain tumor that smelling burnt things signifies? Perhaps I am just so stressed out that I'm imagining things. That has to be it.

Convinced that it was my imagination, I went back to my laptop to work. At least I could put some more items on eBay for sale.

After the third auction I created on eBay, I started noticing it getting significantly warmer in the house. I still heard the air conditioner fans running, and I know it gets sweltering hot in Texas, but my air conditioner always keeps it cool in the house.

I went to look at the thermostat in the hallway. It read 85 degrees. Oh no! Please, God, not the AC! I ran to the backyard to see if the compressor was still running, and it was, so I ran to the master bathroom. There above the shower sits the central air blower, and it was dead.

That smoke I smelled just a few minutes ago? Well, that was the motor on it burning up. I thank God it didn't catch the rest of the house on fire. But now, I have no air conditioner in the heat of the summer and $534.23 in the bank with no incoming income of any type. This was serious.

The temperature in the house was steadily climbing as the sun bore down on the house. It was getting close to 95 degrees inside. Not even rattlesnakes would come out in that kind of heat. I had to do something, or both the dogs and I would die of heatstroke.

Jumping on my laptop, I browsed the Home Depot site. They had window AC units that would fit my front windowsill. The cheapest one that could have enough BTU's or energy to keep the front room cool was a little over $300, but it was closer to $400 when it was all said and done with taxes. That didn't leave much left in my bank account for anything. I had to bite the bullet or risk dying from heatstroke. Death or Life was now being defined by a single window AC unit. Both Rio and Shaggy were also glad I made that decision, as I plugged the window unit in, and the room started cooling off. Finally!

That little window AC became the new norm, but I was still on the super-fast train tour that was headed straight for the pits of hell and beyond.

In September of 2015, I sat down at the kitchen table and wrote a short note to the only people that could help me. Mom and Raymond. I told them that I knew that the relations between the three of us were strained, to say the very least, but I was willing to give it another try. I desperately needed their help.

I signed it with my physical address, my email address, and my cell phone number. I bought a stamp and said a little prayer, "Please, God, let them read it and respond positively." I put the letter in the mailbox. The letter should reach them in two days by snail mail. Two days was a long time when I knew I was going down very fast.

My phone was ringing. I knew it was probably another bill collector wanting their hundreds of dollars that I did not have to give them. Reluctantly I look at the Caller ID. It was Mom! I inhaled a sharp breath, and my heart pounded a little faster as I accepted the call. "Hello?"

"Sandy?"

"Mom!"

"I have missed you so very much!" I heard her tears over the phone. "I have dreamed of this moment for so very long."

"I know, Mom. I am so sorry. I want to change all this."

I agreed to come to their house the next day for the reunion and tell them of my business adventures. Mom and Raymond live 65 miles from me on the south side of Houston. As I left my house, the cloudy skies were just starting to lay a fine mist on my yard. The closer I got to Mom and Raymond's house, the darker the sky got, and the harder the rain fell.

Really God? Such dramatics! I turned down a road I had recognized from my childhood. I was determined to get to their house on my own, but I was met with floodwaters that crept over my tires. My phone rang.

Mom was worried, "Where are you? Are you ok? Maybe we should meet when it isn't flooding."

"Nope, I'm almost there. I think I got off at the wrong exit."

"Where are you?"

"I took the Fuqua exit off the Beltway. I suppose it was the wrong side of Fuqua, but the water is over the curb now, and cars are turning around. I'm going to try to turn around and get back on the beltway."

"Just stay on the phone, so we know you are ok."

"I'm ok, Mom, the car is running, water is not coming in the car. Oh, wait... I see the Beltway. I'm almost there."

The rain poured down harder and faster than ever. My windshield wipers could not keep up, as I was stopped at a red light. I saw the underpass of the beltway, just a short distance away. I knew If I could make it there that I would be safely back on higher ground. "The light just turned green, Mom. I'm going back on the beltway. I should be there soon."

"Raymond and I will meet you at the McDonald's that's on the corner. Do you think you can make it there?"

"Yes, Mom, don't worry, I will be there." It took only ten more minutes as I pulled my car into the McDonald's parking lot and searched for Mom and Raymond's car. And then I saw her!

Mom's face brightened as she recognized me and got out of their car. We hugged and made our way into McDonald's hand in hand. Mom and Raymond ordered a McCafé and French fries. I just had a coke as we spent the next couple of hours catching up on my life and its downfall.

"I've got something else to tell you," Mom said softly.

"What is it, Mom?"

"Your sister Isabella is living with us."

"How did that happen?"

"She's trying to get better." She paused a little too long, "She is better."

No one wanted to say it. No one wanted to say that my sister was bipolar.

CHAPTER 10

The sound of my iPhone ringing disturbed my troubled thoughts. It was my best friend, Deborah. "I need your help. They finally kicked us out into the cold. I have 24 hours to get our stuff out of the house. Can we come to stay with you?"

"Of course! When?"

"Tomorrow."

"What are you planning on doing?"

"I have enough money for a U-Haul. We will pack everything we can into it and head to my folk's house in Iowa. We just need a place to repack and regroup before we leave."

"Not that it matters, but how long do you think you'll be staying?"

"Maybe a week"

Three large dogs and three women crammed into a three-bedroom house for a week. The stress levels would be sky high as none of us knew how to salvage our futures. That decision was already made a long time ago. It was the only thing I knew how to do correctly. "No Biggie, Deb. Ok? I'll start clearing out a room for you and your stuff."

Deborah, Megan, and I made many trips back and forth from her house to mine as we packed everything up and put it floor to ceiling in my house. I cleared out one room for them to use, but it wasn't enough as their things spilled over into the hallways and the living room. Their couches, my couches, and things and stuff everywhere there was empty room to put something.

Stuff piled high on the stovetop and the kitchen counters. The stress from it all was piling up on the three women. I love my friends to death, but the pressure was not good for any of us. Even the dogs were feeling it. "Mind if I listen to the radio?" Deborah asked.

"Not at all! Please do!" That should brighten up our spirits. Deborah put the radio on KSBJ, a contemporary Christian radio station. I enjoyed listening to the music that they were playing. At least it made me think about something other than the perils of life and the pit of hell that I had eagerly landed in.

I watched as they sorted and repacked tubs and boxes, trying to cram everything they had into every inch of air space that was given to them. They knew everything they wanted to keep had to go into the 6x12 foot U-Haul trailer. The decisions they made were not very easy ones.

I watched as they made piles to give to Goodwill and piles to give to the Church. What was left was tightly packed into the trailer. We held one last garage sale to get rid of the rest of their stuff, and hopefully, it would give them enough money to eat on the long trip to Iowa.

Deborah and Megan repacked the last of their tubs, and we crammed them in the last air pockets available in the trailer. I turned to see the fifteen tubs that didn't make it onto it. I could have kicked myself for not thinking about this sooner, which might have made some of their decisions a little easier. "Look, guys, you can leave stuff here. You can come and get it when you're settled. I'm not going anywhere anytime soon," I forced a smile onto my face, hoping against hope that it would be the truth. "We can put it back into the room I cleared out. The rest of this stuff won't take up that much room."

"Are you sure?"

"Yes! It will be a while before they start foreclosure proceedings, and I'll have a job way before that happens. It's no big deal, my friend."

We toted the tubs and stuff they couldn't take back into the room and neatly stacked it in one corner. My heart broke, and tears streamed down my face as I watched them pull away from my driveway and head off to Deborah's folk's house some 940 miles away.

Over the next few months, Raymond and I poured over how to rebuild my business model. Raymond, being a long time salesman, figured it out right off the bat. I had geared my ad campaigns to the wrong people. I was targeting the people who would use the software, not the people who had the clout to buy it for the people who would use the software.

I needed to target the production managers of the production companies. I needed to figure out a way to tell them that this software would save them thousands of dollars in re-work during their pre-production schedules and that they could get their shows up and running error-free. If they didn't use my software, they would literally be sitting in the dark losing money.

Hope for the existence of my company was blossoming as my geek mode went into overdrive. I scoured the web for every name, phone number, and address of every production manager for every production company in every city of every state. That included thousands and thousands of names. Every Ballet Company. Every Symphony. Every Opera Company. Every Performing Arts Group. From Colleges to Universities, to Community Theaters, to Private Schools, to Churches, to anyone that had anything to do with lighting in any type of production company in the US, Canada, and the World. I painstakingly gathered the data and created a clever advertisement for the software, and I sent it to the production managers. Hundreds of the ads went out, and I watched and waited.

In the meantime, I was sending out 10 to 25 resumes a day. Gone are the days when you could snail mail a company your resume and request an audience with a hiring manager. Everything was all online now. Every job offer stated, *Do not call or come by*, and that they would review your application and call you. I suppose that it was cost-effective for the companies that offered the jobs.

By 10:00 a.m. every morning, seven days a week, I applied to at least fifteen jobs. I am registered with eight staffing agencies, including The Texas Workforce Commission. I search on an hourly basis every major job site in the United States. Anywhere and everywhere that has Houston job postings, but I was getting no nibbles. No bites and no phone calls. Nothing except the relentless pursuit of the bill collectors.

After weeks and weeks had gone by, I got *THE* call.

"Hello, Sandy Ryan?"

"Yes, what can I do for you?"

"This is Janet with Artistic Consultants; I have a job I would like for you to interview for."

I almost fainted!

She continued, "The Christian Gospel Church is looking for a Lighting Designer. Are you interested?"

"That's less than a mile from my house! I could walk there! Yes! Yes, I am very interested in the job! Thank you so much!"

"No problem Sandy. I need you to come downtown to my office to finish filling out some paperwork, and then do a short interview with me before I send you to the Church's Human Resource Center."

"I can come tomorrow!"

Things were looking up! I had hope now!

I had gone through four interviews with The Christian Gospel Church and was on the last stage before getting the job. It was an interview with the Pastor himself. Weeks and weeks went by with no word from the church about when I could talk to the great Pastor. I called the staffing agency. "Hi, Janet! Have you heard anything from the Church yet? It's been three weeks since my last interview with them."

"No, Sandy, I haven't. It's unusual that they are taking so long.

I called them yesterday, and they said that the Pastor had a hectic schedule. They are having a hard time setting a date and time. I'm sorry, I'll let you know something as soon as I hear back from them."

The knot in my stomach was growing. I needed this job. I needed money. I needed food. After Deborah and Meghan left, I kept the radio where they had left it, on KSBJ. The station was growing on me. They inspired me. They became my cheerleader, moving me to keep going and never give up. They were not like any old gospel radio station. They aren't bible thumpers. They are everyday people encouraging and lifting people up to God. They tell stories of other people and how God helped them. They talk about the Word of God and what He said in the Bible. Their slogan is *God Listens*, and that is my hope, "If you are there, Lord, I need this job. Please! I'm begging."

Christmas was right around the corner, and I was still dirt broke. I had no money for presents. Having sold almost everything that had any kind of value, I rummaged through what little I had left in the house and searched for gifts I could give to my nephew, my Mom, and Raymond. It's the thought that always counts. Right?

With the little bit of gas left in the car, I drove the 65 miles to Mom and Raymond's house for Christmas Dinner. My sister Isabella answered the door when I got there. I had forgotten Izzy was staying with them, so it startled me a little bit just seeing her there at our childhood house. Especially after all the horrible commotion she had caused our family and friends. Mom had reassured me that she was better, so I gave Izzy the benefit of the doubt.

"Hey, little sister," Izzy said as she opened the door to me. "Come on in! Mom's in the kitchen, putting the last touches on dinner."

"Thanks, Izzy," I said, a little uneasy at the sight of seeing her, but the smell of Christmas dinner shook me out of the troubling thoughts. "Mom! It smells wonderful!" I said as I peeked my head into the kitchen.

"Well, Hi, Sugar! Merry Christmas! Raymond is upstairs getting dressed, and when he comes down, we'll have dinner."

"Cool!" I said as I kissed my Mom's forehead.

Dinner was awesome. On the menu were turkey, dressing, rolls, green bean casserole, herring salad, a German dish, and traditional food for our family's holidays. Afterward, we all headed into the den to exchange our gifts. Isabella handed me an envelope. "Merry Christmas, little sister."

I opened it and found a check for the $500 I gave her the year before. I had written that money off to a lost cause. "Thanks, Izzy! I appreciate this." And I hugged her.

This money could keep my lights and water on for another month or so. Maybe Izzy has changed. Perhaps she was on the road to being better. Mom said she was taking vitamins or some kind of pills. Maybe they were doing the magic. I sure hope so because I could not take any more of the Crazy Izzy.

Tonight was a lovely evening. The food was excellent. The company was even more extraordinary. As the evening was winding down, I found Izzy sitting at Mom's computer. "Whatcha doin', Izzy?"

"Looking for a job, I need to get out of Mom's house."

"You're a nurse. It shouldn't be that hard to find a job. Nurses are always in demand!"

"I've got an interview with a staffing agency next week. They seem to think they can place me pretty easily. The only problem is it's on the other side of town."

"What side of town is it in?"

"Northwest Houston."

"Izzy, that's my side of town."

And then the light bulb went off in my head. I needed money. I needed help with food. I needed to keep the lights on and the Internet running. Izzy gets a job. Izzy has money. "Hey, Izzy? Why don't you come to stay with me? I could use the money and help a roommate could offer. I live closer to your staffing agency than Mom and Raymond. I have a room at my house. I would love to have some company. What do you think?"

"I don't know, Sandy. Let me think about it some more."

The week after Christmas, Izzy gathered a bunch of her clothes and headed to my side of town. She accepted my offer to come and stay with me! Izzy went to her interview with the staffing agency and got her first job through them. She was making $25 an hour. I started to breathe a sigh of relief. I knew that I could dig myself out of this hell hole I had wallowed in for so long with her help.

At the end of this month, my cell phone company would cut off my iPhone service. I could no longer afford to pay for a cell phone, which meant I would not be able to receive calls for jobs. I didn't even have a landline phone number because I could not afford it. That's when Izzy rushed in to help.

She got me a new cell phone with her cell phone company, and I kept the same phone number. That was a Blessing! It meant I wouldn't have to change the phone number on hundreds of job applications that I had already sent out. Most of which I couldn't remember who I sent them to because there were literally hundreds of them floating around Houston.

Yes, this was a Blessing, indeed. It was nice having my sister living with me. She bought groceries, and I cooked. She cleaned as I looked for more jobs to bring in any kind of money. And then I found the world of Scrapping! I finally understood why I saw people dumpster diving. There was gold in them thar dumpsters!

Yep, scrapping was the art of tearing apart electronics, mainly tube televisions, to get to the copper in them. Copper is a hot commodity, and the scrap yards paid a lot of money for it. I spent the day searching for tube televisions in my neighborhood and the surrounding areas. I would drive through the neighborhood looking through people's trash to find electronics and computers too. Nothing was sacred.

When I found televisions, Izzy and I would go out at night and hall them home. I would then turn the radio on KSBJ in the garage and commence to breaking apart the television sets and electronics to get to the copper. It was a great way to relieve a whole lot of stress, but it never made me a ton of money. It did, however, put a few morsels on the table.

Isabella was sent to many different jobs over the next four weeks through her staffing agency. I never really understood why she couldn't keep one. Her excuse was always because "so and so was mean," or "so and so did this to me." And the best one was still "I was railroaded. They have no clue what they are doing."

I didn't snap to the fact that she was headed down the bipolar path again until one morning, I was awoken by the television blaring in the front room. I found Izzy in the kitchen trying to fix herself a cup of tea. She looked horrible. Her hair was a mess, her eyes were sunken in, and she was wrapped up in a blanket.

"Why are you so upset?" Isabella looked at my face and saw I was pissed off. "I've been up all night. I'm fixing myself some tea. Then I'm going to bed."

She left three candles burning in the kitchen as she promptly went to her room. She knows that I am paranoid about any kind of candle or open flames in my house since I have no homeowner's insurance. I went to the living room and turned down the TV that she left blaring. Looking around the room, I found soybean edamame shells all over the floor and the couch.

Then I heard her bedroom door open, and I turned around. Isabella was fully dressed, keys and purse in hand. "I'm going out," she said.

So much for her sleeping.

That was the warning sign I did not want to see. Izzy opened the front door and was off to God knows where. I texted her, "Do not come back. You are not welcome in my house anymore."

Isabella's bipolar rampage was starting again.

As the days grew into weeks, and the weeks grew into months, to my dismay, there were no bites on my software. It was a new year, 2016, and there was not even a nibble. My bank account was bone dry. I could not even afford the $5 a month service charge, so I sadly closed the bank account. All the money I had in this world was now tucked away in a cigar box in my underwear drawer. I had less than twenty bucks and some change.

Artistic Consultants never called me back. It had been over nine weeks since I had heard anything from The Christian Gospel Church. Sadly, I had to give up the ghost for that job. It was difficult to push the thought out of my mind. God has turned his back on me, yet again. The job was with a Church. His Church. I guess I am not worthy enough for that.

KSBJ keeps saying that God listens. I wanted to believe that with all my heart, but I had hit rock bottom at full speed and was continuing to burrow a 20-mile tunnel straight past hell and beyond. It was time to find another source of income. I scoured the internet for opportunities to make a buck.

Just one buck coming in would be one-quarter of what I needed to buy the ten pounds of chicken to feed my dogs and me for a couple of weeks. Even the cheapest dog food at fifty cents a can was beyond my reach. I figured it was cheaper to make the dog's food rather than buy it processed in a can.

Going to the grocery store was super hard. Walking down the aisles and knowing that I couldn't afford even the cheapest box of Roman noodles was excruciating. Everything in the dairy case was way too expensive for me. Cheese became a luxury. Red meat was entirely out of my reach. Even fish was way too expensive. Sadly, I went without those things I couldn't afford.

I did find ten-pound bags of chicken leg quarters at the local market for 49 cents a pound. It was meat. It was protein. I boiled the leg quarters in water then picked the meat off the bones. The chicken fed the dogs and me for almost a week. Spices were out of my reach, even spices from the dollar store. I couldn't even make a simple recipe from the leg quarters. Boiled chicken with a little salt and pepper, along with rice, was the luxury meal for the week. My pride did not want to accept the fact that I was in poverty.

I did not want the help of others. I did not want others to know just how bad off I was, but the pains in my stomach said otherwise. None of my clothes fit me anymore because I was losing weight so fast. The hunger pains come in waves, and at the peak of the hunger pains, it racked every muscle in my body. I could feel the surges of pain way down in the core of my bones. Starvation is real, and it is not very fun or pretty. I would not wish this on anyone.

On a trip down to Mom and Raymond's one day, I was very humbled when their Church friends sent me boxes of food—humbled and overjoyed to see spaghetti sauce, noodles, cans of tuna, cans of vegetables, and peanut butter! Peanut butter was a real treat for both the dogs and me!

Mom keeps telling me, don't give up. Just keep doing what you're doing. The Lord will come through. But it is so hard. Days and days go by where I am so hungry, and my body hurts so bad because I have no food to eat. All I can afford is the salt in the tears that keep streaming down my face.

My phone rang, stirring me out of my poor me pity party for one. "Mom!"

"Hi, honey! Whatcha doing?"

"What I always do, Mom, send out resumes, scheme about ways to make money, send out more resumes, get rejected, send out more resumes, get rejected, send out more resumes, get rejected again." I took a breath in between the sobs, "It's like God keeps slamming all the doors and windows in my face. Everywhere I turn, the door slams shut. Every opportunity finds a way to not work out for me. I spin my wheels, sending out tons of resumes to jobs. I'm either way too qualified or way too old, and some just give no excuse but just say I'm sorry someone else got the job. NO one wants me to work for them. I don't understand why this is happening.

"Even the grocery store turned me down for a shelf-stocking job. Even Walmart shut the door in my face. Walmart Mom! I can't even get a job at Walmart! I can't get a job to save my life, Mom." I started crying for the hundredth time.

"And I just found out the Roland, my ex, just died of a heart attack. I hated him, Mom. I hated what he did to me." And the tears kept coming. "He's probably standing right by me now, mocking me from hell."

"Look, sweetheart, you need to go to Redbox and rent this movie. I'll pay for it. Just go watch this movie."

"A movie, Mom? Really?" I said in between sniffles.

"I think it will help you."

I love my Mom. I will do anything for her. "Okay, Mom, what's the movie called?"

"It's called *The War Room.*"

"I have a couple of bucks, Mom. I can go rent it."

The movie cost me one dollar and some change. I didn't have any money to spare to watch movies, but Mom sounded so insistent that I couldn't refuse her. I went to the Redbox at the Walgreens store on the corner and rented *The War Room.*

I sat down that night to watch the movie. I watched as Priscilla Shirer, who plays a wife, built a War Room. It's a room to pray in. A room she can be alone in with God. She is sitting in the war room and keeps repeating over and over, "*Submit to God, resist the devil, and he will flee,*" over and over again, she says, "*Submit to God, resist the devil, and he will flee.*" (James 4:7)

Then you can see on her face that she finally gets it! She goes screaming from room to room in her house, telling the devil to get out. I don't know if it was because of all my pent up frustration, fear, and degradation or what, but I started screaming too. It felt good!

Then I started yelling at the devil to leave me alone. To get out. My dogs began barking excitedly as their tails went wag-

130

ging a mile a minute. God had closed all the doors and the windows. He left me with the only thing I could cling to. Him and Him alone. He was trying to tell me, "Hey, little daughter, all is forgiven. Just come to me now."

I had to turn my troubled childhood and teen years over to God. I had to forgive myself and those who hurt me. I had to lay my desperation and my helplessness at his feet and trust Him. I had to step aside and let the Lord deal with everything. I had to trust Him. I had to either accept it or go down.

I accepted it. I took all my problems and turned it over to Jesus. I believe in God, and I trust him. I ran from room to room in my own house and yelled out the words that would seal my fate for eternity.

"I believe. I believe in Christ Jesus. I believe that Jesus died on the cross for me and that I am forgiven. I believe he was resurrected and will return. I believe." I screamed these words as I ran through every room of my house. The dogs hot on my heels, barking their excitement.

I stopped in my front living room. The silence was deafening. I am not sure what I expected. A crack of thunder? Lightning? God's booming voice echoing throughout the house? Just silence... you could have heard a pin drop.

I sunk to my knees and prayed, *"Lord, come into my life. In the name of Jesus Christ - Amen."*

That being said, I left the Law of Attraction back in hell where I found it, and my new journey in God's Grace began.

Yet to all who did receive him, to those who believed in his name, he gave the right to become children of God. (John 1:12)

CHAPTER 11

"For our struggle is not against flesh and blood, but against the rulers, against the authorities, against the powers of this dark world and against the spiritual forces of evil in the heavenly realms." (Ephesians 6:12)

Finding faith in the dark when your life has taken a turn for the worse. It's tough. I won't kid you. I do laundry about once a month because I don't want my electric bill to go up any more than its already high price. I run the dishwasher only when the sink has no more room to cram in dirty dishes, and the dirty dishes start to blanket the kitchen countertops.

The house is so dusty I don't even care anymore. "Screw the germs. Just take me Jesus, and if its death by dirt, then so be it." I just don't have the energy. Besides, no one comes over to see me anyway. My best friends, Deb, and Meghan were now in Iowa.

I don't turn on lights unless absolutely necessary. I hate going to the grocery store because everything there is way out of my financial budget. Who's kidding who? I don't have a financial budget. I don't have finances. All I have is my cigar box full of change tucked away in my underwear drawer. It has become an enormous struggle just to buy a couple of bucks worth of cheap toilet paper.

It is now early spring, and my grass is getting overgrown, but I don't want to spend the money on gas for the lawnmower. I don't even have the gumption to go trudging out to the edge of the property to check the mailbox. What was the point? I know I didn't win the Publishers Clearing House.

I do not want to see the piles of hate letters from the tons of companies to whom I owe a lot of money. On the other hand, I didn't want thieves to go looking in my mailbox either. Bracing myself for the worst, I walked out to the mailbox and reached in to grab the 9000 letters. I did not even want to look at them. I didn't care anymore. Bashing my brains against the wall because I couldn't pay these people wasn't going to do anyone any good.

But I had to look at them as I took them out of the mailbox. Of course, the top letter was from the stupid Homeowners Association. *This is a friendly reminder to please mow or trim your yard...* blah blah blah. Fine! I'll mow the grass. I've already sent out 500 resumes today. What else do I have to do?

With a heavy sigh, I dug out my lawnmower and poured some precious gas into it, and cranked it up. After mowing two strips of the high grass, my lawnmower just stopped working. "Oh, just great! What am I supposed to do now, Lord? Get out the scissors?" I yelled.

I have no money to buy another, and no money to pay someone to look at this one and fix it. "Lord, help me," I cried aloud. And that's when the geek in me turned to YouTube. I searched for things like *my lawnmower won't start.* I found tons of videos out there that show you how to clean a lawnmower. How to take apart the carburetor on your lawnmower and clean it— step by step, they showed you how to fix it yourself.

With YouTube by my side, I took apart and cleaned the whole lawnmower engine. It reminded me of scrapping, except I didn't want to tear the mower apart and beat it to death... however stress-relieving that would be for me right now.

On the second try of cleaning the carburetor, I had a running lawnmower. Amazing! I did the Happy Dance! I was smiling at myself as I went to finish mowing the lawn. The small feats of victory kept me going after that, along with KSBJ, the Contemporary Christian Radio Station, who continuously said God Listens! I genuinely believe that now, but I sure wished He would hurry up and land me a job!

I also decided to go to a small church just down the street from where I lived. If I already declared the Lord Jesus my savior,

I figured that I should go and talk to Him in His house. Maybe... just maybe... If I spoke to Him in His church, he would speed up this job thing.

It felt awkward entering the church for the first time of my own will. I wasn't sure how to act, so I picked a seat in the bleacher-like seats way at the top and out of the way. I did not want to draw any attention to myself, but I also wanted to listen intently.

The pastor spoke about their missions to faraway places and the good they were doing there. Then came the sermon, which was mainly about marriage. I am not married and never will be again. Regarding that, the sermon was interesting anyway. I prayed on my own behalf as the Sunday Service was finishing up. "Lord, I need a job. I need my house, the roof over my head, and I need food for my dogs and me. Please help me, Lord, as I need these things to survive here. In your precious name - Amen."

My phone was ringing as I got home from church. I answered it. "Hello?"

"Hi, sweet sugar!" It was Raymond.

"Is everything ok? Is Mom ok?"

"Yes, Yes, we are both fine. I just wanted to tell you about our Pastor's sermon today. You can probably see the whole thing online. It was fascinating."

"Ok, I'll go watch it now. Tell Mom I love her!"

I pulled out my laptop and looked up Mom and Raymond's Church. Their Pastor was giving a sermon called *No Trespassing. You have to prosecute the Devil!*

Raymond was right! This sermon is going to be interesting! I clicked on the link that would start the program.

The pastor was speaking. "You have to prosecute the Devil. You have to make a stand in your life and say, 'That's not how it's going to be.' You have to prosecute the enemy and demand repayment of what he has stolen from you. In Job 22:28, it says, *'What you decide on will be done, and light will shine on your ways.* YOU will speak it out, and it will be established for you! Established means it will arise and come on to the stage of action."

I paused the video. Oh wow! That sounds familiar! *For every action, there is an equal and opposite reaction.* The sermon was indeed getting interesting! I clicked on play, and the Pastor continued. "If you say you're having problems, it will arise and come to the stage of action... and you WILL have problems! You have to change your thoughts, words, and actions. You have to declare, *I am healed!* or *My family is put back together!*"

As I watched, I screamed at the top of my lungs, "I HAVE a job!"

Pastor Don Nordin continued. "...and it will arise and come to the stage of action. As it comes to the stage of action, the light will shine onto your pathway!

I paused the video. OK! You have to think and say positive things. I still do that even though I do not practice the enemy's Law of Attraction anymore. I hit the play button, and the video continued.

"In Exodus 3:20-21, it says *'So I will stretch out my hand and strike the Egyptians with all the wonders that I will perform among them. After that, he will let you go. And I will make the Egyptians favorably disposed toward these people so that when you leave, you will not go empty-handed.'* When you go, you shall not go empty. God is focused on restitution, not the deliverance. It's not "IF." It is WHEN. God keeps good records of what you go through. He's focused on getting payment for what you go through.

"Pharaoh finally said to the Israelites to leave his land, and the Pharaoh would do whatever it took to ante up with the Egyptians. So, the Egyptians opened the doors to their homes, and the Israeli women went on a shopping spree! They took jewels of gold and silver. They were making good on a bad debt, and then they left to camp at the Red Sea with the Egyptians hot on their heels.

"God made the Israelites vulnerable so they could get what was owed to them. Then after God opened the Red Sea for the Israelites and they got to the other side, God shut the Red Sea down upon the Egyptians, drowning them. Then God washed up all the weapons and chariots, which allowed the Israelites to defend themselves for 40 years against every savage and every enemy. No weapon armed against you is going to prosper! And every tongue that rises against you in judgment you shall condemn.

"This is the heritage of the Lord. The power of Life and Death is in your tongue! Verbalize it! Then praise Him for fixing what you verbalized! You have not because you ask not! Declare Victory!"

I stopped the video. Kick the devil's ass with the Word of God! Wow! That's cool! This is one very cool sermon! If Mom and Raymond didn't live 65 miles away, I would go to their Church because Pastor Don Nordin was one cool guy! I loved his sermon.

It wasn't like the Pastor of the Church I was currently frequenting. Pastor Don Nordin spoke to you like he knew you. He talked about the Word of God in terms that you could understand. Pastor Don Nordin was amazing! Unfortunately, I couldn't make the 65-mile journey every week to listen to him, so I settled for the small church I was going to until I could find one that was like Mom and Raymond's.

I don't know *Christian-ese*. You know that language people of the traditional Church speak so fluently with all the Thee's and Thou's and Thou Shalt Nots. I think that the *Christian-ese* is what turns a lot of people away from God and Jesus. It's the formal words that none of us have a clue how to speak.

The people that want to force the *Christian-ese* onto you are wrong. And a lot of us feel like we need to speak these words in order for God to hear us. That's not so. You do not have to speak "Thy will" and "For art" and all the words we have no clue how to say. God hears us when we cry. He hears us when we are mad. He hears us in whatever language we speak. All we have to do is talk to him. Start by saying, "God! Hi! It's me. Look, this is what happened. I know you love me. You died for me. You are amazing. I know you will provide, and I know you hear me."

KSBJ has it right. God Listens!

My sister, Isabella, was now in a full-blown, extremely manic depressant bipolar state as she continued on her path of destruction. Lord, have mercy! On the other hand, I was still selling everything that wasn't nailed down just to keep the electricity flowing. That's when the idea hit me between the eyes to go through the room where Isabella had stayed.

I opened the door to her old room and saw piles of things she had recently purchased on the bed. Izzy bought these things with money she did not have. Most of the items still had tags on them. It had to be almost $200 worth of stuff, and all of it had come from retailers on Mom and Raymond's side of town.

On my next trip down there, Mom and I went to all the stores to return the stuff. To rephrase that, we went to all the stores we thought they came from as we had no receipts for most of the stuff. It made me sad to have to explain why we were returning the things to the clerks. "My sister is bipolar and went on a shopping spree. We are not sure this came from your store, and we don't have a receipt. Can you accept a return?"

Most of them were very understanding, which makes me wonder how often do they hear the same story? Are there that many bipolar shopping sprees going on every day?

Exhausted from the shopping trip, we settled down for some dinner. I started the conversation. "Hey Mom, when I was driving over here, I noticed the house around the corner for sale. Wouldn't it be great if I could move there! I wouldn't have to waste so much gas coming to see you guys."

"You know Sandy," Raymond took on his serious voice. "The houses in this area are worth at least $120,000. I think that is out of your reach, darling."

I was dumbfounded. Somethings never change. Where does he think I have been living for the last 30 years? Under a bridge? Does he believe that I have been unemployed all my life? Does he think that I do not own my own home?

My home's value is equal to the one for sale around the corner from their house. How dare he criticize me like this. Raymond's narcissistic opinions were grating on my nerves. *Push it out of your mind, Sandy. For Mom's sake.*

I was about to tear into Raymond when the doorbell rang. Fast, furious, and repeatedly the bell rang. It was Isabella.

I got up from the dinner table and peeked out the front window as Raymond went out to talk to her. "Izzy, what are you doing here, sweetheart?"

"None of your beeswax Pops. Where's my son?"

"He's not here, Izzy."

Izzy screamed, "His freaking car is in the driveway. Do NOT tell me he is not here."

"Look, darling, believe me. He is not here."

Izzy was having none of it. She wanted to talk to her son. Raymond knew he couldn't calm her, so he returned to the dinner table.

A couple of minutes later, the doorbell was repeatedly ringing again. I couldn't stand it anymore. I opened the door. This time Izzy will have to talk to me. "What are you doing here?"

"Nothing. Where is my son?" My nephew Preston was in his room.

"He's not here."

"Yes, he is. Why is his car here then?"

"Just because his car is here does not mean that he is here." That's when I noticed a cylindrical looking thing in her left hand that she was trying to conceal from me. "What's that in your hand?"

"That's none of your business."

"You need to leave. No one wants you here. That includes me, as well."

Izzy turned to get back in her car and couldn't find her keys. "Help me find my keys. You know I always lose my keys." Her ability to instantly switch her thoughts and actions to something way out in the left-field was extraordinary. Something that a bipolar mind does all the time.

Izzy found her keys on the floorboard and tossed them to me. "Here, Sis, I want to give you my car so you can pay your bills."

"Do you have the title?"

"Yes, I do!" Isabella had this massive grin on her face.

"You can't even pay the car note, and they don't give you the title until you pay off the car note. You can't sell it without the title. I have no use for your car. You need to leave NOW!" I yelled at her.

Unceremoniously, Isabella got in her car, backed out of the driveway, and left. I went back inside to finish my dinner. Preston went outside to see if his mother left any damage. It was only a few seconds when he returned to the dinner table, "She wrote something on Opa's van but didn't finish it." Opa is German, which means Granddad.

Raymond and I went out to look at it. It read *I am a ...* "I suppose she didn't finish it because I interrupted her when I came outside to talk to her. It also explains what she was trying to conceal from me. A can of shoe polish." I said, walking to my car to see if she did any damage there too.

On my back window, it said, *Scrapper Aboard.* "That's just lovely! Yes, I am a scrapper, but I do not need that written on the back of my car." I continued, "In the name of Jesus, chase that devil out of my sister."

Raymond sighed heavily, "Let's all go back in and finish our dinner."

As the evening ended, I said my goodbye's to Mom, Raymond, and Preston and hopped back in my car to head to my side of town. I was halfway down their street when this whirring, screeching, horrible noise made itself be known from the inside of my engine. I knew from the sound that something was fixing to break in my engine. "Please, Lord Jesus, wrap my car in Angels wings, and get me and my car back to my house in one piece." I prayed over and over as I drove the sixty-five miles to my home.

I praised His name and thanked Him profusely when I reached for my garage door remote and drove into the garage, locking me and my car safely in for the night. Yep! God Listens!

The next morning, sipping on a cup of coffee, I remembered that horrendous noise my car was making and cringed, "Well, it's not going to fix itself." I googled car noises and was taken to a site that had audio files you could listen to so you could compare them to the noise your car was making.

I listened to the sound file that was an exact duplicate of the noise my car was making. I clicked on the link for the diagnosis. It came back with: *Your serpentine belt is fixing to break.* Your serpentine belt powers most all of your engine's accessories. That means when your belt breaks, it will take out everything from your power steering to the alternator to the air conditioner, and your expense for the damage will go up considerably.

I sighed, "Oh, that's just great. How many hundreds of dollars is this going to cost me? Hundreds of dollars I do not have. No car means NO job interviews, means NO job, means NO money, means NO food. Oh, Joy." I went out to the garage, armed with a flashlight, and popped open the hood to my car.

There it was. Yep! The belt had more cracks in it than the Grand Canyon. It looked like chewed twine. Chewed up, spit out, and stepped on! It was a miracle I made it home! But I still have no money to fix this.

Not giving up so quickly, I went back inside to google the repair cost estimates for my car type. Just replacing the belt would cost anything from $300 and up with labor at most car repair shops. "That's wonderful. What's my next option?" I asked my favorite search engine. "How much is the serpentine belt?" and "How hard is it to replace the serpentine belt yourself?"

Google came back with, "AutoZone serpentine belt is $30." BINGO! Ok, I can do $30; I just have to have another garage sale. Next stop... YouTube. After watching three videos, I found out that changing out the serpentine belt only involved ONE bolt! I can deal with one bolt!

I got into my car to drive the six blocks to Auto Zone. Now I know what you're thinking if my belt was fixing to break, then why did I drive the car. Well, if you have ever lived in Houston during the summertime, the heat tends to be vicious. One hundred ten degrees in the afternoon is considered the norm. Plus, my bicycle had two flat tires. It never ends!

My car did make it to AutoZone without incident, and I retrieved the belt and made my way back home. Parking the car back in the garage, I now had to wait for the engine to cool off before I could attempt to replace the belt.

It being Sunday, I realized I couldn't make it to my Church Service. "No big deal, I'll watch Mom's Church Service!" I thought to myself as I opened my laptop. I searched for the good Pastor's last sermon that they had listed on their website.

The latest and greatest video stream was Pastor Don Nordin continuing his sermon from last week about *No Trespassing*. Very Cool! I clicked on play and listened.

"Payment by the enemy! This hits on three topics: First, what we have the right to do as Christians. Second, what the enemy is required to do. And third, what God will do on our behalf. In Isaiah 28:5-6, it says, *'In that day the Lord Almighty will be a glorious crown, a beautiful wreath for the remnant of his people. He will be a spirit of justice to the one who sits in judgment, a source of strength to those who turn back the battle at the gate.'* To turn back the battle at the gate means to drive the enemy back beyond his starting place. As children of God, we have been given the power and authority according to the scripture to turn the enemy back to the gate."

I paused the video long enough to exclaim, "He who slings mud loses ground! I WILL defeat the enemy! HA!"

The pastor continued, "This is what we as Christians have the right to do. In Deuteronomy 7:24, *'He will give their kings into your hand, and you will wipe out their names from under heaven. No one will be able to stand up against you; you will destroy them.'* In Deuteronomy 11:25, *'No one will be able to stand against you. The Lord your God, as he promised you, will put the terror and fear of you on the whole land, wherever you go."* In Joshua 1:5, *'No one will be able to stand against you all the days of your life. As I was with Moses, so I will be with you; I will never leave you nor forsake you."* - PRAISE GOD!

"In Daniel 11:32, *'With flattery, he will corrupt those who have violated the covenant, but the people who know their God will firmly resist him.'*

"WOW! That's so cool!" I exclaimed.

"Where it looked like you were going down, then all of a sudden, the tables get turned, and you have Victory! And everybody around you says *Wow!* - Praise God!"

Laughing out loud, I said, "Hey, that's exactly what I just said! I love this pastor!"

"Victory will be so complete that peace will become the norm in your life. When you learn how to fight the enemy, you can have peace in the midst of the battle because you understand your authority is as a believer, and you can just say, 'You know what? The devil picked this fight, but he's gonna be sorry when this is over because this is all going to turn out to God's Glory and my benefit! HALLELUJAH!

"And so, devil, if you want to try it, then just bring it on! Because we are going to rub your nose in it before it all over!

"In the second part, this is what the enemy will be required to do. In Proverbs 6:31, *'Yet if he is caught, he must pay sevenfold, though it costs him all the wealth of his house.'* The enemy comes to steal, kill, and destroy. But if he is found, he must pay sevenfold. Say this, 'I declare and demand that the enemy make sevenfold restitution in my life.' NO MORE MERCY FOR THE ENEMY! Amen!

"God is waiting for you to file the charges to prosecute the enemy! Put your foot down! Draw the line. Do not let this happen any more! Make the enemy pay you back! -Amen!

NO More from the devil! I will prosecute! I laughed out loud!

"In Isaiah 61:7, *'Instead of your shame you will receive a double portion, and instead of disgrace, you will rejoice in your inheritance. And so, you will inherit a double portion in your land, and everlasting joy will be yours.'* Praise God! In the here and the now, we will blow the enemy away.

"In the third part, what God will do on your behalf. But you have to do what is required before God will give us what we desire. In Deuteronomy 30:1-3, *'Prosperity after turning to the Lord. When all these blessings and curses I have set before you come on you, and you take them to heart wherever the Lord your God disperses you among the nations. When you and your children return to the Lord your God and obey him with all your heart and with all your soul according to everything I command you today, then the Lord your God will restore your fortunes and have compassion on you and gather you again from all the nations where he scattered you.'* Return to the Lord and obey His Word. He will give us compassion.

"In Romans: 16:20, *'The God of Peace will soon crush Satan under your feet. The grace of our Lord Jesus be with you.'* -Amen! In Isaiah 54:17, *'no weapon forged against you will prevail, and you will refute every tongue that accuses you. This is the heritage of the servants of the Lord, and this is their vindication from me," declares the Lord.'* -Amen!

"And in Joel 2:25-27, *'I will repay you for the years the locusts have eaten, the great locust and the young locust, the other locusts and the locust swarm, my great army that I sent among you. You will have plenty to eat until you are full, and you will praise the name of the Lord your God, who has worked wonders for you. Never again will my people be shamed. Then you will know that I am in Israel, that I am the Lord your God, and that there is no other; never again will my people be shamed.'*

"You need to declare that your life is off-limits to Satan, and the devil has no legal right to delve into any area of your life! Declare that you are God's property, and you intend on prosecuting him. Amen! Prosecute him to the fullest extent of the law. Declare that you intend to ask your attorney, who happens to be your elder brother Jesus, to partition the court for a change in venue.

"Declare that you have every reason to believe that it will be granted because the Father of your attorney, Your Father, is the Judge! That looser devil doesn't stand a chance! Declare that you intend to throw the book at the enemy and declare you will ask that the maximum penalty be assessed, and the enemy will have no option but to pay restitution on every account.

"Declare that the enemy is going to lose ground every battle because you are aware of your rights against him. - Amen! Praise God!

Very cool sermon! No More devil! I am a child of God! Very, very, very COOL! I smiled! Speaking of cool... my engine should be cool right about now! I moseyed out to the garage and popped open the hood. There it was. The serpentine belt. Joy! "Off you come now!" I gripped the one bolt holding the old serpentine belt on to its track and moved it towards me just like the YouTube video showed.

The belt slipped off its track, and I removed it. Ok, now the hard part, weaving the new belt onto the snaky pattern. I guess that's where it gets its name, serpentine. I tried several times to get the new belt onto the tracks, but there was one tricky part that I just couldn't get my hands in there to push it onto the tracks. I grabbed the longest screwdriver I had and prayed, "Hey, Lord, could you give me a hand, please?" And to my amazement, the belt easily slipped on to the track like it was the most normal thing ever. Just like socks on a rooster! Yep, God Listens!

I went to call Mom and Raymond to tell them the good news and discovered my phone was disconnected. You know, that phone that my darling bipolar sister gave me before I kicked her out of my house. She had it disconnected.

You can't port a phone number over to a new service after it has been disconnected. That means all the 900 kabillion resumes that I have sent out over the months and months of job searching are now null and void. The prospective employer would dial the wrong phone number if they wanted to interview me for a job.

I suppose the only good thing about having a disconnected number was the creditors that hound me a billion times a day no longer call because they too don't have the right number.

It's the little things that keep me amused these days!

144

CHAPTER 12

The only means of communication I had left was by email. So, I emailed Mom and Raymond to let them know what happened to my phone. They were heartbroken.

"Honey, just come over, and we'll go to our phone service provider. They can get you a new phone and a new number fast." Mom always knew how to fix things.

"Alright, Mom. I'll be there in about an hour. Thank you very much. That's going to help me a lot."

As I was driving down to the south side of town, my mind was on how many resumes I would have to redo because I have a new phone number. The short answer was thousands upon thousands. I would essentially have to start all over with the job search. That thought didn't put a smile on my face.

Mom and Raymond were ready to go when I got there. We piled into Raymond's minivan and made our way into the cell phone shop. A very enthusiastic employee met us at the door. "Hi! Welcome! How can I help you today?"

"We are here to get a new line on our service," Raymond said, looking over at me, "It's for my daughter."

I cringed a little at the *daughter* word, "Before you do that, I want to be sure that there is no way I can have the same number that I had before."

"What do you mean?" the salesman turned to me with a quizzical look on his face.

"My sister had my phone number tied to her account. She had my number turned off. Disconnected. Is there any way I can get that number back with a new service here?"

"No, Ma'am. I'm sorry. That would be impossible."

"That's what I thought, but I wanted to make sure anyway."

"Do you have an idea of the type of phone you want to use?"

"The cheapest flip phone you have would be great."

The salesman hooked me up with a cute little flip phone. Nothing fancy. All it did was text and make phone calls. At this point, that's all I needed. Driving back from the cell phone store, we passed Isabella's storage unit.

Mom points to the storage lot, "Sandy, look! That's where Isabella's storage unit is. We got a phone call from the manager the other day. He is giving us a week to either let the storage unit go up for auction or pay the past due bill of $1200. Raymond and I would just let it go, but your Grandmother's things and Preston's things are in there too, and we want those things back."

"Oh, Mom, that's horrible. Where are you going to get that kind of money?"

"Well, I'm going to go talk to the manager, who is a good friend of ours, and see if he will drop the past-due bill down a bit. Hopefully, he will drop it down enough to where we can afford it." Raymond was just pulling into the driveway of their house.

"Well, keep me informed. I wish I could help out, but money is as tight as a wet boot right now."

"I know, sweetheart. That will eventually change. Just keep the Faith."

"Mom, if a trip around the world costs one dollar, I might make it to your house from mine with the money that I have right now. That's how broke I am."

"Well, you have a new phone number that works and isn't going away, so that should help."

"Yes, it will. Thanks again!" I hesitated, " And on that subject, I should head back to my side of town and start retyping the kabillion resumes I sent out to reflect the new number. Let me know how the storage unit pans out."

Mom gave me a big hug in their driveway, and off I went to my side of the world. With a new phone number in hand, I started a new quest for jobs. I occasionally came across some of the jobs I had applied to before, which still had my resume on file, so it was merely a matter of changing the phone number.

This job hunt is all very frustrating, and the rejection is overwhelming. Every day, I pray that any kind of job will present itself to me, even if it's not *the* job. Lord, I just need something to keep the lights on, the water running, and my dogs fed.

In February of 2016, I was still sending out five kabillion resumes a day when I came across an ad on the internet about a company called Appel. It advertised a job that you could do working from your own home, and all you needed was an internet connection. I immediately signed up for it. A week later, they accepted my application, which made me as pleased as punch.

The job paid $370 a month, which didn't go very far. But what it did do was keep the lights on, the water running, and my dogs fed! Thank you, Jesus! It was the first step in the right direction, and that gave me hope!

I've learned to fix a lot of things around my house during my stay in hell. I learned to fix the things that I would usually hire someone else to fix because they knew how, and I did not. Back then, it was just easier to hire someone than figure it out yourself.

Being broke and needing things fixed is pure, by God, motivation to figure it out by yourself because you need things to work. It is just the things that cost a lot of money that I can't do right now. The dogs have an electronic dog door that lets them in and out by themselves. One day it stopped working. The dog door motor had burned up.

I can fix it, but the new motor and motherboard would cost me over a hundred bucks to replace. Even if I had a hundred bucks, I couldn't afford to spend it on dog doors. I ended up putting plastic in the hole of the dog door to cover the opening. I hoped and prayed that a varmint wouldn't find its way into the house.

I continue to have garage sales, but I have nothing left of value to sell. I would sell all my furniture, but it's over 20 years old. I would have to pay the sanitation worker to take it off my hands. The only thing that keeps my sanity going these days are my dogs and the Internet. My only friends are in Iowa now, and the only family that cares enough about me are my Mom and Raymond.

My sister is nuts, and the rest of my step-siblings... well, I wouldn't want to contact them if hell froze over. They showed me how they felt about me way before I left Mom's house when I was seventeen. I do not care to dredge up those feelings again.

My daughter will not talk to me. She is mad because I let my only blood sister come live with me after she caused so much hurt and ruckus to all the family members. My daughter is mad at me because I tried to help my crazy sister. I doubt she even knows the dire straits that I am in right now.

My only blood sibling, Isabella, my sister, well... her cheese done slid off the cracker, and she's running from the law. Her drama is what probably keeps me from being anxious and worrying all the time about my own problems. And by drama, I mean soap opera-style drama, except this isn't TV. It is real life. This was happening now. This was all happening to my poor, dysfunctional family.

The sound of my phone ringing shocked me out of these disturbing thoughts. It was Mom.

"Hi, sweet sugar!" Mom was always cheerful, no matter what the circumstances were.

"Hi, Mom! What's new?"

"I called the manager of Isabella's storage unit and made a deal with him."

"Really! You are amazing, Mom! What's the deal?"

"I talked him down to $500 instead of $1200 that Izzy owes for past bills, but we have to clear her stuff out by the end of the week."

"Wow! That's awesome!" I paused for a second, "But wait! Where are we going to put all that stuff?"

"Well, darling, I haven't thought that far in advance yet."

"Mom! I have an idea! We could put her stuff in the room that I let her live in my house. It's ten feet by fourteen feet. It should be enough to pack all her stuff into it. I can cram it in from floor to ceiling. We just need a way to get it here."

"Are you sure, honey?"

"Yes, Mom, It's just the dogs here and me. Besides, Deb and Meg's stuff are in the other spare room. We can put some of Izzy's stuff in there if it doesn't fit in the second spare room. I don't use either of those rooms, so it's ok with me."

"Let me talk to Raymond about it, and we'll try to come up with a plan to get it there."

"Ok, Mom sounds good. Call me back when you know something."

"I will, sweetheart. Love you!"

"Love you more, Mom!"

The sun was just starting to come up one cold pre-dawn morning in February when my sister, Isabella, after another sleepless night, decided she wanted to kill Mom and Raymond by setting their house on fire. She knew that her son Preston would be in the house sleeping along with Mom and Raymond because he had been living there since his very early childhood. That was right about the time that Isabella started showing bipolar symptoms. Back then, no one snapped that she was a manic depressant. No one put two and two together. No one knew she was bipolar.

In the back of Isabella's mind, she knew she did not want to hurt her son. She loved him and tried to protect him, but she also wanted to hurt Mom and Raymond. She wanted to punish them for some twisted thought that the enemy had placed in her mind.

She knew she had to warn her son to get out of the house, or he would become a victim in her diabolical plan of murder. Preston had a full-time job working for the local grocery store. He managed the grocery carts in the parking lot the evening that his mother came to warn him. As Isabella pulled into the parking lot, she spotted her son and sat watching him for some time.

Finally, she got out of her car and approached him. "Preston!"

"Mom?" Preston said cautiously. He knew of his mother's bipolar antics all too well.

"Look, son, you can't go home tonight. Promise me you will not go home tonight."

"What's this about, Mom?"

"Just promise me you won't go home tonight."

"Whatever, Mom, just go away now. I'm working."

Isabella was satisfied that she had adequately warned her son to stay away from Mom and Raymond's house that night. She pulled up to a convenience store, borrowed a customer's phone, and called Raymond and Janice. Raymond saw the incoming Caller Id on his phone. He did not recognize it, so he let it go to voice mail and listened to the enraged Isabella.

"Raymond, you are an arrogant, self-centered, narcissistic, controlling pedophile and should not be breathing my air. If you ever hurt my mother, make no mistake, I will hurt you. Go back to hell where you came from. If you need directions, just ask. Better yet, I will send you there myself. I bought a 9mm colt, and it has your sorry ass name written all over it." - Beep.

As the night was giving way to the predawn hours of the morning, Isabella drove to Raymond and Janice's house. She proceeded to set small fires around the air conditioning unit located on the side of the house, just under her son's bedroom window. Satisfied that the flames were going on their own, Isabella set fire to Janice's birdbath and garden closest to the front door. Taking a plastic clothesline, she tied it to the mailbox that hung on the wall, inches from the front door. "This should start the door on fire," she thought as she took her cigarette lighter from her pocket and set the clothesline ablaze.

As the fire started, she looked down at her feet and spotted the welcome mat. "And that should help immensely!" She lit all four corners of the welcome mat on fire and watched as the flames started to kiss the bottom of the front door. She turned and saw the mulch in the garden just catching fire. Satisfied, she stuffed her cigarette lighter back into her pocket and left the premises.

CHAPTER 13

As the sun was just coming up, Raymond finished fixing himself a cup of coffee and headed to the front door to grab the morning newspaper. As he opened the door, the ash that was still smoldering from the welcome mat blew into the house's entryway burning small holes in the carpet around it. Raymond called the police.

The ringing of my phone woke me from a dead sleep. "Hi, Sweetheart, I'm sorry to wake you so early."

"That's ok Mom, what's wrong?"

"Your sister tried to burn the house down this morning."

"Oh my God, are you guys, ok?"

"Yes, we are fine. Raymond called the police. The police said that we have no evidence that it was Izzy, so they can't arrest her for it."

"You have got to be joking! We all know she did it. We all know she is capable and sick enough to do it. Did you let them listen to the phone messages she left?"

I had started a file of recorded phone messages that Isabella had left for them on their answering machine. All of the messages were vile and disgusting. In all of them, she clearly threatens to kill both of them. "Those phone messages are rock-solid proof she wants to kill you guys."

"Yes, we let the Arson Investigator hear some of them, but he said all they could do was issue a warrant for her arrest for a *terroristic threat to the family* just because of the phone messages. They can't get her on arson because we have no solid proof that she did it. If we knew where she was, we could at least get the police to go and issue her the warrant and get her behind bars.

Then maybe she could get the help she so desperately needs."

"Oh my God, Mom, I'm so sorry. Do you need me down there to help?"

"Not now, sweetheart, let the police do their thing."

"OK, I love you guys."

"We love you too, honey."

I hung up the phone as chills ran down my spine. Lord, you have got to stop this insanity before Izzy kills someone.

A week later, we learned that Isabella was currently staying close to one of the only friends she had left on this planet. Alecia was a sweet, kindhearted soul. That is until Izzy threatened her too. Late in the night, I got a text message from Alecia.

Hi, this is Alecia. Please call. Izzy attempted to taser a friend of ours last night and has threatened me. She has a friend impersonating a Webster Police Officer and has been trying to get into my apartment. Our friends called the Houston Police Department, and they are looking for her. I love her very much and know that this is just her disorder. I am not angry, but I want you and the family to understand what is happening.

Webster is a small city just a few miles south of Houston. I'm not sure what the Houston Police Department can do but impersonating a police officer was a serious offense. I called Mom and Raymond in the morning. "Hi, Mom!"

"Well, Hi, Sugar!"

"So, Izzy's friend Alecia texted me last night. Izzy tried to taser one of her friends and threatened Alecia. Izzy's on the run again."

"Oh, Lord! Well, we got a voice message from Officer Andrew Byrd with the Webster Police Department. He was furious and called Raymond all kinds of horrible names."

"Mom, Alecia said that Izzy had a friend impersonating a Webster Police Officer. Do you still have the voice message on your recorder?"

"Yes, we do."

"Let me hear it, Mom, and I'll record it. Impersonating a police officer is a felony. That guy is going to get the book thrown at him when they catch him."

Mom turned the answering machine on and put the phone up to the speaker, as I grabbed my phone and hit the record button.

"Yes, Mr. Davis. I don't even want to put the sir in front of your name. This is Andrew Byrd. Deputy Andrew Byrd with the Webster Police Department. You need to call me back, and when you do, you will take a little ride with us. We will do a few extra-curricular activities, and nobody in their right mind would approve of it. You weak ass pedophile freak."

There was a short pause, and the fake cop continued, "Answer the phone! This is the Webster Police Department. If you think you have the guts to rape a little kid, wait till you talk to my troops and me. I can't wait to get my hands on you. You should be a little scared now, huh!" Beep.

Mom let the answering machine continue, and the next message was from Izzy's x-husband Thomas. "Raymond, this is Thomas. A Webster Police Officer just called me and told me that you guys need to get to safety and clear the house until a situation is cleared up. Ok? I'm going to call Preston now." Beep.

I yelled into the phone, "Mom, this is crazy stupid." But the next message was already playing, and it was from Izzy herself.

"Just a little by note. Ms. Alecia is going to be calling you and telling you that I am out of control. I am out of control because she pissed me off. I broke her freaking phone, so she took mine." Isabella was breathing heavily as she angrily continued her rant. "I've called the police, and I've knocked on her door. She won't give me my phone back, so I reported it stolen. That's OK, Raymond, because I am a productive member of society, and I have freaking insurance on my phone."

Izzy's voice was starting to shake. She was losing control. "Anyway, the other piece to this is that I called David Walker. He's going to help me acquire property in San Leon. When I am finished with that, I will ask him to help me file a lawsuit against you. I don't know how long it's been since you raped Sandy, but I am going to ask him to take care of it personally."

My ears perked up. *Raped Sandy?* Is Izzy confusing Raymond Sr. with Raymond Jr.? And if so, how did she know? Did the two twin brothers molest her too?

Izzie's bipolar mind sort of had those facts right. The big difference was Raymond Senior did not rape me. It was Raymond Junior and his twin, Dan, that sexually molested me during my teen years. Raymond Senior and my Mom still had no clue about that.

Isabella's mind went back to her childhood. She remembered the family lawyer Mom had way back when she was divorcing our father. David Walker was a good Christian man who attended the same Church that Janice and Raymond attended. He had always helped Mom through her legal problems with gentle kindness.

Izzy continued her phone rant, "Oh yeah, it will go something like this, Raymond. *Mr. David Walker? This is Isabella Jenkins Schmidt. I'm Raymond Davis's stepdaughter. Oh, Hi there! How are Janice and Raymond doing? My Mother is fine, but my stepdad is a pedophile. I'm going to file charges on his freaking ass.*"

Isabella was in a rage now, "Raymond, I'm going to humiliate you all over this town. Do you hear me? Starting with every freaking post office there is in the state of Texas. Do you understand me? You are done. I will take you down. You pedophile. I am taking you down."

Finally, Mom came back on the phone, "There are a bunch more San's. They all accuse Raymond of being a pedophile."

"I'm so sorry, Mom. Just keep them on the answering machine until we get them all transferred to a flash drive."

As I weather this poverty hell storm, I now had to deal with this horrible hurricane of bad memories that surfaced and continued to attack my brain. All I can do right now is to try and push those ugly memories out of my brain.

Isabella needed food, shelter, and money to survive on the streets. But none of these things gave her any worry. She was high on life, and there was nothing that could cross her path to bring her down off her manic state. "Nothing and NO one," she thought to herself as she sped down Highway 3 to Clear Lake City.

It was nearing 2:00 a.m., and she had not slept in days. Her bipolar brain told her she did not need to. She pulled into the lot of a convenience store and sparked up a conversation with a female hanging out near the entrance. "Hey there! How's it going?" Isabella was walking towards her.

"Pretty good! I'm just waiting for my boyfriend to pick me up. He's late as usual." The prostitute was dressed to the hilt in high heels, bright red lipstick, and all that.

"How would you like to make a quick couple bucks?"

"What do I have to do?"

"Just call this number and tell them you're a police officer and you found me on the side of the road out of gas."

"Seriously?"

"It's a joke I'm pulling on my parents! They are going to love it!"

"Well," she said with a slight hesitation, "How much?"

"Five bucks for two minutes of your time, but you have to use your phone."

"OK, you've got a deal."

After several rings, the phone finally woke Raymond out of a dead sleep, "Hello?"

"Hi, this is Officer Samika with the Houston Police Department. I found your daughter Isabella stranded on the side of the road. She's out of gas, and her car is dead. She asked me to call you and see if it was OK for her to come to your house for the night. She said she would fix her car in the morning."

Raymond wasn't convinced that she was a cop. Not after the fake Webster Police call. "If you get Isabella to sign a statement saying that in the morning, she will admit herself into Ben Taub

Hospital for manic depression, then she can stay at my house overnight."

"Sure thing, I'll let her know and get back to you." She hung up the phone as she reached out her hand with her palm up, demanding payment from Izzy.

"Wow, that was awesome! Great Job! Thank you!" She dug in her purse, searching for the money she had promised the fake Officer. "I'm going to have to go to the bank down the street to get you the cash." She said as she hopped into her Honda Accord and sped away laughing. She never had any kind of intention to pay her.

Driving down Highway 3, she thought, "I think it's time to visit my darling ex-husband. I'm sure he's worried about me." She turned the car down State Highway 288 South, then took Texas 35 to Bay City some 95 miles away.

At 4:30 a.m., Isabella pulls into the Apartment Complex where her ex-husband Thomas lives. She strolled up to the door and knocked. Thomas wasn't answering, so she started banging on the door and screaming at the top of her lungs, "Tom, let me in. Let me in!"

Thomas ran to the door to quiet her down so she would not wake up his neighbors. "What do you want?"

"I need a place to stay. I need some food too. What's for breakfast?"

"You are not welcome here. Leave now, before I call the cops."

"Come on, Darling-poo, at least give me some money. You know you owe me money, and I have come to collect."

"Go away, Isabella." He dug his phone out of his pocket, "I'm calling the cops."

"Call the freaking cops! I don't care! I'm going to wake up your neighbors so they can watch you be an asshole to your wife." Isabella started banging on all the doors and windows within 40 feet of Thomas's front door. Screaming and hitting, fast, hard, and furious. Thomas dialed 911.

"911, what's your emergency?"

"My ex-wife is disturbing the peace. She's banging on my

neighbor's doors and windows, screaming at the top of her lungs. I need an officer here immediately."

Isabella overheard Thomas' conversation. She ran to her car in the parking lot and left the complex. Isabella turned into a dirt road that was a few yards past the apartment complex entrance and waited. It didn't take long as she watched two police cars pull into the complex.

Getting out of her car, she walked in the shadows back to Thomas' apartment building. She was crouched down behind a large bush as she watched the officers talk to Thomas. "Take as long as you want! I have all the time in the world!" She thought to herself as she watched the body movements of both the Officers and her ex-husband.

She was just close enough to hear them speak. The Officers had taken out pencil and pad and were furiously writing down everything Thomas was telling them. "I'm sorry, sir, but she didn't do any damage. The best you can do is charge her with mischievous behavior."

"Isabella left the property. I'm sure she is on her way back to Houston by now." He sighed, "I won't press charges because there are no damages. Thank you, Officers, for coming out so early."

Isabella watched the Officers leave the complex and waited another 30 minutes in the dark. "No damages! HA!" Izzy thought, "I'll show you damages, Tommy-Poo-Poo."

She walked to the parking lot where Tom's car was parked and took out her keys. "No Damages! How do you like this?" As she slashed deep scratches into the door panels of Toms car. Her twisted mind wouldn't let her stop there. She ran back to her car and grabbed all the packets of ketchup that were on her floorboard.

Taking the packets, she wrote the most obscene message she could think of on his front windshield and down the hood. She was satisfied that her artwork was perfection. She got back into her car and drove back to Houston. Thomas filed a charge of mischievous behavior with the Bay City Police Department.

CHAPTER 14

T he sun had been up for just a little while as Isabella pulled into the Goodwill Store parking lot that was just around the corner from her parents' house. She decided she wanted to go on a shopping spree. "What the Heck," she thought, "I need some new clothes."

She spent hours in the store trying on clothes but didn't find anything she liked. Then she saw a purse and said, "This is Mine!" She turned and promptly walked out of the store without paying for it. As she sat in her car parked in the Goodwill parking lot, a Houston Police Department cruiser pulled in and blocked her exit.

Two officers got out of their vehicle and made their way towards Isabella. She was sitting in the driver's seat. "Ma'am, can you please step out of the vehicle?"

"What's wrong, Officer? I haven't done anything but sit in my car."

"Ma'am, I am not asking. Step out of the vehicle NOW."

"Oh, all right, but I see no reason for this." Izzy unlocked her door and stepped out.

The Officer grabbed her and spun her around. She landed face down on the hood of her car. The Officer pulled her arms behind her back and slapped on the handcuffs. Isabella had no time to think as the Officer threw her in the back of their car and hauled her off to the Harris County Jail for petty theft. Goodwill called a wrecker service to haul off her car.

Two days later, the Judge released her from jail for time served. Isabella left the jail with no money or possessions, as everything she had in this world was in her car, which is sitting in the impound lot.

Isabella walked across the street from the police substation and met Rick, a 65-year-old Christian man who gave her $330 to get her car out of hock. As soon as she had the money in her hands, she ditched him. That was only the beginning.

Once she had her car back, she went to an old family friend's house, who, out of the graciousness of their hearts, let her stay with them for a little while. That is until Isabella threatened their family, and they kicked her out. She knew they still had some of her things, and she wanted them back.

At 3:00 a.m., she drove to their house and banged on their door. "Michelle, let me in." She yelled, knocking on the front door. "Come on. You still have a lot of my things. Let me in."

Silence.

"Let me in now, or I'm going to bang on every one of your neighbor's doors and tell them what an asshole you are."

Michelle called the police.

The police show up minutes later. Michelle and her husband had already boxed up what little possessions that they knew belonged to Isabella. They gave the box to the police officers, who gave the box to Isabella with a warning. "If you go back to this house or threaten this family, they will file criminal trespassing charges against you. Stay away from this family, Isabella. Or face criminal charges."

"No problem, officers," she said as she threw all of her stuff into the back of her car.

Isabella cruised the neighborhood until she was barely out of gas. By some kind of magic, she found herself back at the Goodwill parking lot. The car was sputtering on the last little bits of fumes. Isabella came to a stop, not caring if it was a parking spot or not. Out of gas and nowhere to go, she left her car with the driver's side door open, the windows rolled down, the headlights on, and the parking lights blinking.

In a daze, she started walking. She had not gotten too far from the car when she thought of Mom's 84-year-old best friend who lives alone. Her house was just a few blocks from where she was right now. Her pace quickened as new possibilities formed in her mind. Ms. Lee should have a gas can and probably gas too. Hell, there's food and water there also. The more she thought about it, the faster she walked. There's no way she could turn down one of Dear Janice's children.

It was no time at all before she found herself knocking on the front door of Ms. Lee's house at 6:00 a.m. In the meantime, her car's battery died since she left everything on that would drain it. And there it sat, driver's door open and windows rolled down when a Goodwill employee saw it and called the cops. Her car was towed yet again.

"Isabella!" Ms. Lee said, very surprised to see her.

"Hello Ms. Lee, I need a place to stay for a little while. Do you mind if I stay with you?"

"Well, Heaven's no! Come on in!"

"Also, my car ran out of gas at the Goodwill parking lot. Can you drive me back there with some gas?"

"Oh, My! Well, there should be some gas in the can that I use for the lawnmower. Let's go get it, and I'll drive you up there."

"You're the Best!"

When they got to the parking lot, Isabella's car was gone. "I don't see it here," she said, scanning the parking lot. Isabella looked up and noticed a sign that was on one of the light posts. If your car has been towed, please call the Charter Wrecker Company at 1-800-999-5757.

Isabella was furious. "Oh, my Gawd. I cannot believe the stupidity of these people at Goodwill. They KNEW that was my car."

"Come on, Isabella, let's go back to the house," Ms. Lee coaxed as she threw the car in reverse and headed back to her own house.

Settling down finally in the warmth of Ms. Lee's home, Isabella made herself comfortable on the couch as Ms. Lee went to make some tea for the both of them. Isabella eyed the phone in the next room and decided it was time to give her ex-husband Thomas a good piece of her mind.

Thomas was in the habit of screening his calls by sending them straight to voice mail.

"Hello Tommy-poo," she said in her sweetest voice as she began her voice mail message. "I do not know why you are the way you are, and I do not care anymore. There is someone in this world that deserves you. It just is not ME. Why do you not care about me and my relationship with Preston? What possible positive, warm fuzzy do you attain by watching my heartbreak and ache? Why can you not give me his phone number?"

She is getting angrier just thinking about the abuse she has suffered at her ex-husband's hand. "And now I have been wrongfully accused of stealing my very own purse from Goodwill. I was consequently jailed for two days and now I find my car has been towed at a $330.00 expense."

She's seething now as she continues, "Then..." taking a deep breath, "I tried to sell my car from the Goodwill parking lot alongside other cars that had for sale signs on them. Goodwill called the Houston Police Department, who called the Charter Wrecker Company to tow my car, YET AGAIN, to the Houston Auto lot on Old Galveston Road." She's so mad now she is shaking as she continues her speech. "Three Houston Police Department Officers accompanied me to the car lot, but to no avail. The Auto Lot insists on an ID for proof that I am who I am. I can't do that because my ID is IN MY FRIGG'N CAR!"

She's yelling at the top of her lungs now, as her bipolar mind spits out the venom, "I've lost two weeks of pay, and now I've lost my job. My parents have put out an all-out bounty on anyone aiding and abetting me in any way. I got out of the Galveston County Jail on Sunday, late afternoon. I was barefooted. I had no monies, and I had no credit card."

She calms down a little bit, "I called Janice, our dear Mother, and asked nicely for help. I told her that my income tax refund is back, and when I could get transportation, I would have $1200.00 to pay her back. OR, she could just come to get me, OR ask Preston too." Izzy takes a deep breath, "But NOOOO-OOO. Janice responded with; *We're having Church home group*

162

right now..."

Back to yelling at the top of her lungs, "How does a MOTHER do that to her daughter? How does a son see his mother cold, barefooted, and in need? ...and not care?"

Thomas was listening as she spoke these hateful words. Furious, he picked up the phone, "I only know that you came to Bay City and banged on my door at 4:30 in the morning after sending me threats. You were told not to come back, and you keyed my car, which cost more than 1000 dollars to repair. I know you have sent death threats to your parents and tried to burn their house down while they and Preston were asleep inside. I also know that felony charges have been filed against you."

In the lowest voice he could muster, he continued, "You cannot expect people to help you when you do not apologize for the threats and damage you have done. Your best bet for help is to go to a hospital. There is no excuse or reason to justify the things you have done. Do not come to my apartment again! I will not answer the phone if you call until I hear and see that you are genuinely sorry for what you have done. You will be arrested if seen on this property, and while I have not pressed charges for property damage on my car, I can. Go to a hospital! "

Isabella was taken aback. How could he? "Have a nice friggin day!" She slammed the phone down. "Ms. Lee? Do you mind if I use your computer? I need to check my email."

"No, darling, go right ahead." Isabella opened the internet browser and searched for the Houston Police Department's website. "I'll fix this deceptive trap that they have set for me. Right now. Right this instant."

Scrolling down to the bottom of the webpage, she found the Contact Us form and clicked on it. She entered just her first name and gave my address. She entered her phone number but gave them my email address. Then she entered in the comments, '*my 2004 gold Honda Accord was stolen from Fuqua and Sabo Road, approx. eight days ago. It has been harbored at the Houston Auto Center, on Old Galveston Road. I have had to pawn my James Avery jewelry to eat and stay in a hotel. I have lost eight days of pay.*

Due to not being able to work. Never mind the humiliation that went along with it, I NEED MY CAR BACK... eight days ago.'

Of course, the Contact Us form generated an automated response, and since Izzy used my email address, I did what any computer geek would have done. I responded to it!

> Hello,
> My sister, Isabella Jenkins, aka Isabella Schmidt, aka Isabella Jenkins Schmidt, generated this email from an unknown IP address. She is extremely mentally unstable, violent, and currently at large. The car she speaks of was repossessed due to failure of payment. She does not and has not held a job since the beginning of February. The phone number she gives in this email used to be her phone number; however, they have stopped service due to non-payment. The address she gives is mine, but she does NOT live here. I repeat, she does not live with me at my address that she listed as hers. She is currently living on the streets. She was last seen and heard from in Galveston. The email address is mine, though. I am guessing that's one of the few email addresses that she can remember. However, this email that she generated will be used in my case against her for computer fraud. Any help or evidence you can supply me with would be much appreciated. My sincerest apologies for any inconvenience this might have caused.

Still, on Ms. Lee's computers and not finding anyone that can empathize with her, in a fit of anger, Isabella decides to write several threatening emails to her niece who lives in Pearland, Texas. "That'll teach her to mess with me," she said as she hit the send button.

Isabella had enough. With no car, she could do nothing about it, so she hailed a cab. Isabella asked the cab driver to take her on a tour around the Fuqua area as this was where, in her mind, her enemies were. Besides, she thought, it was such a magnificent sunset that shone directly over her subdivision. I am sure many peoples will be Blessed with His magnificence on this day!

Shaking off a shiver that ran down her back, she said to the

Lord, "Why are you so nice to me after all I've done in my life?"

She believed that God spoke to her spirit and said, "Because I Love you!"

As the tour around her subdivision continued, she was racking up a pretty hefty cab fare. It was $150, to be exact. Losing his patience, the cab driver pulled over and asked for payment. Isabella had no money to give him, as she had no money to her name. The cab driver took her to a Houston Police Department substation where she was booked for Theft of Service.

Isabella sat in the Houston Police Department jail waiting for her judgment from the Court. After hearing Isabella's side of the story, the Magistrate placed a $5000 bond on her. Isabella only needed to pay ten percent of that to get out of jail right at that very moment. That boiled down to $500. Since Isabella couldn't remember anyone else's phone number but Mom and Raymond's, she continued to call them over and over again.

She pleaded with them to pay the $500 bond to get her released. Mom and Raymond refused. They had no intention to pay the bail money, knowing full well that she would just run and never show up for the court date.

I kept up with her jail records through the VINE system, the Victim Information, and Network Everyday system. You can find offenders in any state by searching for their name or other features of interest. Her name popped up, and her offense from the jail. It said that Isabella had a court date with the Judge that very morning.

The next day the judge found her guilty and, because she couldn't come up with the $500, Isabella was sentenced to five days in jail to pay for her cab ride. As sure as the sun rises, the morning of the fifth day came, and they released her from the Galveston County Jail for time served.

Lord, I pray that the Houston Arson department picks her up for attempting to burn down Mom and Raymond's house with them in it. To me, that's attempted murder as well as arson. However, she had warned her son the night before not to go home. In my book, that should make it premeditated attempted murder.

Isabella is out free now and still on a rampage. The police are doing nothing. That is until my niece read all the hateful, threatening emails that Isabella had sent her. My niece called the police. She ended up filing a *Terroristic Threat to Family* along with restraining orders against Isabella. Now that gave the police something to do. Those orders put Isabella back on their radar.

As the morning progressed, I started doubting myself. Today is one of those days where it takes all my strength to push the enemy out of my head. The pressure of finding a job, losing the roof over my head, having the car repossessed, living on the streets, my dogs, food, electricity, water... it all came down on me today.

It feels like your boxed into a very dark corner with no way out. I curled up in a ball in my darkened house and cried out to the Lord. "Why am I going through this, Lord? Forgive me, please. I need food, Lord. I need a job. Please help me. Why aren't you helping me? Your dog's, Lord, they need medicine that I cannot afford. Please, Lord, keep them healthy until I can get them to a vet." Tears were streaming down my face, and my voice was getting hoarse from screaming at the Lord when I finally fell asleep, completely exhausted.

When I woke up, I decided to punish myself and look into the mailbox to see my hate mail from the creditors. At the top of the pile was a letter from the credit union that loaned me the money to buy my car. The statement said I only owed 50 bucks on the car loan. I could come up with fifty bucks if it meant not worrying about the car getting repossessed. That's one less burden I had to worry about.

In the same pile of letters was a postcard from the Community of Faith Church. They were advertising for their Easter Services. I've been looking for a new church. I'm going to go check them out! My day was getting brighter!

I spent the rest of the day, applying for more jobs. I found a job posting for a call center in town. The starting rate was $11.50 per hour. But guess what the joke is... The position is for bank card collections. I think I'll be calling myself a lot if I get the job! HA!

Yep, I heard that door slam shut way before the rejection letter hit my email. Of course, I didn't get the job.

Mom and Raymond are not sleeping. Raymond rests on the couch next to the front door waiting for Isabella's next horrible twisted trickery and assault. She's already tried to kill them once, and nothing is stopping her from trying it again.

Preston and Raymond are keeping their guns loaded and at their sides. I decided to call and check up on them. "Hi, Mom!"

"Hi Honey, what's happening?"

"Not much over here. Same old thing. Send out resumes, door slams in my face. I smile and send out more resumes."

"Look, Honey, keep on doing what you are doing. The Lord is working on it."

"I know, Mom. It's just getting harder and harder every day."

"Just hang in there, darling, don't give up!" She pauses for a second, "So we had another visit from your sister last night."

"Oh my God, Mom! Are you guys ok?"

"Yes, we are ok. Your sister decided to help me pull some weeds out of my garden last night."

"OK now I am confused. What really happened?"

"Isabella pulled up every plant in my front garden and then proceeded to take globs of the dirt from the garden and cake it on top of our van. Preston is outside right now trying to get the dirt off the van's roof."

"Did you call the police?"

"No, there's nothing they can do about it."

"You guys should get a camera installed to video her antics.

At least it will be proof that she is destroying your property and trespassing on it too."

"That's probably not a bad idea, sweetheart."

If I thought about it using my old self, I would say that Mom and Raymond brought this on themselves because they thought negative thoughts at some point in the past. But the new me said that the devil wrote the Law of Attraction. The enemy. The evil one.

For years, the enemy isolated me from people. For years, the enemy separated me from what was happening in the world. I fell into the enemy's trap... hook, line, and sinker. God teaches us to love one another and to help one another.

Proverbs 18:1 says, "*One who has isolated himself seeks his own desires; he rejects all sound judgment.*" And in Ecclesiastes 4:12, it says, "*A person standing alone can be attacked and defeated, but two can stand back-to-back and conquer.*"

The Law of Attraction teaches you that watching the news is bad. The News pounds into your mind all the negativity of the world. Negativity brings about negativity. Think negative and get negative. Who got shot. Who got robbed. Who got raped. Who died, multiple car pile-ups on freeways, people dying, tsunamis that kill thousands of people somewhere on the other side of the world, terroristic attacks, all the hate, all the death and destruction everywhere you turn, everywhere you look.

The Law of Attraction says that all that negativity is not good, and the negativity will bring more negative things to you.

'*And no wonder, for even Satan disguises himself as an angel of light.*' (2 Corinthians 11:14)

The Law of attraction says to not think about the people around the world and their destruction. That all that mass thinking about them and that mass praying for them would only bring about more mass destruction. This is how the enemy stops you from praying and talking to God and Jesus. '*The enemy comes only to steal, kill, and destroy.*' (John 10:10)

The Law of Attraction would like you to believe that what it teaches comes from the Bible. It's a perfect trick the enemy uses to persuade you into believing the wrong things. In Luke 4:9, the devil tried to tempt Jesus to fling himself off the temple. *'The devil led him to Jerusalem and had him stand on the highest point of the temple. "If you are the Son of God," he said, "throw yourself down from here.'* (Matthew 4:6)

The devil used Scripture to try and persuade him. Satan will do anything to divert your path away from the Lord, including quotes from the Word of God. Including making a Law of Attraction that twists the Word of God. There are tons of cults out there, just like The Law of Attraction, that disguise the truth of God's Word from you. They want to reprogram your subconscious. They want you to heed the enemy. They dangle that elusive carrot out in front of you. The '*You can have Wealth, Health, and Purpose*' carrot. The *'all you have to do is this...'* carrot.

Be warned. The evil one is not asleep at the wheel. This tactic that the enemy uses is one of the oldest tricks in his book, and he knows it works just about every time.

So, what does all this mean? That I was had, and that I fell for the trap of the enemy. For years I was under the rule and thumb of the devil. I was tricked into not talking to Jesus Christ. But God changed this to where he sent a storm so big, and so bad, and so horrible that the only thing I could cling to was Him.

Jesus used this illustration: *"If you had a hundred sheep and one of them strayed away and was lost in the wilderness, wouldn't you leave the ninety-nine others to go and search for the lost one until you found it?"* (Luke 15:4)

All I can say It worked. Amen! I traded in The Law of Attraction for Jesus Christ, my King! Don't get me wrong, I am still broke as dirt, with no prospect of a job in sight. But I believe the Lord will provide until he is finished with whatever he wants me to do. So, I try not to worry or be anxious. Like Mom says. "Don't give up. God is NEVER late, and he is always on time."

But I digress. Back to the story...

As Izzy's escapades became increasingly violent, we all began to worry about the trip down she will have. People with bipolar disorders get on this high where they believe that everything they do is good and right. They believe they can't get hurt if they fall off a 20 story building.

People with bipolar disorders believe that everything and anything is attainable. And when they come down off that natural high, they go lower than when they started. Their emotions are so depressed that suicide is not out of the question. What causes this in bipolar people is they have a chemical imbalance in their brains. It is a disorder of the worst kind. But with today's modern science, drugs can put the imbalance back in balance, and those suffering from bipolar disease return to a normal state of mind.

In Izzy's case, the family's biggest problem is trying to get her to realize that she has a problem. When she is on the high side, she does not want to come down. Quite frankly, who wouldn't want to? She is having such a good time on the high side! Fearless good times! That leaves the downside when Izzy finally swings back further than whence she started.

The downside is almost the only hope our family has of getting Isabella any kind of help. After Izzy's last bad episode, she was so depressed she allowed Raymond to take her to a Psychiatric Clinic to get her re-evaluated. She protested about going, which made Mom and Raymond question why she was going there in the first place. I believe that she went solely to shower, have a place to sleep, and eat regularly.

However, Izzy knew how to beat the system. Because Isabella spent many years as a psych nurse, she knew all the answers to the doctor's questions. The answers were not Izzy's answers, but the answers that she knew that the doctor would accept and diagnose her as not being bipolar. Thus, no medication and no diagnosis. Izzy would continue on her merry bipolar way.

As the years progressed, we noticed that her horrible episodes with the 'high feeling' part of the disease would worsen.

Her destructive and violent behavior became exponentially worse after each episode. And the 'high feeling' episodes would come at a faster pace and last way longer than any previous episode.

Isabella was at her worst stage yet. Her confused mind was now insistent on murder. The only way we knew she would be forced to get help was when she landed in jail. That is if we can get the police to pick her up again.

CHAPTER 15

I sabella knew that all of her possessions were in her car that was towed from the Goodwill Parking lot, including her purse and her driver's license. She needed her driver's license to cash checks and get money. In her bipolar mind, she believed she had $12,000 that the IRS owed her, but the accountant at HR Block needed her driver's license to release the money. Her bipolar mind did not tell her that this was not true.

Standing on the side of the road that leads to the Department of Motor Vehicles, Isabella stuck her thumb out to the passing cars. "Someone will stop for me!"

And just as she thought this thought, a nice young man pulled off the side of the road and rolled down his window. "Where ya headed to?"

"Just to the DMV about five miles from here. Can you give me a lift?"

"Sure thing, Miss, I'm headed that way anyway. Hop on in." He opened the door from the inside to let her in.

"Thank you so much! That's very kind of you to bless me this way."

"No problem." He said as he sped away down the road, making it a very short trip.

Isabella got out of the car and thanked the young man for his kindness. She stood just outside the doors to the DMV office and knew this was going to be her day. All she had to do was ask for a copy of her driver's license, and upon receipt, most of her problems would be solved.

She stepped through the front doors and moseyed up to the first available service window.

"How can I help you, Ma'am?" the young officer asked.

"I need to get a copy of my Texas Driver's License. Mine was stolen."

"Sure, just give me a second." The officer turned to his computer and made his way to the file that would run a search on any Driver's License number. "Do you know your Driver's License Number?"

"Yes, I do!" Isabella rattled off the eight-digit number to the officer as he diligently typed it into the search box. It didn't take long for the computer to spit out the red warning that indicated to the officer that there was a warrant out for her arrest.

The DMV officer typed in a message to the dispatcher in the next room, who in turn radioed a Houston Police Department Officer that was standing a mere ten feet from where Isabella was waiting.

The HPD officer made the distance between himself and Isabella a short one. "Ma'am, step away from the counter."

"What's wrong, officer? I'm just here to get my driver's license. I have done nothing wrong."

"Please, Ma'am, just step away from the counter."

Isabella made no indication of moving, so the officer grabbed her left arm and swung it around to her back. He forcefully pushed her face down against the counter and slapped the cuffs on her hands. "You have a warrant out for your arrest in Pearland."

"Look, Officer, I told them that the emails to my niece were not terroristic, and they agreed. My entire family is out to get me. This is a witch hunt! They want to keep me silent. My stepdad conspired with my sister-in-law's ex-husband, who is the Pearland Detective David. This is all a mistake."

"Tell it to the judge, Ma'am." The officer took her to the Pearland Jail, where she spent three days before they transferred her to the Brazoria County Jail, charging her with a *terroristic threat to family*.

Isabella sat on her bunk bed in her new home that she shared with ten other inmates. It was called a tank. There were five sets of bunk beds, one toilet, one sink, and shower stalls that everyone shared. Frieda Lee and Gladys Jane sat near Isabella, eating the lunch that the guards had brought them. Lunches in jail usually consisted of peanut butter and jelly sandwiches with apple slices on the side.

"You know Frieda. It has been nine weeks since I was innocently jailed."

"Ain't nobody innocently jailed Sugar. Ain't nobody," Frieda said, popping another apple slice into her mouth.

"That's right, Izzy, I was innocently jailed too," Gladys Jane laughed so hard she could barely get the rest of the sentence out, "after I put a knife in my low life cheating husband."

The whole tank burst out laughing. Izzy remarked, "Well, at least I have the Holy Spirit on my side. I would not trade that for the world."

"Amen! To that, Sugar! Amen!"

Izzy continued, "You know, it hurts when the people I love, and I could never hurt, belittled and attacked me. They have abandoned me and hurt me deeply. But you know what? God loves me, and that's all that matters."

"Even if He put you in jail?"

"Yep, He did it to slow my roll down. He put me in jail to get my undivided attention. But you know what? I'm going to get to Galveston as soon as I am released."

"What's in Galveston?"

"I have nine lawsuits pending against those that jailed me," Isabella went off on another tangent, which is something a bipolar mind does quite often.

"Only nine child?" Gladys Jane laughed out loud.

Izzy counted them out, "Yep, one in Houston, one in Galveston, one in Bay City where my stupid X is, and one in Pearland."

"That hardly makes nine Izzy, didn't ya mamma teach ya how to count correctly?"

Izzy was getting irritated, "Just shut up and eat your sandwich Freida, no one asked you." And off on yet another tangent, she continued, "I would like to stay in Galveston or Bay City until I can go to Florida. My tentative plan is to reorganize, repack my storage unit in Houston, and clear out my garage in the house I sold. I need to gather my clothes from two places I was living before all this. Then load a moving truck and drive to New Orleans. I'll stay awhile till Kamron can come to drive me to Tampa Bay."

"Now, who the heck is Kamron?" Gladys asked, genuinely amazed at this developing story.

"Kamron and I met at a psych hospital where he did the intake, and I was the charge nurse for the PTSD Unit in 1989. And we have been close friends ever since."

"Lordy mercy," Freida laughed, "who needs TV when we have a real-life soap opera right here!"

"He also was a SEAL." Isabella continued without skipping a beat. "I will feel very safe there for a while. I need to rest, and heal, and wrap my head around all that has happened. I can unpack and feel like I'm in a safe place with the ONLY male I know I can trust. And the sooner, the better."

"The only male I thought I could trust was the one they found face down floating in the river."

"Gladys Jane! You really should stop talking like that."

"Who cares? Izzy, it is why I am locked up in this hell hole."

Izzy rambled on, "I have so many wonderful things to be grateful for even in this hell hole. Let's see now, my health, the renewing of my mind, body, and spirit. My son, Preston, who I claim, will eventually want to talk to me again. Unemployment checks for about four months at least. That's $6000.00 just waiting for me to collect since Feb.! And an IRS check I haven't cashed. Sharon and my dear new friend of 1 and 1/2 years now, Mr. Randy Miller. He is an LCADC counselor I met in 2014 while doing community service at the Bay Area Club in League City, Texas. It's an AA Meeting Center. He befriended me when I was a sad sack at the time."

"If you ask me, you're a sad sack of…"

Izzy interrupted her, "Shut up, Freida, no one is asking you. Randy believed in me when I couldn't. He believed in me when he hardly knew me. He shared his experiences and his time with me. I hope and pray that I can still trust him. I'm a tad on the leery side, though. We'll see, I guess."

"I know that's right, sugar. You just keep believing' everything's gonna be just fine."

Isabella's attorney in Brazoria County was a red-headed barracuda from Houston who assured Izzy that the case would be dismissed. However, while Isabella was still in the Brazoria County Jail awaiting trial, Janice and Raymond filed arson charges on her in a last-ditch attempt to get Isabella off the streets and in jail so she could get the mental health help she so desperately needed.

Since Isabella did not recognize that she was bipolar, the family believed that a mandatory in-house medical facility could force her to get better. That all spelled out Felony Mental Health Court. After her trial and sentence from the Judge in Brazoria County, Isabella would be transferred to the Harris County Jail in downtown Houston to face arson charges, which is a felony crime.

"Can you believe the nerve of my parents! They are assholes. They just charged me with arson. Who the hell does that to their children?"

"Calm down, Izzy. Ain't gonna do you any good gettin all dialed up and all." Gladys Jane did her best to calm Isabella down.

"There is zero evidence of soot or embers. There is no call to the fire department. Zero to the police. Zero arson reports. My attorney spoke to my so-called friend, Alecia. The snake not only gave my cell phone and tablet to my Mom and Raymond, she told my attorney, 'We (Me, Janice, and Raymond) just did that because we want her to get help.' The nerve of that slime. Arrrrrggggggg"

Isabella let out a scream that would curdle milk. "Hopefully soon, my attorney will gather enough discovery and speak with the District Attorney in Houston to get the charge reduced or dropped. Hopefully, she will also speak with my Pastor to coax him to speak to my parents about dropping the charges."

After sitting in her jail cell for 43 days, the Brazoria County Judge proclaimed that Isabella had served time for the crime. She was now to wait in her cell to be transferred to the Harris County Jail in downtown Houston to face arson charges, a Class B Felony crime.

"Just who the hell do you think you are, Ms. High and Mighty? Ain't nobody here wanna hear your stupid mouth flap all night so just shut the frack up." Freida was tired of hearing Izzy preach to everyone within listening range. She was tired of Izzy period, and she was in a mood to fight.

"Oh, just go to sleep, ass wipe. God's not going to save you with that kind of attitude."

That remark hit an already severed nerve, and Freida leaped out at Izzy, striking her in the face, which made Izzy twist to her right, throwing her off balance. Izzy went to steady herself by grabbing the top bunk with her left hand. Just as her fingertips scraped the edge of the bed, Freida pushed her from behind, bending her left hand back to her forearm, which snapped the bone. Izzy blacked out.

Freida put her in the lower bunk and covered her up with a blanket. "That shut miss pride right the frack up!"

Isabella awoke in a cloud of pain. She begged the jailer for aspirin and to be taken to a surgeon. But the jailer did not believe that anything was wrong with her, so her request was denied.

On the second day after the fight, the Harris County Sheriff's Office transferred her to downtown Houston's jail. Upon her entrance exam into the new jail, she was seen by a real doctor who declared her wrist broken.

They took her into surgery the next morning. Izzy woke up in her new jail cell in downtown Houston with her left arm in a cast.

By March 2016, I was still putting out 15 to 25 resumes a day and scrounging the internet to find more ways to make a buck or two. That's when I came across a website called WeLook4U. It was a company that started its business from online car auctions. People who wanted to buy a car online, but lived far away from where the vehicle was, needed a way to see and verify that what the seller stated about the car in their classified ads was true.

That's when WeLook4U was born. They employ people to go and take pictures of cars or videos of cars. The photos and videos are sent back to the WeLook4U headquarters and then transmitted to whoever requested the verification. As the company grew, they extended this service to the insurance companies. WeLook4U paid $25 for every mission that was successfully completed and uploaded to their servers.

I was bringing in about $100 bucks a month from them. So, on top of what I was making at Appel, that brought my monthly income up to $430 a month. That was enough to keep the water running, the lights on, the cable bill paid, and food for the pups. Unfortunately, it did not leave much else for anything that resembled real food. So in between taking pictures of cars, I still scrapped TVs and small appliances for copper. Mom and Raymond were still sending me boxes of food from their church. Amen!

Spring was in the air as I sat on my tattered couch tossing a tennis ball to *The Boys*, Rio, and Shaggy when I remembered the flyer from Community of Faith Church about their Easter Services. Easter was a couple of weeks away, and I didn't want to wait until then to check them out.

The next Sunday, I hopped in my car and drove the twelve miles to the new Church. My jaw hit the floorboard as I turned into the parking lot. This place was huge! But it also looked very welcoming and not daunting at all. There were people in the parking lot waving at me with huge smiles on their faces as they directed the cars to park. I waved back at them. Everyone was so friendly here!

As I walked to the main entrance of the Church, I saw a gentleman that looked to be around the age of 60-something greeting everyone as they passed by. He was wearing a fishing hat and a light-colored Hawaiian shirt with tan khakis. On his feet, he wore flip flops. This guy looked comfortable! With a giant smile on his face, he instantly took my hand and shook it as he welcomed me into the foyer.

"Good Morning! And welcome to Community of Faith, my friend!"

"Thanks!" It was about all I could get my mouth to say as I was overwhelmed.

The foyer of the church had small kiosks that were selling books, t-shirts, and coffee cups. There were small kiosks that housed the coffee bars. And just off to the right was a small kitchen that was selling everything from doughnuts to burgers. Every church that I had ever been in was all so stuffy and formal, but this one. Well, this one just looked and smelled like home.

And what was that sound? Could it be a band playing? I distinctly heard a guitar player and drums! And beautiful voices that were singing. You're kidding me! A Band? Just off to my left was the entrance to the worship hall. And that's where I headed as if the music the band was playing was drawing me closer to them.

I approached the double doors to the worship hall and was again greeted by two very nice ladies who handed me a pen and a service pamphlet. This was no ordinary church! There was no alter. But what was there gave me goosebumps. On stage was a seven-piece band, and they were singing the songs that KSBJ, the contemporary radio station, had played for me over and over again. Right behind the band was a giant projection screen. And on the screen, they were projecting the actual words to the song.

Even the lighting was worthy of a rock band: nice shiny silver truss, moving lights, and colored lights over the audience. Yes, I think I found my new home, as I smiled to myself and made my way up to the very top of the stadium seating. The worship hall could easily fit 5000 people in it.

The band played on as a lot of the congregation held their hands up to the sky. Most swayed back and forth as the sound of thousands of voices filled every corner of the hall, praising Jesus. It gave me goosebumps!

Just as the band stopped playing, Pastor Mark walked on to the center of the stage. "Today, we are going to continue the discussion about when you feel like giving up. Let's look at what it says in Matthew 6:25-34. *"Therefore, I tell you, do not worry about your life, what you will eat or drink, or about your body, what you will wear. Is not life more than food, and the body more than clothes? Look at the birds of the air, they do not sow or reap or store away in barns, and yet your heavenly Father feeds them. Are you not much more valuable than they? Can any one of you worrying add a single hour to your life? And why do you worry about clothes? See how the flowers of the field grow. They do not labor or spin. Yet I tell you that not even Solomon in all his splendor was dressed like one of these. If that is how God clothes the grass of the field, which is here today and tomorrow is thrown into the fire, will he not much more clothe you? You of little faith? So do not worry, saying 'What shall we eat?' or 'What shall we drink?' or 'What shall we wear?' For the pagans run after all these things, and your heavenly Father knows that you need them. But seek first his Kingdom and his righteousness, and all these things will be given to you as well. Therefore, do not worry about to-morrow, for tomorrow will worry about itself. Each day has enough trouble of its own."*

You've got to be kidding me. Does the good Pastor know who I am? Who told him what I've been going through? Pastor Mark talked, but I felt like it was God speaking directly to me. How does he know so much about what's going on with me right now? All of this was blowing my mind.

God was talking to me through Pastor Mark. "There are three things to remember when you're discouraged. Remember God's goodness to you in the past. Remember God's closeness to you in the present. Remember God's power for your future. In Psalm 119:25 it says, '*I am completely discouraged; I lie in the dust —Revive me by your Word*'"

Revive me by your Word! Oh, man! Revive me, God!

Pastor Mark concluded the sermon. "*You need to go on the offense and fight for your brothers, your sons, your daughters, wives, and homes!*" *(Nehemiah 14b)*

I'll fight God! I'll never stop fighting! I won't give up! I stood up after Pastor Mark was finished speaking. I knew that I would continue to do as he asked and fight through this misery that I put myself in.

Yes, I found my new home in the Community of Faith. The music, the people, and even the sermon… which isn't a sermon as far as the traditional church sermons that usually put folks to sleep… all these things were awesome. I was amazed! This Church talked to me personally. God spoke to me personally. I left stunned and in awe. I knew I would be back next week just to hear more.

CHAPTER 16

Sometimes it's just hard to wrap my head around Izzy being in jail, let alone trying to kill my Mom, Preston, and Raymond. But the sad fact is that it's all true. As Izzy sat in the Harris County Jail in a tank with convicted criminals, she waited and waited for the court system to do something.

The judge set her bail at $30,000, which meant that she would have to come up with 10% of that to make bail. A whopping $3,000. Even if we had the money, no one in the family wanted to give It to her because we knew that she would not make her court date. Izzy would run, and that would forfeit the bail money.

While Izzy waited, the courts did find her very mentally unstable and put her on generic medication for her bipolar symptoms. Still, her only chance for getting effective mental health treatment was to get into the Felony Mental Health Court system (FMHC), where she would be separated from the general jail population for treatment. Felony Mental Health service would be in the form of an in-house treatment at the jail or a separate inpatient facility.

I knew it was time for me to go and see my sister in jail. I was nervous, anxious, and even a little scared to even go there, but I knew I had to. Knowing that I didn't have enough gas to get me downtown and back left me with the only other option. The Metro Bus Lines!

I've never ridden on a bus that travels to downtown Houston, but I did know that they travel there every hour on the hour. I searched the web for the maps of bus routes to downtown Houston leaving from the Metro Park and Ride Stations closest to me.

Riding a bus there and back was only a couple bucks each way. I could handle a couple of bucks!

I purchased a Metro Bus Pass and loaded it with two passes. One for each way. There and back again. I found a Park and Ride that was less than five miles away! I could ride my bike there if I had to but riding five miles in Texas heat was not something I wanted to do. Instead, I opted to take my air-conditioned car to the Metro Park and Ride Station.

I parked my car in the Metro lot and made my way to the platform where the bus would be leaving. This isn't so bad after all! Eyeing a bench just off to my left, I sat down and waited. The Metro schedule said the next bus would be leaving for downtown at 3:30 p.m. It was only 3:10.

A few people were waiting for this bus along with myself. Some were well dressed, and others were not. The variety of people who rode these busses came from all walks of life, making me feel a little better about being there.

Ten very long minutes later, I spied a Metro bus rounding the corner to the platform where I was sitting. As it came to a stop, the doors opened, and tons of people started piling out. I stood up and just watched as the flock of people disembarked the bus and walked quickly to their cars. I watched the last person exit off the bus.

The driver finally acknowledged those of us waiting to board. I had no idea what to do, so I watched the others. Each boarded the bus and stuck their pass into an ATM looking machine before they were allowed to find a place to sit down. OK! That didn't look too difficult for me to do. That is, if your Metro Bus Pass worked properly. Which, of course, mine didn't.

I couldn't get it to work like the others to save my life! I looked over my shoulder and saw the frustration in the people's eyes that were lined up behind me, waiting for their turn to board the bus. The Bus Driver sadly looked at me. She took my pass from my shaking hands. Turning it upside down, she stuck it in the machine. The machine dinged and displayed a big green checkmark. The bus driver turned to me and said, "Go, sit down."

How embarrassing! All I could do was mouth the words, "Thank you." Live and learn, I guess! I promptly made my way to the back of the bus to watch the others that boarded. Ten minutes later, the bus was turning into the Metro Only Lanes on the freeway that headed into downtown Houston.

I settled in for the 25-minute one-way ride into downtown and wondered what kind of conditions I would find Isabella living in. All of Mom's stories about the times that she and Raymond visited her sounded horrible.

I could hear Mom's voice in my head, "You need to take as little as possible with you. And pack some hand sanitizer to wipe your hands, and you'll need it to wipe down the phones too."

Wait! Wipe down the phones? Images of television crime shows flooded my mind. Surely, that was all just for television. That couldn't be how it is in reality. Could it? I found a small backpack that I packed a bottle of hand sanitizer, my wallet, and my phone in. That should be all I needed.

In my mind, I went over the many questions regarding Izzy's mental health and what kind of facility she would end up in, but there were more immediate questions that needed to be addressed as well. If we got her charges reduced, would she get dropped from the Felony Mental Health Court System? Would she just get probation? And where would she serve that? At a halfway house?

If she got out on probation only, are there conditions that Isabella must follow, and if she does not follow them, does she go back to jail? Who decides that she is not following the requirements set forth? Would a psychiatrist be a part of the conditions along with seeing a probation officer? But if she gets into the FMHC program, does she immediately get out of the General Population? Where exactly would she go to wait for a bed to open up in the Felony Mental Health Court System? Where exactly are the beds at FMHC once she gets in? Are they in the same building that she is in now?

I looked out the busses window to find that we were near

downtown and my drop off point. The skyline of downtown Houston was incredible. Tall majestic buildings looked like they could touch the moon. I took in the absolute beauty of it all and wondered which building was holding my sister.

It was time to look at my map and see which streets I needed to walk down to get to the jail. According to the downtown Houston map, the bus would make five stops at different street addresses before heading back to the Metro Park and Ride Station. The third stop that the bus would make would put me closest to the jail.

The busses intercom crackled on "Preston and Smith Street... Ding. Preston and Smith Street... Ding" That's my stop! All those that were exiting the bus stood up in preparation. I took the cue and stood. Once the bus came to a complete stop, the doors opened, and like a herd of cattle, we exited the bus.

The jail sat five blocks east then three blocks north from where I was deposited by the bus. The sun was shining, and the streets were crowded as most of the downtown workers were ending their day and making their way back to their homes. I looked at my watch, which said it was 4:00 p.m. The jail visitations were just beginning. I had plenty of time to trek the eight blocks, check-in, see my sister, and make it back to the bus pick up spot before the last bus leaves for the Metro Park and Ride Station.

With firm steps, I made my way to the jail, as thoughts of Isabella returned to me. Izzy was convinced that she would still be in the same jail cell that she is in now if she went into the Felony Mental Health Court System. She was convinced that nothing would change other than being on a new medication.

Isabella was also deathly afraid that if she screws up just once, the Judge will sentence her to prison, whether she was in the general population or FMHC. In her mind, it all didn't matter. Making my way to the jail's front entrance, I saw the line to get in the building was wrapped around the outside of the building. Oh, my God! You have got to be kidding me! Mom never mentioned a line.

My heart sank. This was going to be more challenging than I had ever imagined. The closer I got to the entrance, I could now see that four different lines were entering into the building, not just one. Then the big red sign came into view:

Visitation for inmates on floors 2-3 Line #1
Visitation for inmates on floor 4 Line #2
Visitation for inmates on floor 5 Line #3
Visitation for inmates on floor 6 Line #4

No Phones, No Drinks, No Food, No purses beyond this point.
Place all belongings in the lockers provided in the lobby area. The only thing allowed is your ID.
Fill out a card for inmate visitation before getting in line.

The cards you were supposed to fill out were on a small table just to the left of where the police officers sat behind very thick bulletproof glass. I picked one up and started to fill it out.

Name: Isabella Jenkins Schmidt
SPN: How the heck am I supposed to know that?
Floor Number: No idea!
Driver's License Number: Seriously?

I spotted a rather large book sitting in the corner on the table as I watched someone else look up the SPN number of their loved one that was also behind bars. The book showed the inmate's name, SPN, and floor where they were currently located. Bingo! I promptly filled it out and made my way to Line #2 since they kept Izzy on the 4th Floor.

I looked at my watch. 5:00 p.m. I still had plenty of time! Take a deep breath! By 5:30, I finally made it to the policemen behind the thick bulletproof glass.

"Hi!"

"Please hand me your ID and your card."

"Sure thing." I dug out my Texas Driver's License and the card I filled out and handed it through the little slot in the glass.

The officer took my license and card, punched a bunch of

numbers in the computer, signed the card, and said, "You're clear to stand in the search line. No Phones, No Drinks, No Food, No purses beyond this point. Place all belongings in the lockers over there." He pointed to all the lockers that were located to his right. "Here is a token to be used in the lockers. Place the token in the locker, open the door, place your belongings in, close the door, and take the key. NEXT."

My head was swimming as I took the token that the officer placed in the slot and took a few steps towards the lockers. There was not one locker that was available for use.

"Hey Missy, the line starts over here."

"What?" She really couldn't be talking to me, could she? "The line for what?"

"For the lockers, lady. For the lockers."

Oh no, not another line! There were six people in front of me waiting for a locker.

"Don't worry. This line goes pretty fast."

And indeed, it did. People came back down from seeing their loved ones in large groups. They would put the key in the locker, grab their things, and leave. I only had to wait another fifteen minutes before I had the chance to grab a locker, secure my backpack, and take my license, Izzy's card, and the key. I looked at my watch—5:45 p.m.

The next line was the search line, and it was almost out of the front doors. It wasn't moving as fast as the locker line. There was an officer that would let five to ten people through to be searched, as he repeated over and over, "Remove belts, earrings, jewelry, and anything metal. Empty all pockets and place all the contents in this basket. Proceed through the metal detectors. Once you have cleared the metal detectors and retrieved your belongings, you may proceed to the proper inmate floor."

As I waited in line, I got a chance to look at the people around me. They were all kinds of people you could ever have imagined. Some looked like ordinary everyday people, and others, well, they kinda scared the bejeezus out of me. I had to keep reminding myself that Jesus died for them as well. I'm sure they all had stories to tell about why they were here. I shivered even to think about how gruesome they could be.

Another 30 minutes went by before I was allowed through the metal detectors. It was now 6:15 p.m. The last bus leaves for the Park and Ride Station at 9:00 p.m. Oh Lord, don't let me get stuck down here. Grabbing my precious locker key, my license, and the card that had Isabella's info out of the basket, I made my way to the fourth floor.

As the elevator doors swung open, I was faced with at least thirty people standing and sitting on the floor facing a small glass-enclosed room. It looked like a fishbowl. There were about ten inmates in the fishbowl, each in a separate compartment. They all held a phone to their ear. On my side of the glass, people also had a phone to their ear.

Oh, my God! It's true. It's not just something you see in the movies. Each inmate only had fifteen minutes to talk to their loved ones behind the glass. After fifteen minutes, the guard would open the door to the fishbowl and lead the inmates back to their cells. The fishbowl would remain empty until the next group of inmates was ushered in.

I waited through at least four rounds of inmates, and finally, by 7:30 p.m., the guards ushered in Isabella. I was shocked to see her dressed in the orange jail jumpsuit. I sat down at one of the partitions, and Izzy made her way to me. She picked up the phone on her side of the fishbowl. I picked up the phone on the other side and looked at her through the glass that separated us. I tried not to show how utterly shocked I was at seeing her like this.

"Hey, Izzy! Mom seems to think you have a real good chance at getting into a halfway house. That is if we can get you into Felony Mental Health Court."

Izzy had tears in her eyes, "If I get on probation and go to a halfway house, they will not care for me there. It's just a lonely place to stay. I would have to ride a bus to get to the probation officer. I don't know how to ride a bus, Sans." And the tears were turning into waterfalls.

"Izzy! Riding the bus is not all that difficult. I will go with you for the first couple of times so you can be comfortable with it." I smiled. It wasn't that far from the truth! I made it here, ok, didn't I?

"But I don't have any clothes. I don't have anything to my name. I have nothing."

"Izzy, that's not true. You have us. You have me. You have Mom and Raymond! And together, we will help you."

I wasn't about to tell her that we had rescued all her stuff, and it was all crammed into a spare bedroom at my house. I was still not sure that her mind was in Crazy Izzy or Normal Izzy. "Look, Izzy, I don't have much time. You have to start taking your meds that the guards are giving you. You have to do what they tell you. Please, Izzy. It's the only way to get into Felony Mental Health Court."

"Sans, you have no idea what it's like in here. There's a slime that runs out of the faucets. There are real criminals in here. People who have murdered other people."

"Izzy, I know it's hard, but you won't get out of there until you cooperate."

"How can I cooperate when I can't even trust my court-appointed Defense Lawyer. He is not working for my best interests."

"Just try Izzy. I can talk to Mom and Raymond to see if we can get you another attorney. Please, Izzy, just try." I pleaded with her and cried with her, but all my words were falling on deaf ears.

The guard came into the fishbowl and called time. Izzy and I both had a hard time hanging up the phone. My heart broke watching her being ushered out of the fishbowl into the other parts of the jail that the public could not see or go.

I looked at my watch-7:40 p.m. The minutes had flown by way too fast. It seems like you should get more time with your loved one for having to jump through so many hoops to get there. But I was grateful for the fifteen minutes at whatever costs. By the time I made my way back down to the jail's lobby to grab my things and relinquish my locker, it was almost 8:00 p.m. That gave me an hour to get to the bus stop that would take me to my car and finally home. Home seemed like it was on the other side of the galaxy. I was exhausted.

The next day I met Mom and Raymond at the Criminal Court House in downtown Houston. This 20 story skyscraper is known for its wide granite steps that lead up to the main entrance. Very grand and very old. Just inside the entrance were the security stations where you had to remove any belts, shoes, jewelry, and take out everything from your pockets and place them in a small plastic bin before you were allowed to walk through the door that scanned you for weapons. The line to get inside the building was out the entrance and wrapped around the corner. What is it with courts, jails, and never-ending long lines?

Finally, I made it through the security station. I made my way to the elevators. Isabella's courtroom was on the 17th floor. My stomach muscles lunged at the thought of being cramped in such a tiny elevator to get there. There couldn't possibly be enough air in that little elevator compartment for all the people that they crammed into there. I tried to get my panic attack under control.

Taking a ride in a tiny cramped elevator was the worst, and to my dismay, it stopped on every floor. Lawyers would get on, and Lawyers would get off. In the whole ten second ride to the next floor, they would tell each other about their cases. If I weren't so claustrophobic, I would have enjoyed just riding up and down in the elevator listening to all the drama. But no, I held my breath, shut my eyes, and thought of all the wide-open spaces in Texas as the elevator took me to the 17th floor.

When I got off the elevator, I found Mom and Raymond sitting outside the courtroom. They were engaged in a rare conversation with the FMHC's advocate, Melisa Danbury, who is in charge of Isabella's case. Melisa motioned for the three of us to take a seat on one of the benches outside the courtroom.

"One of the deciding factors as to if Isabella would be admitted into FMHC will be determined if Isabella cooperates with taking her meds. It also depends on the way she takes care of herself right now. Isabella's actions would be considered when the judge decides on putting her in either outpatient care or in-patient care." And then Melisa said the unthinkable, "If Isabella could stay with one of you, it would go a long way with not only the Judge but with her mental health as well."

I cannot believe she just said that! She tried to kill Mom, Preston, and Raymond. No way was I going to let that happen. But if Izzy stayed with me, she would have no vehicle access. If she needed to get around, she could use my bicycle. If she needed to get on the internet, I could also restrict it being the Geek I am.

And I sat there rolling the possibilities of Izzy staying with me. I could probably get her on the Appel Ad Project that I was working on through the internet, which could likely bring another $400 a month in income. That alone had my wheels turning. But not enough that I wanted Crazy Izzy staying with me again.

The conversation ended as the court clerk came out to tell us that Isabella's trial had been reset yet again. Isabella was not cooperating with anything or anyone. We all knew that this was the road to prison for Isabella if she did not change her ways.

The next week I went down to see Isabella in the fishbowl. After standing in all the way too familiar lines, fighting for lockers in the atrium, and going through all the metal detectors. I finally made it to the inmate's fourth floor. I saw Izzy through the double glass window and went to a phone to talk to her. "Izzy!"

"Hey, Sans."

"Izzy, you have to rethink how you are doing things in there."
I was starting to beg now. "You have to take your meds. You have
to take showers. You have to eat. You have to obey the guards.
Izzy, if you don't do this, you might go to prison. Felony Mental
Health Court is the only thing that will save your life."

"Look, Sans, I know you mean well. I know for a fact that
FMHC will give me multiple medications. The meds will knock
me out so much that I will not be able to see anyone ever. The
people, the nurses, they all do not care. All the medications that
they will prescribe will keep me like a zombie."

"Izzy, you watch too many movies. Your starting to quote
One Who Flew over the Cuckoo's Nest."

"No, I am not. I have worked in places like that. It's the God's
honest truth." The waterworks flowed freely down her face. It
broke my heart to watch her as she continued, "Even in here, if I
refuse to take the stupid meds, they place you in a rubber room
where there is only a hole in the floor to poop in and no toilet
paper."

The guard came into the fishbowl and called time. All the inmates had to stop mid-sentence, get off the phones, and proceed
back to their cells. If they didn't follow this rule, they would
be put into detention and refused visitation rights for a week.
Disobeying Guard's orders will also get them more time on their
sentence.

Isabella had been serving time in the tank for over five
months now. Her court-appointed defense lawyer was a complete jerk, and she did not trust him. She did not believe that he
is working for her best interests. That alone could hinder her cooperation in getting her into FMHC. The big question was... can
we get her another one?

Mom and Raymond went to visit Isabella. Because they are
both in their 80's, they were excused from having to stand in
the lines and wait with all the other people waiting to see their
loved ones behind bars. Mom sat waiting behind the double
panel window with the jail phone to her ear, waiting on her oldest daughter to be escorted into the fishbowl.

When Izzy made it to a phone, Mom saw how sunken her eyes were. She tried to fight back the tears. Izzy looked like she must have lost at least 50 pounds. To begin with, Izzy never weighed much, so losing 50 pounds took her weight down to 85. Rio, my beautiful labrador, weighs more than that.

Mom immediately started crying at the sight of her. "Isabella! I've missed you so much, honey."

"I miss you too, Mom."

"Look, sweetheart, you have to start eating something. You have to hang on. The Lord is working for you. Please, Izzy, eat something."

"Mom, the food here is horrible. The bread is moldy. The fruit is overripe. I can't stand to smell it."

"Oh, Izzy, they are going to force-feed you if you do not start eating on your own."

"Mom, I'll try. But this place is retched. There's mold everywhere. I won't take a shower because there are no showerheads. It's just a pipe that has a one-foot string of algae growing out of it. It's disgusting. Everything is filthy in here. "

"Honey, I'll see if the good Pastor can come to see you. Maybe he can do something about the conditions in there." Mom paused for a few seconds, took a deep breath, and continued. "Sweetheart, you need to start taking the medication that the nurse brings you. FMHC won't take you if you won't even take your medication here."

"Oh, Mom, I won't take my evening meds because they give them to me at 3:00 p.m., and they put me to sleep. I am afraid that the other inmates will take what little stuff I have when I am sleeping. The general population tank where I am kept is so noisy. I can't think straight, let alone sleep at night."

Tears started to well up in Izzy's eyes as she continued, "and the criminals are physically threatening me and stealing my personal items. There's no way I can be fully compliant with the requirements for acceptance into the FMHC."

"Isabella, you have to try."

"Mom, I have to sleep on top of my toothbrush so no one in

there will steal it. It's one of the few things that I have left. The thieves stole all the things I bought at the jail's commissary in here. I can't even take a shower because I don't want to leave my things out to be stolen from these thugs."

Mom was crying now, "Please, Izzy, you have to try. It's your only chance. Please, Isabella."

Because Isabella had been a Psychiatric Nurse for over ten years, she had seen firsthand when patients were over-medicated so the nurses could control them. It explained how mentally ill patients get lost in the mental health systems. Isabella was very fearful this would happen to her.

Finally, the day came when the FMHC Psychiatrist evaluated her condition. He suggested to the Court that Isabella be released to an inpatient facility. But the way Isabella was acting in her jail cell made the court think twice about offering her the option. It seemed like Izzy was acting like this on purpose.

CHAPTER 17

Isabella sat in the tank with her new friends and waited for the next court date to discuss admitting her into Felony Mental Health Court. She passed the time by dreaming and scheming up business deals. But what impressed her fellow inmates even more, was Izzy's tall tales recounting what she told our family when we came to visit. "Yep, they believed me when I told them that y'all were thieves, and this place was unfit for a dog, let alone a human."

Miss Wendy burst out laughing, "Did ya tell them about the broken water shower that has strings of algae growing on it? You know, that was my idea!"

"My acting abilities could have gotten me the starring role on Broadway. I was that convincing!"

"Did you tell them how bad the food is here?"

"I did indeed! Slime in the ice machine and moldy bread!" And her bipolar brain switched her thought pattern instantly. "You know, Maybell, when I was little, my Grandmother and Grandfather owned a Domino Parlor. I am going to recreate that when I get out of this dump."

"Whatcha gonna call it?"

"The Domino Parlor! Family-owned since 1936."

"Well, ain't that original!"

"I know, right! My husband, Schroder, and I will live upstairs above the Parlor. I can see the newspapers now, *The Domino Parlor, in Fredericksburg, Texas. Owned by Walter and Elsa Marguerite Klaus in 1936. Restored by Granddaughter Isabella Jenkins and Great Grandson Preston Chase Vignovich, 2016.*"

"Just what's so special about this Parlor that folks would

want to come to visit?"

"It's gonna have hardwood floors throughout, except in the kitchen, of course. And a super long bar for drinking, eating, and chatting."

"Go on, child, I'm picturing it all in my head!"

"Okay, listen to this... there will be two 70 inch Hi-Def TVs. One will be at the bar, and one on the patio outback. There will be a special area for my Grandmother's kitchen table. It's a table like the one you would see in an old-timey soda fountain shop. That'll be where everyone can play dominoes, cards, Uno, chess, or checkers. And the table in the center has a silver plate in the middle of it that says, *Reserved for Knoche and Guests*. I am having James Avery make it for me!"

"Now I like the James Avery stuff! Very highfalutin!" Maybell sat back and opened her bag of apples, ready to hear some more.

"You know those old fashioned cash registers? I want one of those at the bar and electronic games that everyone can play. And there will be a bowl of munchies every two feet so all the gamers can have something to chow on."

Maybell could almost taste it now, "Bowls of peanuts and pretzels, and maybe those little Melba toasts? That's one of the things that I miss the most in this hell hole."

"And wait till I tell you about the back porch!" Izzy paused all dramatic like. "It's gonna have the fanciest outdoor lounge-type furniture for smoking cigars and cigarettes with Bose speakers in the rafters that'll play all the great country music. And the best part is gonna be a giant waterfall that comes off a tin roof that spills into a fishpond. And, of course, it will have a water wheel spinning around just like the one at the little park across from Bethany Church. "

"Lord have mercy! It sounds just wonderful, Izzy!"

As the night wore on, Isabella continued to tell everyone who would listen precisely where tables and chairs would go. Exactly which beer brands she would sell, what was on the food menus, and what she would sell in the gift shop, including everything from dominoes to salt scrub to t-shirts to candy, to bumper stickers and posters.

I could hardly wait for the next Sunday Service at Community of Faith Church. I hopped in my car and drove the twelve miles, not even thinking that I was burning up precious gas in the process. As I got out of my car, there he was again. It was the same gentleman who looked to be around the age of 60-something. He was wearing his fishing hat, a bright colored shirt with tan khaki's. On his feet, he wore flip flops.

With a giant smile on his face, He took my hand and hugged me! "Good Morning! And welcome back!"

"Thanks!" It was about all I could get my mouth to say as I was amazed that he even remembered me out of this 3000 person congregation.

I could hear the band playing as I walked into the foyer where tons of people were getting their coffee ready to take into the Worship Hall. I picked up on that clue and grabbed some java as I headed into the Worship Hall.

I went through the double doors, and the prayer team handed me the service pamphlet and a pen to take notes. I eagerly grabbed them and made my way up to my spot at the top of the bleachers. Settling down in my seat, I opened the pamphlet. Pastor Mark was going to talk about Easter Gifts! Easter was just a mere week away.

"Where do you find yourself today?" Pastor Mark started his sermon. "Easter is a gift of power. In Ephesians 1:20, '...How tremendous is the power available to us who believe in God. That power is the same divine energy which was demonstrated in Christ when he was raised from the dead...'"

I sat there mesmerized by every word Pastor Mark said. It felt like his words were coming through my heart to rest in my brain. Everything just made sense to me.

Pastor Mark was wrapping up the sermon, "In Isaiah 43:18-19, 'Forget about what has happened; don't keep going over old history. *Be alert; be present. I'm about to do something brand new. It's bursting out! Don't you see it?'*

And my jaw dropped yet again. Does this guy read minds too? Or was it God talking to me again? That gave me goosebumps that followed me all the way back home.

Isabella sat in her jail cell, wondering if she would ever be able to leave its filth. Maybell sauntered up to her, "Watch you doing, baby girl?"

"Hey, Maybell! I'm stewing on how to make hell tremble with my lil' part in life."

"Girl, you just get on with ya bad self."

"Maybell! You know my stupid X-husband Thomas Schmidt? How can he lay his head on the pillow that I worked overtime to buy us? Downright knowing that I have been cold, lonely, scared, and hurting for the last eight weeks?"

"Seems like he's a real winner."

"Look, Maybell, I found this pamphlet down in the commissary. I think it was left there for me to see."

"What are you talking about, silly girl?"

"See, it says, *'Don't be afraid of anything you are about to suffer. Listen! The Devil will put you to the test by having some of you thrown into prison... Be faithful to me, even if it means death, and I will give you life as your prize of victory.'* (Revelation 2:10)

"Look, Maybell, I underlined the part in this verse that says *The Devil will put you to the test by having some of you thrown into prison!*" Isabella looked up at Maybell expectantly, "That's totally us, Maybell, we are being tested! That's why we are here!"

Isabella took a pen and wrote next to the passage, "I believe I passed this test, could you, Raymond?" And Isabella's bipolar rage was ramping up again.

Isabella was given a Bible when she first came to jail. It was the only thing she regularly read. Isabella took her pen in a fit of rage and started writing a letter to Janice in the margins. Just as she was putting on the finishing touches, Ms. Wendy pulled up a chair to talk to Isabella.

"Ms. Wendy, I'm so glad you stopped by, darling."

"Why's that crazy girl?"

"I just finished writing a letter to my Mom. Wanna hear it?"

"Sure thing! I could use a little soap opera right about now."

"Here it goes then!

To Ms. Janice Y. Davis:

Thank you for helping to get my warrant and bills to my attorneys. I will NEVER understand why a mother could demand her firstborn daughter to not receive any assistance from her friends, family members, places of business, or any living person on this planet. However, I do, and have recognized, since living at your house from January 2015 to January 2016, just how much the narcissism, control, verbal abuse, and neglect of your known second-husband has on you! But you know what, Janice? I forgive you. No one could endure such deranged love and be any different.

Which brings me to my point of this note, I am preparing a MAJOR lawsuit against Raymond. I decided not to include you as I still respect you as my mother. Your husband is planning to put you in a nursing home, and you ought to be ashamed of the compromising position you placed Ms. Lee in! Absolutely disgusting. She is hurting, and I understand her pain and her loyalty to you. Ms. Lee believes you are her friend. What type of friend denies basic needs in life to their offspring? Huh? Perhaps a review of this chapter is in order? John 15:6, 'Those who do not remain in me are thrown out like a branch and dry up; such branches are gathered up and (and she circles this next part) thrown into the fire where they are burned.' *This is the FIRE you should heed!*"

"That should get their attention, don't ya think, Ms. Wendy?"

"I dunno Izzy seems like you just want to piss them off more.

Aren't they trying to convict you for arson?"

"They don't have any evidence against me. All my parents want to do is lock me up and drug me for life."

"Well, seems to me it's your funeral you're writing," and Ms. Wendy turned on her heels and left.

Izzy never saw her leave as she frantically kept writing her letter to Janice.

Janice, you have the power to stop all this. Just DO IT! Drop the fraudulent charge of arson, IMMEDIATELY! In John 15:18, 'If the world hates you, just remember that it has hated me first.' John 15:20, '...If people persecuted me, they will *(and she circles the next part)* persecute you too.' John 15:25, '...They hated me for *(and she circles)* No reason at all.' *HELLO!?!*

DROP THE CHARGES. Janice, PLEASE drop the charge of Arson. Why didn't you charge me with the destruction of property? I wrote rapist in ketchup and chalk. I put your flower bed on top of your van. I chalked up the neighbor's driveway. I wrote in shoe polish on your cars. But arson? Really?

And Izzy went on and on twisting the Word of God to her use and abuse.

The next Sunday, as I pulled into the Church parking lot, I saw my favorite greeter. He was still wearing his fishing hat and a light-colored Hawaiian shirt with tan khaki's. He even wore the same flip flops on his feet! As I approached, his face lit up and took me into a giant bear hug. "Good Mornin' Sans!"

"Good Morning," was all that fell out of my tongue-tied mouth. How did he know my name?

I walked into the Worship Hall just as Pastor Mark had taken the stage. I was more than eager to listen to what he said.

"Today, I want to talk about The Law of the Harvest! In 2 Corinthians 9:6-11, it says, *'Remember this: Whoever sows sparingly will also reap sparingly, and whoever sows generously will also reap* generously. Each of you should give what you have decided in your heart to give, not reluctantly or under compulsion, for God loves a cheerful giver. And God is able to bless you abundantly, so that in all things at all times, having all that you need, you will abound in every good work. As it is written: "They have freely scattered their gifts to the poor, their righteousness endures forever. Now he who supplies seed to the sower and bread for food will also supply and increase your store of seed and will enlarge the harvest of your righteousness. You will be enriched in every way so that you can be generous on every occasion, and through us, your generosity will result in thanksgiving to God."'*

What does this all mean to me? I have to give, and when I give, God will increase what I have so I can give more. That's very cool!

Pastor Mark continued his sermon, "In Malachi 3:10, it says to *'Bring the whole tithe into the storehouse, that there may be food in my house.'* What is a tithe? Simply put, the word tithe means ten percent. *'Test me in this, says the Lord Almighty, and see if I will not throw open the floodgates of heaven and pour out so much blessing that there will not be room enough to store it.'*

Wait! What? Test me in this? Does it actually say that? Interesting! But I have nothing to give. I have no money. How am I supposed to tithe? Ten percent of my garage sale money? The money that barely keeps the lights and water going? The money that buys what little food I have to survive? Ten percent of *that* money?

Pastor Marks words drew my attention back to him as he said, "In Mark 12:41-44 it says, *'And he sat down opposite the treasury and watched the people putting money into the offering box. Many rich people put in large sums. And a poor widow came and put in two small copper coins, which make a penny. And he called his disciples to him and said to them, "Truly, I say to you, this poor widow has put in more than all those who are contributing to the offering box. For they all contributed out of their abundance, but she out of her poverty has put in everything she had, all she had to live on."*

In this beautiful Church that I had found, God was talking to me again. I will test Him. I will give ten percent of what I earn from now on. I can always stop tithing if His Word is not true. Right? I will put His Word to the test!

As the sermon concluded, and Pastor Mark spoke a prayer over the congregation, an image began playing on the two giant video screens. It read, "In remembrance of Jerry Goldstein. Our well-loved greeter and driver of Community of Faith. Feb. 23, 1956 - April 14, 2014."

The video screens displayed a picture of Jerry Goldstein. There he was! My fishing hat, Hawaiian shirt, flip flop guy! But wait! It says he died in 2014. That couldn't be right! I just saw him before I came into the worship hall. The goosebumps ran up and down my arms as my hair stood at attention. I had seen Jerry Goldstein. He was an angel. God had sent Jerry to welcome me into His Church.

CHAPTER 18

June 2016 had finally rolled around, and I was still unemployed. I couldn't figure out why Jesus denied me. What little I made from my garage sales, I was giving ten percent to the Church. I didn't mind because I knew the Lord was still helping me. The Lord saw that I had food and a roof over my head. Mom continued to tell me, "Don't give up. He's working on it!"

All my life, I begged for a normal life with a normal family, but I was denied all of it. Sentenced to a life of solitude, and now it all came down to this. I was still afraid to check the mail, and when someone came to the door, I was scared to answer it for fear it might be the cops coming to throw me out of my house.

I was running and hiding from everything and everyone. I felt like I was sub-human. Like I wasn't part of everyday things. I felt like I was genuinely wallowing on the bottom of the pond. I was a bottom feeder. I was crying all the time now and screaming at the Lord, asking him why can't you help me? I found prayer lines online and asked people to pray for me because I felt like the Lord wasn't listening to me and that maybe He would listen to them.

I was overwhelmed with defeat, and I humbly was still accepting food from charity as I still could not afford to feed myself. I was spending sixteen hours a day, filling out job applications. The rejection from it was devastating. Father's Day fell on Sunday, June 19th of 2016. As I made my way to the seat at the top of the worship hall to listen to Pastor Mark's sermon, I felt something tugging at my heartstrings.

Pastor Mark would always talk about following one of God's

commands to be baptized. He always said it wasn't the fact that you were dunked underwater, but God said to do it. And we all should obey. I don't know if it was because today was Father's Day that I chose to honor the Lord, but my heart pulled me to the foyer's front desk as I told the young attendant that I wanted to be Baptized.

Just as I spit out the words, her face lit up, and her smile was from ear to ear. She gave me a form to sign, and to this day, I don't even know what I signed. I just knew I had to do this. She was saying something to me and handing me this bag of clothes, "If you don't want to get the clothes you have on wet, you could change into these."

I handed the bag of clothes back to her, "I'll be fine, thanks. Where do I go?"

"Just outside the main entrance is the baptismal pool. Pastor Mark will be there."

"Thank you!" I said as I headed in the direction of the baptismal pool. Pastor Mark was in the baptismal pool, helping a young woman getting out. He turned to me and held out his hand, "Welcome! What's your name, miss?"

"Sandy," I paused, "Sandy Ryan."

"Welcome, Sandy!" He took my hand and led me to the center of the pool. "Sandy, I now baptize you in the name of the Father, the Son, and the Holy Spirit, for the forgiveness of your sins, and the gift of the Holy Spirit."

He gently put his arms around my shoulders and dunked me backward into the pool. I was a bit stunned when I came back up for air, but I was grinning from ear to ear. It was done! I am a Christian now!

Pastor Mark helped me out of the pool. My soggy clothes were clinging to me. My shoes squashed when I stepped. I was dripping wet from head to toe as I walked back to my car in the parking lot. Strange though, I thought that I would feel different after I was baptized. It was The Gift of the Holy Spirit, after all.

I got in my car without concern for my dripping wet body getting the car seat wet. I drove off the Church lot and onto the freeway heading home. That's when I felt it. It was the same feeling I felt when my Grandmother visited me after she died. I sensed this force coming straight at me, and before I could react, I felt this force go right through my chest. It made every hair on my body stand at attention. My whole body tingled with the sensation. I knew who it was this time!

I welcomed the Lord Jesus into my life.

During one of my darker days of searching for a job, I came across an ad for Texas Pre-paid Legal Services and Identity Protection Plans. It was sort of like insurance. It was prepaid lawyer help if and when you might need a lawyer or help if your Identity was stolen. I was convinced I could sell this to every person with which I came in contact.

I told myself I would go door to door selling this because I was that desperate for something, just anything, to work in my life. For hours and hours, I practiced my spiel. I knew I only needed five people to sign up for the services to get me to the level that might start bringing in money for me.

That's when Raymond said I needed to talk to my stepbrothers. "Dan and Ray Jr. can sell just about anything, Sandy. You should go talk to them and ask for their help."

"I don't know, Raymond. It's been a long time since I have talked to them."

"That's ok. I'll call Ray Jr. and Dan and tell them you're coming. I'll even give you money to take them out to a fancy lunch. That will impress them. What do you say?"

Knowing this could be my only hope to make some decent money at selling stuff, I reluctantly agreed to try. But Raymond had no idea he was sending the lamb to the lions. I fought every urge to run and hide. I fought every inch of my body repelling. I fought off every memory I had of my stepbrothers molesting me. I had to try and talk to them as it seemed like it was my only hope.

On a scorching June day in Houston, I drove the thirty-mile one way trip to my stepbrother's place of work. I had not seen or spoken to either one of them for over thirty years. As I pulled into the gravel parking lot behind the building, I spotted my stepbrother Dan walking towards my car. I was shocked to see him. His hair was silver-grey, and it looked like he had put on at least a hundred and fifty extra pounds. There obviously was no food shortage at his house.

I got out of my car, and he wrapped his chubby arms around me, "Hey Sis, you look great! What's it been about twenty years?"

I resisted the urge to run for my life, "Ya, something like that."

"Ray's in the office. Let's go get him, and we can go to lunch."

"Cool, lead on," I said as the images of Jabba the Hutt from Star Wars kept popping into my head.

Dan led me into the building where we zigged and zagged down many hallways before we came to Raymond Jr.'s office. Raymond Jr. was just as overweight as his twin Dan. He looked up from whatever he was doing behind his desk just as I was entering, "Hey Sandy."

"Hey, Ray. How goes it?"

"Good. Did you know that your daughter is getting married?"

"Yes, I do." My daughter's getting married? I wasn't going to give him the satisfaction of gloating that over me.

He turned to me and said, "Ok, whatever. Let's take your car, Sandy."

"Sure thing." *Of course, I can waste more precious gas on you two fat...* "My cars in the back parking lot. What's a good place to eat around here?" I patiently asked.

"There's a chicken place right down the street. We only have thirty minutes for lunch. So, we should make this quick."

We pulled into a dinky little roach trap called the Chicken Hut. I could smell the grease as soon as I opened the door to get out of the car. Yep, this was Raymond Sr.'s fancy lunch I was promised.

"This is a great place to eat," Dan said, grinning from ear to ear. "We shouldn't wait so long next time to get together."

The three of us made it to the counter, and they both ordered a four-piece chicken meal, complete with a basket of French fries and biscuits. I, on the other hand, felt like I was about to puke. "I think I'll just have a small chicken sandwich, no dressing, please."

As we took our food from the sales counter, we made our way to the cleanest table we could find and settled down to eat. Just as I sat down, all the horrible feelings about them came flooding back with a vengeance. I couldn't hold it in any longer. Spotting where the lady's room was, I got up and made my way there.

Opening the door, the smell of excrement hit my nose, and I ran to the sink as it was the closest vessel I could throw up in as my guts were coming out of my mouth in massive heaves. Without looking at the mess I made in the sink, I turned on the water and held my right wrist, palm up under the cool water. This was that trick that I used before I almost died back in 2005. Holding my wrist in this way usually helped me to stop heaving.

I knew I had to make myself think of something else other than the two I came to see. Slowly I got my heaves under control and my face looking back to normal. I made my way back to the table. I knew any conversation with these two hogs was going to go nowhere. There was no way I was going to beg them for anything. I knew right then and there that it was time to put out the fire and call in the dogs. It was over. But in my heart, I also knew God was still working on it.

As both of my stepbrothers were wiping the grease off their faces, Dan said, "Sandy, Dad said that you are trying to sell insurance."

"It's not insurance."

"Well, it's like insurance, and I don't think you have what it takes to sell anything."

I felt the bile forming in my throat as Raymond Junior piped in, "Well, it's time we get back to work, Dan. Our thirty minutes is almost up."

We piled back into my car, and I drove them back to their

jobs. Just as I was pulling into the parking lot, a Metro bus passed by us. On the side of the bus was an advertisement-*Hiring Now*. "Hey Sans, look at that sign! You should call them!" Raymond Junior said with a laugh.

I wanted to tell them that I already did and that I had sent Metro over twenty applications from everything from being a janitor to a bus driver. I wanted to say to them that even they had slammed the door in my face. But I couldn't. I knew they didn't give two hoots about anything concerning me or my plight.

"We are here. Y'all have a good rest of the day at work," I said gloomily.

"Sure thing Sans, keep in touch," Dan said as we exchanged phone numbers and email addresses, which was pointless since neither of us would ever use them. When I finally made it back home from the ill-fated lunch, I took the boys Rio and Shagz for a walk to clear my head and my heart.

Just as we turned a corner in the neighborhood, Rio saw a cat and took off after it. I was still attached to the leash. Unfortunately, I saw the broken cement on the sidewalk way too late and tripped over it. As I fell to the ground, my little finger on my right hand crushed underneath me, not bending in the direction it was supposed to. My right elbow took the rest of the blunt force. It felt like my little finger was broken, and the blood vessels in my elbow had burst and now was turning my entire elbow a pretty shade of purple. I had no health insurance and no way to pay a doctor. If my finger is broken, I guess it stays broken.

Broken seems to be the normal now.

CHAPTER 19

Have I not commanded you? Be strong and courageous. Do not be afraid; do not be discouraged, for the LORD your God will be with you wherever you go." Joshua 1:9

Sunday's service had just concluded, and I was driving home pondering today's sermon. It never ceased to amaze me how each sermon spoke only to my heart. That God was speaking through the good Pastor Mark just to me. Today's sermon was about Matthew 17:20, *'If you have faith as small as a mustard seed, you can say to this mountain, 'Move from here to there' and it will move. Nothing will be impossible for you.'*

Lord, if you're listening, a mustard seed is pretty small, and I have faith that is bigger than a mustard seed Lord, and I don't want to move a mountain. I just want a job that will pay the bills, buy me food, and get me out of this hole I dug for myself.

On the way home from church, I saw this guy selling tamales out of the back of his car. That got me to thinking. I can make tamales! I'm a good cook!

I promptly went home and researched how to sell tamales in Texas. What I found was the Texas Cottage Law that went into effect in 2013. The Cottage Law says it is illegal to sell tamales in Texas without being made from a processing plant. However, it did list the things that you can sell legally without licenses and packaging plants.

That born the idea of Texas Jam-N-Jellies! I can make jams for little to nothing, Unusual jams, and jellies. And sell them for five dollars a four-ounce jar at farmer's markets. Or better yet, I could sell them at my garage sales. I found a couple of unusual jam recipes online that had cheap ingredients and decided to try them out.

One was called Watermelon Jalapeño Jelly, and the other was a Strawberry Mint Jam. I ended up making about a dozen four-ounce jars of each of them. I had some leftover Christmas ribbon that I taped around the jars' necks and deemed them ready to sell.

Friday was the first day of my two-day garage sale and the first day of my Texas Jam-N-Jellies sale for my Watermelon Jalapeño Jelly and my Strawberry Mint Jam. As it turned out, both are a big hit. I even had one lady come back to tell me that she couldn't stop eating the Watermelon Jalapeño Jelly. Hallelujah!

By the end of the second day, the Texas Jam-N-Jellies garage sales had great reviews, and I have sold almost 3/4 of what I made. But I figured the time and effort to make the jellies and the money needed to buy the ingredients outweighed what I got in return. So, I gave up the ghost on that little project.

At this point, I was ready to try just about anything to make a buck or two. The last time I was brave enough to check the mailbox, I found a letter from a University study group studying knee pain. It said that participants would not only get free prescription medicine, but they would receive up to a grand for just participating.

I filled out the form for the study group online, but they denied me. God had blocked that adventure and that medical help. I am starting to feel like I am cursed.

Mom and Raymond went religiously to visit Isabella in jail at least twice a week. On their last trip, they brought her new reading glasses because she had told one of Mom's friends that she couldn't pass the Felony Mental Health Court tests because she couldn't see very well. As Raymond was still parking the car, Mom went to the fishbowl to talk to Isabella.

"Hi sweet sugar!" Janice tried to sound cheerful, "I brought you a pair of reading glasses. The guards said that they would give them to you."

"Thanks, Mom."

"How are you, sweetheart?"

"Mom, the conditions in here are so bad I can't stand it. People are lying in the halls, and they had shat all over themselves. Mom, people are fornicating in the halls and everywhere."

Janice let the tears flow freely. She couldn't stand the thought of her oldest daughter being locked up with these criminals. "Honey, you have to hold on. You have to pass the Felony Mental Health Court tests. Then you will be in a better place."

"I can't, Mom. Please get me out of here. Do you still love me?"

"We are trying, Izzy. We are trying, and yes, we love you very much."

"Mom, I'm scared that I have nowhere to go and that I'll be lost in the system."

"Oh Izzy..."

Without warning, the guard called time, and Isabella was lead from the room.

I woke up to a typical Monday morning. I turned on the laptop and sent out another kabillion resumes to jobs that I thought I might have a smidgen of skills to perform. By the time I had finished that task, it was time to treat the dogs to a romp in the dog park. I saddled Rio and Shaggy up, packed them into the car, and off we went.

As soon as I stopped at the first stop sign, I heard the brakes moaning in protest. It sounded like metal grinding on metal, or worse, like fingernails being drug down a chalkboard. My brakes were getting worn by the hour. I knew I had to do something soon or risk my life by not fixing them.

In previous years I would just take the car to a mechanics shop, and they would charge me hundreds of dollars to fix them.

My bank account couldn't handle a car repair bill. Who's kidding who? I had about $80 bucks in my cigar box that was tucked away in my underwear drawer. That was my bank account.

Sixty bucks later and several YouTube videos on how to repair my brakes, I was confident that I could do this myself. It seems like it is all just a matter of a few screws. If I had known way back how easy this was, I wouldn't have paid for the convenience of letting a mechanic doing it. Live and learn, I guess. At least now I could make it to the bus stop without everyone cringing when I applied my brakes next to their cars, which was where I was headed this very day.

I had found a participant's manual to Felony Mental Health Court that I wanted Isabella to read. I thought it might make her feel a little better about what she could expect when she got there. However, you can't take anything in with you when you talk to the inmates in the fishbowl. The next best thing was to write on my arm and hands the highlights that I wanted to point out to her, and I only had fifteen minutes to deliver the message as that was the time limit that the guards gave each visitation.

I waited for Izzy to enter the room with the other nine inmates. "Izzy!" I picked up the phone.

Izzy sat down and picked up the phone on her side of the double glass window. "Sans, you have to get me out of here."

"Izzy, we are trying, but you have to do your part too. You have to get into Felony Mental Health Court."

"Sandy, Felony Mental Health Court won't get me away from these evil people. It won't get me away from the murderers, and rapists, or drug dealers. Even if I get in, I will still be in this very building. Nothing will change."

"Yes, it will, Isabella."

"That's where you are wrong. I will still be in danger. I can't think in here anymore, and I fear for my life. Please, Sans, you have to get Raymond to drop the arson charges."

Izzy was crying hard now, which in turn made my waterworks start to flow. I tried wiping my tears away with my hands and arms, which in turn smeared the notes that I had made on my arm. I suppose it didn't matter anymore. Izzy was a basket case, and she was in no mood to hear me lecture her about Felony Mental Health Court anyway.

When I got home, I called Mom and Raymond. "Hi Mom, I just got back from the jail."

"Hang on a minute, let me get Raymond on the phone too." I heard her screaming his name to pick up the phone.

"How did it go, Sandy?"

"Izzy is worse. She asked me if you, Raymond, were the one that filed the arson charges on her. Did you?"

"No, Sandy, I didn't. The prosecutor for the State was the one that filed the arson charges on her." Raymond sighed loud enough for me to hear him on the phone.

Mom chimed in, "The assistant District Attorney is filing the papers today that will get Isabella into Felony Mental Health Court, but the judge needs to hear it out of Isabella's mouth that she wants to go there."

"I get it, Mom. Izzy isn't budging. She won't tell the judge that's where she wants to be. She believes that nothing will change."

I could hear Mom sniffling between her words, "Isabella's trial is set for tomorrow morning. I pray for a breakthrough."

"We all do, Mom. Get some rest. I'll see you guys at the courthouse in the morning. I love you."

"I love you to sugar."

It was 7:00 a.m., and I didn't want to get out of bed to face the horrors of another day in the criminal courthouse. The weight of my world was pressing down on my heart and soul. I still didn't have a job to support myself and my dogs. I hardly keep the lights on just to keep the electricity bill down to a low roar. I wash my clothes once a month because I can't afford the water bill either.

God, please give me a job. Open the door. Let me be human again. I can't take this anymore. I am begging Jesus. Please help me.

The ringing of my cell phone jolted me out of my morbid

thoughts as I rolled over in bed to answer the phone.

"Hi Sweet Sugar!"

"Mom! Is everything ok?"

"Yes, sweetheart. Raymond has been on the phone all morning trying to find out more information on what might happen to Isabella today. It seems like it boils down to just three options."

"What are the options, Mom?"

"Well," she paused for an unusual amount of time, "If she continues not to eat or shower, she will be deemed incompetent, and they will ship her off to the State Mental Hospital."

"That's a bit extreme, don't you think?"

"It's better than her getting sent to prison for arson, which is the second option."

"What's the third option?"

"She gets re-evaluated and gets deemed competent. Then she gets transferred to the Felony Mental Health Court who will eventually put her in a halfway house."

"That's what we want. Right? For her to be in a halfway house?"

"At this point, yes, that is what we want. Oh, by the way, the courthouse called. Her trial this morning has been reset for next week."

"Why am I not surprised?"

Mom laughed, "I know, sweetheart."

"Well, that will give me time to go down and try again to convince her to get re-evaluated."

"OK Sweetheart, call me afterward and let me know how it goes."

"I love you, Mom."

"Love you too, darling."

Riding on the bus headed back to downtown Houston, I knew I had to convince Isabella that regardless of the conditions she is living in, she had to show the judge and her lawyer that she can eat and shower by herself. Isabella had to prove that she wanted to be re-evaluated to go into the Felony Mental Health Court system.

I had prepared a much smaller version of the FMHC manual. I had written notes up and down my arm again so I wouldn't forget anything. On the thirty-minute bus ride, I recited over and over what I wanted Isabella to hear. I wasn't going to take no for an answer. Isabella would see that I was right and finally get into the FMHC system.

After I navigated through all of the jail's lines and procedures, I made my way up to the fourth-floor fishbowl and patiently waited for my sister to be ushered in by the guards.

"Isabella!"

"Hey, sis."

" Izzy, please, you have to get re-evaluated. You have to try."

"No, Sans, I have decided that I want to go to prison." I was dumbfounded as she continued, "It will only be for two years. I can handle that."

"Where do you get the two years from?"

"That's what all the inmates are telling me in here. The guards too."

I had this sinking feeling in my gut. Was I talking to Crazy Izzy? Or Normal Izzy? Is she making this up as she goes along? " Izzy, prison would be a lot worse than what you are experiencing right now. The guards are not going to care for you. The doctors will not care either. No one in prison will help you."

"That's just not true, Sans." She had this dreamy look on her face, a big sign indicating Crazy Izzy was in the house.

"Do you think you're going to chase butterflies in the courtyard at the prison? Do you think the guards will have the dinner table set and dinner prepared for you promptly at 7:00 p.m.? Each night?" I was getting mad and fervently continued with my rant, "Do you honestly think you are going to have your very own room and shower in prison? Do you think there will be no rules to abide by there?"

"Sandy, that just isn't true. I will have all that and more."

As I was about to protest, the guard came into the fishbowl and called time. I slammed the phone down and watched Crazy

Izzy with this massive grin on her face. She turned to file out of the fishbowl with the other inmates.

God Help US! Here we go again.

CHAPTER 20

The next week, on the same day as Isabella's court hearing, I had landed a job interview with a Limousine Company. It was a dispatch job that paid $18 an hour. The problem was that it was located in a very sleazy part of town. I would not feel very safe going there every day, but it was a job, and I needed the money. I sat through the interview, but my mind was on Izzy and the Judge.

"Thank you, Ms. Ryan. I will be in touch if we decide to hire you."

"Yes, Sir, Thank you for the opportunity and for your time."

Just as I walked out of the limousine office, my cell phone was ringing. "Hello?"

"Hello Ms. Ryan?"

"Yes, this is Sandy."

"Hello Ms. Ryan, I am Isabella's lawyer."

"What can I do for you, Sir?"

"Isabella desperately needs to be on probation, but she needs to have a place to stay before the Judge allows that to happen."

"Well, she is not going to stay with my Mom, that's for sure."

"Ms. Ryan, can she stay with you? She will be on probation for two to five years and will have to check in with a psychiatrist once a week. She will be forced to take her meds. She just needs a place to stay."

The silence on the phone was deafening. There was no way I could let Izzy stay with Mom, not after she tried to kill them. Crazy Izzy or not, that was not an option.

"Ms. Ryan, I need an answer."

Izzy has stayed with me before, and it turned into a nightmare. This time I knew she would be on medication, so that was a plus. Perhaps this time it would be different. She was my sister. She was my only sister. Crazy or not, I knew in my heart that I had to help her.

"She can stay with me," I said in a low whisper.

"Thank you, Ms. Ryan. The jail will process her out this evening." He promptly hung up, not allowing for any rebuttal.

When I got home from the interview, I read everything I could find on the net about inmates being released into the streets after they were set free. I read all kinds of horror stories about thugs preying upon the women being released. They would give them rides, then drugs, and then only God knows what else.

These articles scared me so much that I decided to go down to the jail and wait for her release. It couldn't take all that long, could it? It was 6:00 p.m. now. She had to be getting close to being processed out. I knew that the busses didn't run past midnight. My only option was to use my car and its precious gas.

Not thinking about it, I hopped in my car and drove to the jail to wait. In the first thirty minutes, I figured out that all the inmates that were being released would come through just one door. It was a door that was located on the loading dock of the jail. It was right next to the door where officers brought in people who had just committed crimes.

After about two hours, I was becoming impressed with how many squad cars pulled up to the jail carrying two, and sometimes three or more people in handcuffs. Some of them came from as far away as Austin.

After the fourth hour, I became friends with many of the inmate's relatives who were patiently waiting for their loved ones to exit the jail. Each time we heard the door being opened on the dock, we all looked expectantly towards it. Hoping that it would be the one person you were waiting on.

After the eighth hour of waiting, a seventeen-year-old walked out of the door and searched for her family. I sat on a ledge that bordered the loading dock watching her. She looked so young and innocent. It was impossible to imagine her in jail, much less committing any kind of crime.

The young girl spotted me watching her, and she started to walk towards me. "Hi! Are you waiting for someone?"

"Yes, I'm waiting for my sister. She was supposed to be processed out several hours ago."

"What's her name? Maybe I saw her in there. "

"My sister's name is Isabella. She is short and super skinny. Older too."

"I did see her in there. She should be out in an hour. That stupid Desk Sargent is slower than molasses. Hey, can I borrow your cell phone to see where my Mom is?"

I thought about what could be the harm in that? "Sure, here ya go." I handed her my cell phone and watched her every move as she dialed a number and started speaking. I prayed she wouldn't bolt with my phone in hand.

"Ya, they just released me... How far away are you? I don't have any money for a cab... No, she's still in the tank... Ok, just hurry up." She handed me back my cell phone, "Thanks, my mom should be here soon."

"So why were you in jail if you don't mind me asking?"

"I was caught stealing from a jewelry store with my Aunt."

I was speechless and shocked. I guess they like to keep it in the family.

On the tenth hour, just as the sun was coming up at 6:00 a.m. Isabella stepped through that infamous door on the loading dock. Tears were streaming down her face when she spotted me. I ran to grab her and hug her tight. She was shaking from head to toe as I led her to my car. All she had with her was a plastic bag that contained everything she had been arrested with and all the things she received during her incarceration. It was all she had left in the world.

Well, almost all she had left in the world. I didn't have time to clear out a room for her. Both of my spare bedrooms in my house was packed floor to ceiling with everything Izzy had in storage along with my best friends' stuff that they couldn't take with them to Iowa. I wasn't sure how Izzy would react when she found out that all of her belongings were intact and safe at my house.

I put that thought to the back of my mind. The only thing that was important at that very moment was getting Izzy safely to my house, where she could decompress and cleanse herself of the filth that was left from the jail.

I pulled into my driveway. Izzy got out of the car and started walking down the street. Tears were still streaming down her face. I sprinted after her. "Izzy, what are you doing? Where are you going?"

"Sans, I just want to relish the sky and the stars and the sunrise. It's been a very long time since I was free. It's been a very long time since I could breathe fresh air."

"I know, Izzy. I'm sorry that you went through all that."

We walked around the block at least two times before Izzy was able to drag herself inside my house to settle in.

With my business dead in the water, I only had one social media account that I still used. It was my personal Facebook account. But even that was depressing. I couldn't face my friends and tell them that I had failed, that I was stupid to chase my dreams. I couldn't tell them that I was so broke and that I couldn't feed myself. I was too ashamed.

When I went to see my stepbrothers, they made a flippant comment about my daughter getting married. I had to see if the news was on her Facebook account. I logged in, and that's when I found a message from my only daughter Renee.

Renee was very angry with me. In this letter, she told me that she was getting married and I am not invited because I had housed my only sister Isabella. As I read each and every angry word, tears were streaming down my face.

I can't take this anymore—all this hatred. If my daughter truly wanted to talk to me, she knows where I live. I have lived in the same house for the last thirty years.

I navigated my way to the *Delete Your Account* settings on my Facebook account. I prayed that my only daughter would one day understand. I hit the Delete Permanently button. My social media days were over.

Everyone in my extended family, excluding my parents, kept telling Izzy that she needed to get help, but they offered absolutely no way of how she should do that. They just judged my sister and turned their backs on her forever. Then persecuted me for offering Izzy a way to get the help that she so desperately needed.

I pray that my daughter will soon see the light of the truth and speak to me again. Until then, all I can do is turn it over to God.

Everything was going well for the first couple of weeks that Isabella was staying with me. She would clean the house, and I would cook the meals. Before dinner, I would present a glass of water and her bipolar medication and watch her swallow them. I was confident that she was taking them.

I was confident up until the point that she started staying up all night and sleeping a little bit during the day. That is the sure-fire sign that she's ramping up a bipolar rage. I'm not sure how she's doing it, but she is not ingesting her medication. Maybe she's hiding them under her tongue or inside her cheeks. Either way, the only thing I could do now was brace myself for what was to come.

During the day, Isabella was continually talking to a man named Jake Wheeler on my landline phone. For hours and hours, she sat on my back patio and talked to him. I knew she was scheming and planning for God only knows what.

It was Sunday morning, and I had a couple of hours to kill before my church's last service started. I decided to walk out to the backyard and play with the dogs. Isabella sat on my patio with her ears glued to my phone. "I know that sounds lovely," Isabella paused for a few seconds as she was listening intently. "...today? I would love to!"

I tossed a tennis ball to Rio and moved a bit closer to the patio to hear better.

"I'll talk to you in a little bit then," and she hung up.

Isabella declared, "I've decided that I do not want to go to your church anymore. I want to check out my own church."

"Ok, how are you going to get there," I said as I watched Rio go chasing after the bouncing green tennis ball.

"I'm going to walk silly. It's the church that's just down the street from here."

"What time do you think you'll be home?"

"Before dark thirty, I suppose."

It was only 10:00 a.m., and I knew Izzy had been up most of the night.

Izzy opened the patio door leading into the house. "I'll be leaving shortly. Don't worry so much about me, Lil' sister."

I was more suspicious than worried. I could smell the deceit in the air as Isabella went to her room to get dressed to go check out her new church that was just down the street. Thirty minutes later, I heard the front door open and close. I knew Izzy was up to something, and I was going to find out. I did not believe that she was going to a new church, but I couldn't figure out what was next.

The clues had to be in Isabella's room. She was a writer. She made notes and wrote down everything that she wanted and everything that was happening to her. I waited a couple of minutes before I was confident that Izzy wouldn't be returning anytime soon. I locked the front door and headed to Izzy's room.

Piles and piles of letters were stacked neatly in a large brown box. I found writings to and about a person she just called "J." Isabella mentions that he is the only friend she has left. And in another letter, she writes, "J. will pick me up anytime, anywhere. He will take me away from this."

After reading some of the letters in the box, I put two and two together, which made J ...Jake Wheeler. Jake Wheeler was probably picking her up somewhere in the neighborhood and taking her God only knows where. Izzy was going AWAL, and Jake Wheeler was helping her.

I had let her leave the house without fully knowing her intentions. I knew I had to chase after her. I also knew she was on foot. It hadn't been more than fifteen minutes when she walked out the front door. I ran to get my keys and slammed the front door, not even checking to see if it was locked or not.

I looked up and down the street, but there was no sign of Izzy. If she were going to the church down the street, she would still be on foot walking there. I hopped in my car and went speeding through the neighborhood. I headed in the direction of the church, but there was no Izzy to be found. "OK," I told myself, "she must be closer to the church than I figured."

I sped to the church. There were no cars in the parking lot and no sign of Izzy. The only thing I could do now was to go back home and wait.

As I neared my house, I realized that this whole situation was staged. Izzy was playing some kind of game that I had no clue what the rules were, but I needed to find out fast if I was going to keep up with her bipolar mind. It was time to do some more digging through her room again.

Rustling through more letters that Izzy had written in jail, I came across a letter that she wrote to her inmate friends after she was released from jail and was living in my house. I started to read it.

Hello, Mrs. Alice and all me other Bunkie's, Sista's in Christ of 4H2 Cell Block!

Whew! I made it to Sandy's at approx. 6:00 a.m. Yep, I was trip'n in my bunk after court till I heard the Gorilla guard squeak, "Hurry up now!!" And I still wasn't ready to go after at least ten hours of shuffling all my stuff, read and re-reading all the papers as if the words were going to change, move and remove and move stuff again, put back and take out. But none of that surprised any of you because you all took the time to get to know me.

Court beyond overwhelmed me. I was blown away by the claim of my Jerk-ass Attorney. Parents didn't want me to have a misdemeanor? So, now I'm a first-degree felon? Don't mess with me! Especially with matches in my hand. I know, not funny, but I have to joke, or I would crack. If you sing a wrong note, my choir director always said, at least sing it loud and proud!

So, the good news - Wow! What a beautiful clear starry night it was. Stars were out everywhere. Saw the Big Dipper too! My sweet sister had been waiting for me since 8:00 p.m. at the jail! She brought, don't laugh - a PBJ for a snack in case I was hungry and some raspberry tea, cold, with ice! Sans brought some of my clothes and shoes, cuz she wasn't sure what I had or if I ate. My attorney just told her that I'd be out by 8:00 p.m.

I did not cry as I was leaving the jail, although I had numerous reasons too. All the guards, mostly females, were rude and ugly to me all the way out. But when I saw Sandy, I cried almost all the way to her house. We got to her house, and I stood outside for at least an hour, looking at the sky, trees, hearing acorns fall to the ground. So peaceful, and I am so de-sensitized, I could hear people in their homes! Sandy went inside to let the boys out (Shaggy and Rio), and I stretched my arms to heaven and said, "Lord, If you can see fit to do anything with this life that I've messed up - It's yours."

And it was getting close to sunrise. Beautiful white fluffy cotton balled clouds began to form, as it was to rain this afternoon. Soooo Pretty. Jet streams turned pink/orange when the sun rose. I finally went inside about 7:00 a.m.-ish. I was a little leery of being locked in all night, but when I entered, my dog, Shaggy (Sheep Dog), greeted me, and I melted with a lot of "peace" in her home.

I sat in a recliner and had homemade chicken and sausage gumbo, fresh green beans, cornbread, and mint iced tea. Seasoned food! Heck - Food! I ate two plates. I also haven't had any meds in three days, which means that I'm having electric buzzes throughout the body and leg jerks. But that's ok because I'm not taking that

poison anymore! I already feel better, having good nutrition, water,
and back on my green tea and nutritional supplements!

Tell ya more later. Gonna crash because it's 3:30 a.m. I'm pray-
ing for you all! I wish I could get you all out tomorrow, but I can't.
God can, and he will. Oh-Oh!! I've been listening to KSBJ non-stop. I
could and did sing along and know most all the words! What a gift!
I was so worried I had lost the ability to worship! Praise Him. Lord,
whatever you bring to my memory from the Word is exactly what
I'm going to "act on." I'm going to be obedient to every Word and
command of Jesus that you bring to my mind.

Big Daddy God Our Father: Be with Diamond, Alice, Shamika,
Ashley(Bunkie), Money, Toni, Jessica, Ba'Bra, Ora, Baby Mama's,
Shy, Ada, Kalixa, Angela T, Granny, Ashley F-cell, and all the ladies
of 4H2 Cell Block. May they bless you, Lord - Oh, may their souls
bless you, and may they not forget your benefits. The Lord forgives
our sins, heals all our diseases, redeemed our lives from destruc-
tion, crowns us with kindness and tender mercies, and satisfies
our mouths with good things - so that our youth is renewed like the
Eagles! Don't be a chicken!! B-gaw B-Gaw!

So much for her being scared to death of the other inmates.
Yep! We had been scammed by the best! Mom, Raymond, and
I had been played like a sweet-sounding fiddle. Every syllable
that had come out of Isabella's mouth while she sat on the other
side of that double pained glass in jail was a lie. A ploy. All the
alligator tears were fake. Isabella's performance had to be given
a standing ovation because she succeeded in pulling the wool
over all of our eyes.

Her statement about not ever taking meds anymore scared
me to the core. Without her meds, her bipolar rampages would
continue to worsen each time she had them. Isabella was now
on the run with Jake Wheeler. I was sure of it. I picked up the
phone and called her probation officer.

"Hello, you have reached the Community Justice Assistance
Division of the Texas Department of Criminal Courts. If you
know your party's extension, please dial it now or hold for the

next available operator."

Oh, this is just great. Come on, come on! Pick up the phone.

"Hello, this is Ms. Mandy. How can I help you?"

"I believe my sister just went AWAL."

"Who's her probation officer?"

"I have no idea."

"Do you have her SPN number?" The SPN number stands for the System Personal Number, which is given to inmates to identify them within the jail system. The SPN number follows them for the rest of their life.

"Yes. I do have her SPN number. It's 26GR34."

"Thank you. One moment." I could hear her typing in information. "That would be Isabella Schmidt Jenkins?"

"Yes, that is my sister."

"What the problem, Ma'am?"

"Please tell her probation officer that she has gone AWAL from my house. I believe she is with a boyfriend of hers. I do not believe that she is coming back." I paused for a second, "Let me rephrase that she is not welcome in my house anymore. I do not know where she will end up, nor if she will make her next meeting with her probation officer."

"Thank you. I will give Isabella's probation officer the message."

The only thing left to do was change the locks on my doors, as Isabella had the keys.

It was nearing the evening when there was a persistent pounding on my front door that steadily got louder and louder. The dogs were going nuts. I knew it had to be Isabella. She couldn't get in due to the new locks on the doors. "What do you want, Isabella?" I yelled through the closed front door.

"Let me in, Sandy."

"No. You betrayed me. You do not have a home here anymore. Go away."

"At least let me come in and get my meds."

I couldn't help but burst out laughing. "You mean the meds you don't take?"

I peeked through the front window, spying Jake Wheeler's car parked in front of my house. I ran to my room, where I kept her bipolar meds that I diligently gave to her each night. The same meds that she never ingested. Grabbing the bottle and my keys, I opened the door and not so politely pushed her aside and stormed to where Jake was parked.

Jake's driver side window was already rolled down, so I tossed the bottle of meds in his lap, "Good Luck with that. Now get her off my property before I call the Harris County Sheriff's Office. "

I turned and went back inside, as Izzy got into Jake's car and they left. How can Isabella love God so much, read His Word, praise His name, and still be like this? The enemy has a death grip on her, and I failed to help her.

I failed miserably.

God, please forgive me.

CHAPTER 21

I t only took Jake a few days to conclude that Izzy was off her rocker again. He vowed to put a lot of distance in between the two of them. Putting Isabella in a cab, he sent her packing to my side of town. Jake knew Isabella had made some friends when she was staying with me. He didn't care who they were. He just needed Isabella gone from his life.

In the meantime, I went through her things that she left at my house and found even more letters Izzy had written. I found letters to the fake cop, which were never mailed. My guess would be because she didn't have the address or the postage fees. Either way, they were her confessions to her friend named Kerry, who played the fake cop in Raymond's phone call.

Kerry, I am sorry that I put you up to playing the cop that called Raymond. You and I both know that it was a joke. Kerry, I have tried at least four times to see a psychologist or a psychiatrist since Dec. 2014! The last time I wanted to see a psychiatrist was back in Feb. But as you know, Goodwill arrested me for stealing my own purse and had my car towed, so I missed the appointment!

I am beyond sorry that I made, or should I dare to say, my "stunt" made both of my parents feel like their life was in danger! I never intended to terrify either of them by burning a newspaper in the cement birdbath in the front yard garden! I was HURT! Angry even! And again, I reacted! My stepdad lied to my sister, and she threw me out of her home! Before that, I was happy, happily employed, and driving my car with one payment left. I was taking care of my sister AND me!

Well, I messed up bad! I have a bond of thirty thousand dollars!

That's 3000 dollars bail money I have to pay to get out.

I was shocked and mad all at the same time to read the hard evidence that my sick sister did indeed try to terrify Mom and Raymond. It was also evidence that she tried to burn their house down to the ground.

As the days wore on, it became evident that Jake had given her a phone as the crazy texts and angry, threatening voice messages began again. The best we could do was pray that she didn't kill anyone.

It was now nearing the end of another year, but more importantly, it was a mere thirty days before the bank would start foreclosure proceedings on my house, and without a job, there was no way I could stop them. The last time I had to claim bankruptcy was when I racked up tens of thousands of dollars in medical bills that I couldn't pay.

I knew from that experience that the court would need me to have a job to relinquish funds from to pay off the creditors. Without a job, I couldn't pay the court, which meant that I would be kicked to the streets to survive.

Jesus, please help me! I need to keep a roof over my head. You said to test you. I have been obeying your command to tithe. I'm down to the last wire and hanging on by my fingernails. I need you now. Please! In the Name of Jesus! Help me! - Amen

Twenty-five days after I said that prayer, I woke up at 7:00 a.m. with my cell phone ringing off the wall. It was the Human Resource Department at Forest Ranch Independent School District.

"Hello?"

"May I speak to Ms. Ryan?"

"This is Sandy Ryan."

"Ms. Ryan, Forest Ranch ISD would like to make you an offer to come and work for us."

"I accept!" Nope! I didn't have to think about that one!

"Ms. Ryan, they would like for you to start on November 28th. Is that acceptable to you?"

"Yes, Ma'am!"

"The Human Resource department would like for you to come in to sign a contract and get your badge made. Please report to the Information and Technology Building on November 27."

"I'll be there with bells on! Thank you!"

God had done it! A year and a half after my fall into the very pits of hell, God had given me a job that was less than two and a half miles from my house. This job paid enough to pay the bankruptcy lawyers. It paid enough to pay the bills. It was also just enough to get the dogs to the vet.

God is good! All the time!

The Forest Ranch Center is a sports facility complex for the Forest Ranch Independent School District and the community that funds it. It has a 21,000 seat outdoor stadium, an indoor 10,500 seat arena, and a 16,000 square foot conference center. It also houses a 500 seat performing arts theater, and I was in charge of it.

As I walked through the theater on my first day, I believed that I could help them and that this job would be fun. I would be helping the students learn about theater. I was back in my element. Granted, it was a tiny part of my element. But it was a theater!

I walked onto the stage for the first time and imagined plays from the high schools being performed there. All the kids would be learning from my past experiences working for an Opera Company. I knew there would be concerts and comedies.

It was such a small theater. One could even call it an intimate setting. God had given it to me. And I was finally happy. Happy for a job, happy for a paycheck, and entirely happy that I didn't have to worry about where my next meal would be coming from.

As the days wore on, I kept getting weird vibes from the people that worked there. Something was amiss, but I couldn't put my finger on the problem. Once the Forest Ranch Center employees got used to me, they told me horror stories about the management there.

The General Manager of the Forest Ranch Center was a lady named Olga Swendle-Gaylord. Olga comes from a long line of white-collar criminals who delights in everything evil as they masquerade as someone of noble character. They demand mercy but give none themselves. They demand warmth, forgiveness, and intimacy from those they have harmed with no empathy for the pain they have caused and no real intention of making amends or working hard to rebuild broken trust.

Olga is no different from her ancestors, except she takes their evil deeds many steps further. She rejects feedback and real accountability. Olga makes up her own rules. She is all smoke and mirrors.

In 1997, Before coming to the Forest Ranch Center, Olga managed the Nashville Coliseum. It was a venue that was home to the Nashville Professional Wrestling League. It was also a venue for Rock 'n' Roll concerts. However, all was not well with the Nashville Coliseum.

A professional wrestler told the press, "Olga Swendle-Gaylord did everything she could to force wrestling out of the venue. She raised the rent and mandated an expensive security force be hired to control the rowdy wrestling fans. The same fans whom she always looked down upon." Laughingly, he added, "it was pretty funny watching the passive-aggressive conversations between other wrestlers and Olga backstage. They both clearly thought the other was vile and insignificant, masking their hostility with smiling faces."

In April of 1997, Olga courted the satanic band *Marilyn Manson* to perform at the Nashville Coliseum. The pressure was put on Olga by religious, civic, and political leaders who criticized the group's image. There were many sworn affidavits by teens attesting to satanic church services, naked female guitar players, drugs being passed continuously out, and real and simulated sex on stage by band members. Despite the public's rage for the satanic band, Olga still allowed them to perform at the Nashville Coliseum.

Before the band took the stage, an associate pastor of First Assembly of God told the press that members of the Christian community oppose the concert for various reasons, including the fact that the singer calls his album the *Antichrist Superstar* and makes analogies to himself as the Antichrist, as well as promotes suicide. All of their albums are covered with warnings of explicit language and violent content.

After the band had performed onstage, Olga Swendle-Gaylord told the press, "The show was about as plain as a rock 'n' roll show as I've ever seen. There was nothing wrong with it."

This led to a former WWF Wrestler publicly stating to a news reporter that Olga Swendle-Gaylord was none other than *Lady Satan* and that she and her minions frequently treated them like crap.

Olga has this "do whatever it takes" attitude. She hands out directives to achieve her aggressive goals, which leads to unethical tactics. Olga delegates ambiguous demands to others on the campus then turns a willfully blind eye to the consequent questionable and unethical behaviors. Olga's current crimes include misrepresentation of the Forest Ranch Center's finances, in which she consistently deceives the school board and the community.

Olga likes to think that she is smart, and being in the position of power, she knows how to avoid getting caught. She is driven by greed, invincibility, and a desire to win at all costs. Her heart is so evil you could drive a wooden stake through it, and I doubt it would kill her. Her soul is so corrupt it reeked of venomous poison, and I could smell it a mile away.

Mass exodus started taking place at the Forest Ranch Center. Within two weeks, sixteen people had quit their jobs, but I still didn't want to believe that this job was a bad one. After all, God had given it to me. This job saved my house.

I kept telling myself that this job can't be all that bad. God wouldn't put me in a horrible situation. Not with what I had to go through to just get to this point. God wouldn't slap me in the face that way. Would He?

It wasn't long, though, before I started experiencing the horrible decisions from the Forest Ranch Center Management, and the "I care" and the "I can help" attitude quickly got beat out of me in a very short six week period. The management wasn't there for the employees. They were only there to line their own pockets with the taxpayer's money. Nothing else mattered to them.

I concluded that the Forest Ranch Center was run by the evilest hearts on this planet and that the management team was experts at creating confusion and conflict. They are masters at fooling others with their flattering words and smooth speech. They do not know the Lord as their highest authority but only recognize themselves as the law of the land.

Their hearts are cold and black, just like the dark black pyramid I saw in my coma dreams years ago.

They have no conscience.

They have no remorse.

As the weeks went by, I started noticing the corruption in the Forest Ranch Center management. The micromanaging and the poor leadership skills. They were like that annoying fly that got stuck in your car, and you can't seem to swat it away.

Then there was Edgar Sewers, my supervisor, and the Forest Ranch Center's Technical Manager. He is a sour, unpleasant creature. All his life, he has battled his short, rotund body with no success. At age 40, weighing in at 450 pounds, he found himself going bald and his teeth rotting. All of which never gave him any real confidence. Edgar constantly fears that he will be outshined, outdone, and overshadowed, which is why he cowers when he is confronted with anything. It also made Edgar Sewers the worst manager I had ever worked for throughout my life. I trusted him about as far as I could throw him.

Edgar makes it a point to make me as miserable as possible every hour of every day. His favorite thing to do is to send out condemning emails on late Friday afternoon just before my shift ends. He knows that I will stew on it all weekend, thus ruining any chance for peace in my life. That alone made me feel lower than a gopher hole.

Edgar slowly moved up the ranks at the Forest Ranch Center. He started as a lowly video operator. Then Edgar studied long and hard to get a certificate in AV Technologies. A test he failed six times before passing it by the skin of his teeth. With his certification in hand, Olga saw his potential and promoted him to AV Technology Manager.

He now spends most of his time playing the puppet of Lady Satan's politics just to get to his next promotion. Edgar's heart turned to stone as he aligned his values along with Olga's. The two of them became as thick as fleas on a hound dog.

Over the years, Edgar made sure he hired people that had less knowledge than he does. Edgar is paranoid that the A-players will be smart enough to see that he shouldn't have gotten his position. But he never tries to better himself as a manager. Who has time for all that self-help crap anyway? He gets results, and that is what counts - period.

He tolerates lousy work and lets chronic under-performers go unchecked. He never says thank you. He never gives praise, and he consistently plays favorites. He knows that a few folks on his team probably shouldn't be there, but they're old friends, and they've been loyal. Hey, loyalty does count for something these days - right?

Edgar doesn't see the world in black or white. In his twisted little mind, there is no right and no wrong. There are only shades of gray. He thinks that the gray areas are easier ways to find a practical solution to any problem. But make no mistake, he is never wrong - about anything. He takes all the credit for the AV team's hard work, and when mistakes are made, he quickly blames them.

Being a very vindictive man, he never forgets past wrongs

against him and thinks it is healthy to go back and rub his staff's noses in the mud to show them who truly is the boss. He lies about anything and everything, and that puts him in Olga's spotlight of praise. He's the type of person who will beat you senseless and tell God you just fell off the horse. His attitude is, "I get paid the same regardless."

Edgar is very indecisive when it comes to making plans about anything. He requires mountains of information just to decide simple matters. Every time he's confronted with a decision, he questions himself. "Why do I need to decide now, anyway? Let's wait. Maybe the team could do some more research. Maybe I could talk to Charles to see what he thinks. I don't have to rush a plan now. The team doesn't have to be updated yet. I'll just keep the information from them. They are on a need to know basis anyhow. They just need to keep doing their jobs, and I'll handle the big picture stuff."

Edgar continues to withhold information from the team, and the team complains that he just doesn't listen. He believes that people on his team are always talking or whining about something irrelevant, and he's not sure where the whole idea that he's not a good listener comes from anyway, but Edgar doesn't care because he gets paid the same anyway.

Edgar dumps more work on the AV team than he gets done himself. At the end of the day, he knows he is the boss. He knows these people work for him. Edgar justifies this by telling himself, "What am I supposed to do? Do the work for them? I need to be out having dinner and hobnobbing while the worker bees back at the office do stuff. That's just part of being a leader."

That's all pretty inspiring, right? Edgar believes that he doesn't need to inspire the team at all. It's not like they sit around all day singing campfire songs.

As the weeks of my employment turned into months, I started begging God to find me another job. The cute little theater that I was in charge of was used mostly for district meetings. Only ten percent of the time, the communities Dance Schools held their recitals there.

The theater was not used for performing arts. There were no plays or musicals, except for the UIL One Act Play competition. That was the only bright spot in my employment. It was my opportunity to watch and teach the young theater students about an ancient craft called Technical Theater.

In the UIL competition, each High School must perform a play in one act. What that means is each school must set up their play in seven minutes. Perform the play in 45 minutes, then load their set off the stage in seven minutes. All students would then be judged on their performance and technical skills.

The One Act Play competition was fascinating to watch, but unfortunately, it only came once a year and lasted for only two weeks. Afterward, I went back to the drudgery of meetings and poorly rehearsed dance recitals until the day came when I had to manage an Arangetram.

An Arangetram is a classical Indian dance performed by just one student who has spent many years studying the art. During the opening ceremony, the student must pay tribute to the teacher and their gods. That gave me the creeps.

Their gods were represented as a golden idol that looked like a small elephant with many arms. The golden idols were adorned in many fine silks that the parents of the student purchased. The student placed a bowl of fruit before the idol as she kissed its forehead. My heart sank. These people did not believe in God or Jesus. They worshiped idols and demons.

It was fascinating to watch, but it scared me to death. Olga Swendle-Gaylord was allowing this satanism to happen, and I knew in my heart that the entire Forest Ranch Center management team was as evil as this golden demon idol that sat front and center on my stage.

From that day forward, I started praying to God that although I was extremely grateful for the job that was getting me out of the debtor's prison that I had sunk myself in, I couldn't work in this den of evil any longer. I pleaded to God to find me a new job where I could be happy and content.

Why did God put me in this Forest Ranch hell hole? What was the purpose? Why did God want to slap me in the face like this? Was this some sort of punishment for not knowing him all my life?

And the more I asked questions, the fewer answers that I received.

I found out that Izzy stayed with a friend of mine that she had met during her last stay at my house. Gabriel lives only a few miles from my house. Knowing that Izzy was in another rage and staying on my side of town unnerved me.

I didn't have to wait very long before Gabriel kicked Izzy out as well. With nowhere else to go, Izzy called a cab and rode to the only friend's house she had left that would still talk to her.

"Alecia!"

"Izzy, what are you doing here? Last time you were here, you smashed my phone."

"I'm sorry, Alecia, I was furious at you."

"OK, I know it is the disease, so all is forgiven. Come in."

"Can I first borrow some money to pay the cab driver Alecia? I didn't know where else to turn for help."

As Alecia went to grab her purse, Isabella made her way into the apartment, grinning from ear to ear.

The ringing of my phone startled me out of brewing over my job. "Hello?"

"Sans!"

"Gabriel! What's going on, my friend?"

"I kicked Izzy out. She's nuts, Sans. I couldn't handle her anymore."

"Gabby, you know she's bipolar, right?"

"Oh, no. Really? Holy ...aww snap... it now makes perfect sense."

"Yep, she's not taking her meds either that's why she seems nuts."

"Well, she left most of her things at my house. What do you want me to do with it all?"

"I can come and get it. Gabby, I'm so sorry that you had to be put through all this drama."

"It's not your fault Sans. It's a disease."

"I know, I know... Look, I'll be over in about an hour. We can catch up then."

"Cool, I'll be waiting."

As I hung up the phone, I could only imagine what I would find when I sifted through the things that Isabella left at Gabby's house.

It didn't take long before I was walking up Gabriel's driveway.

"Her suitcases are in the spare bedroom." I followed Gabby through her house. "She left a lot of things that still have tags on them. I don't know where she got the money for them, though."

"Gab's, she stole them. It's what she does. Her brain doesn't comprehend that she is stealing. She just takes what she wants like everything is hers."

"I should have seen the signs, Sandy. I had a brother who was bipolar. Except he took his meds, so it was bearable. I did not see this coming."

"It's ok. Not many people do. Just by the way she is acting, I know she is not taking her medication. It's only a matter of time before she ends up back in jail."

"That's so sad."

"I know. But for now, because Izzy is an adult, there is nothing we can do to stop her."

"Please, Sandy, let me know if there is anything I can do to help."

She gave me a big hug. "I will. I promise."

I made my way out to my car dragging along two full suitcases and a couple of small boxes of Isabella's stuff and drove back home. What's a few more bags and boxes? My two spare rooms are already jam-packed floor to ceiling with Isabella's things.

As soon as I got home, I plopped Izzy's things on the living room floor, and Rio and Shaggy promptly went to inspect all the new smells emitting from the suitcases. "There's no time like the present, I guess." Rio and Shaggy's tails were going 90 miles a minute as I opened the first suitcase.

In it were more clothes that were never worn, and all of them had store tags. There were more letters Isabella wrote that were never mailed. And then I felt a hard bump under the mound of clothes. It was her bipolar medication. The prescription said that there were 63 pills in the bottle. There were only six missing from the bottle, and Izzy had the prescription for at least a month. That told me she was definitely off of her meds.

God help us.

CHAPTER 22

In a shopping center north of Houston, two young Spanish males, Santiago, and Alejandro, had just finished pumping gas into their truck and were heading out of the parking lot when Officer Amandeep spotted their vehicle. Their back taillights were out.

Turning on his police car lights, he put his car in drive and pulled them over. Officer Amandeep got out of his vehicle and walked up to the suspect's car.

Santiago rolled down his window. "Hello Officer, what's the problem?"

"Your taillights are out. Can I see your driver's license and insurance, please?"

Santiago was on the run for a very long list of crimes. He knew that if the Officer ran his driver's license number, he would be arrested and sent back to prison. He slowly handed over his driver's license and insurance papers.

Officer Amandeep turned to walk back to his squad car to verify the information that he was given. As Officer Amandeep took three steps away from the suspect's vehicle, Santiago grabbed his .45mm pistol, got out of his car, and shot Officer Amandeep in the back of his head. Officer Amandeep never knew what hit him. He was dead.

Santiago and Alejandro fled the scene only to be captured by the police several blocks away. The Forest Ranch community was in mourning. Officer Amandeep was a beloved peace officer that continuously helped the community. He was also a Sikh, who wore a full turban and beard honoring his religion.

Two days after his death, Olga Swendle-Gaylord offered the

family of the fallen officer full use of the Forest Ranch Center completely free of charge. The family was grateful and agreed to have the funeral service there.

They held two services for Officer Amandeep back to back. The first was a Sikh ceremony, and the second was a ceremony for the Officers in Blue. They did not call it a Christian ceremony. The Chaplin for the police officers said a speech but never mentioned Jesus Christ.

It was the last speaker at the funeral that shocked me. With a scarf covering her head that showed honor to the Sikh Religion, Amy Parks sauntered up to the podium. "Good morning. You may be wondering why I am here speaking to you today. I am a member of the community subdivision where Officer Amandeep lived. He was my friend. Officer Amandeep never hurt anyone. He loved to check in with the elderly and play with the kids. I am very grateful to have known him."

On and on, Amy Parks spoke about the loving ways of the fallen officer, until she came to her conclusion, "It is so wonderful to see so many different religions coming together to honor this man. This Sikh Officer. My Friend. Jews, Muslims, Christians, and Sikhs." She paused to let her words sink in. "You are all sitting next to one another in union. This union is bridging religious and cultural differences. This union is proof that we are working together for the good of communities and the world promoting daily interfaith cooperation."

The crowd applauded as she continued, "We need to end religiously motivated violence and create cultures of peace, justice, and healing for the Earth and all living things. It is what Officer Amandeep did. This is what he wanted. We should all be like Officer Amandeep. Thank you."

Everyone was standing and clapping. Some were openly crying, as others hugged the strangers next to them. The Sikh banners flew just above the casket.

One Universal Creator God, Truth, and Eternal is the Name. Everyone is equal, regardless of caste or gender. Love, unity, mutual

*respect, service, and dedication to all of humanity. - Guru Namhak
Sahib*

Sweet Jesus, get me out of here! This was prophecy. She is talking about a One World Religion. That sent the heebee jee-bee's up and down my spine. The one-world religion is described in Revelation 17:1-18 as "the great harlot."

The term harlot is used throughout the Old Testament as a metaphor for false religion. It's the false religion of the Antichrist in the end of days. This false religion will permit and even encourage the death of Christians during the tribulation.

Christians everywhere need to wake up and smell the roses. *"And do this, understanding the present time: The hour has already come for you to wake up from your slumber because our Salvation is nearer now than when we first believed" (Romans 13:11).*

The Federated Religions Initiative was founded in the year 1999 by a guy named Larry Ferguson. In attendance at the conference that kicked off the Federated Religions Initiative were Catholics, Protestants, Jews, Hindus, Sikhs, indigenous people, and Wiccans. The FRI is an international grassroots interfaith network.

The FRI was the beginning of the One World Religion of the Antichrist that Jesus talks about in the Word of God. *"For false Christ's and false prophets will arise and perform great signs and wonders, so as to lead astray, if possible, even the elect." (Matthew 24:24).*

The One World Religion is the interfaith cooperation that Amy Parks so profoundly spoke of and rallied all 5000 people at the funeral to be like. This event was the Enemy knocking on all Christian doors. This event was prophesied in the Bible. This prophecy was coming true right before my very eyes, and Lady Satan Olga Swendle-Gaylord had orchestrated it all.

Just sitting in the room with all 5000 people that came to say goodbye to this fallen officer made my skin crawl. I could sense the evil, and I wanted to run far, far away. But it was my job to be here. It was the job that Jesus gave to me to do three years ago. I prayed that my time spent at the Forest Ranch Center would end soon.

The evil that dwells here literally makes me sick to my stomach. *Lord, I am witnessing your prophecy. Please, Lord, get me out of here! I can't take much more of this evil. Amen.* And then my mind went back to the time when I was watching Pastor Don Norden's sermon about No Trespassing.

I remembered the part where he said, "Victory over the enemy will be so complete that peace will become the norm in your life. When you learn how to fight the enemy, you can have peace in the midst of the battle because you understand your authority is as a believer, and you can just say, 'You know what? The devil picked this fight, but he's gonna be sorry when this is over because this is all going to turn out to God's Glory and my benefit! HALLELUJAH!

"And this is what the enemy will be required to do. In Proverbs 6:31, *'Yet if he is caught, he must pay sevenfold, though it costs him all the wealth of his house.'*. The enemy comes to steal, kill, and destroy. But if he is found, he must pay sevenfold."

Pastor Don Nordic words were true, but I am still extremely nervous. "Sevenfold!" I screamed aloud, "Jesus, my King! I declare and demand that the enemy make sevenfold restitution in my life." I paused for a second, "And I also declare and demand that I have a new job, one where I can go and be happy to be there. A job where evil doesn't freely walk down the halls and stare at you in the eyes. A job that I can be proud to work at. In your name Jesus, I pray. -Amen"

A Harris County Sheriff's Officer was cruising through a small shopping center one foggy morning when his radio came to life. "Officer is needed at the IHOP on Texas Hwy 35."

That IHOP sits where the Brazoria County line meets the Harris County line. It wasn't all that unusual for Harris County cops to sometimes be near or even patrol the area. He responded to the call and sped down the road to the IHOP.

The manager was standing outside the front door waiting. "Hi. I'm the one who called you here."

"What seems to be the problem, Ma'am?"

"We have served this older lady several cups of coffee, and she can't pay. But she won't leave either."

"I can arrest her for trespassing. I just need you to sign this form." The officer took out his book and started writing down the facts. "Please, sign here." He handed the papers for the manager to sign.

"Great, now can you point her out to me?"

"She's the older lady sitting next to the window."

The officer headed in Isabella's direction, popping the top of his handcuffs as he slowly walked. "Ma'am, could you please come with me?"

"What for Officer? I have done nothing wrong."

"The manager of this facility would like for you to leave. Please come peacefully with me now."

Isabella wasn't having any of it. She just sat there furiously staring him down. The officer wasn't having any of it either. He grabbed her left arm and not so gently pulled her away from the table and led her straight to the front door where his squad car was parked. "Ma'am, do you have any identification?"

Isabella only had an old social security card, but it did have her name on it. "This is all I have." She handed the officer the card.

"You're under arrest. Turn around and put your hands behind your back."

"I haven't done anything wrong."

"Ma'am, the manager of the IHOP, has charged you with trespassing and failure to pay your bill."

"I was going to pay it in due time. I just wanted to sit there for a few more minutes. Officer, this is ridiculous!"

He slapped the handcuffs on her and placed her in the back seat of his cruiser, locking the doors. The officer took Isabella back to the Harris County Jail in downtown Houston where she was booked for theft and trespassing.

"Raymond, come look at this!" Janice yelled from their downstairs office. She had been looking on the internet for halfway houses that would accept Isabella.

Raymond came into the office.

"Look, Raymond!" She pointed to the computer screen, "It's a place called Grace of Yahweh."

"How do we get her in there?"

"The article of acceptance says that they only accept new residents if it's court-ordered. And she has to arrive at the program after seeing a psychologist and has 90 days' worth of medication prescribed by the said psychologist."

"Well, Janice, we can present the Judge with this new information next week at Isabella's court hearing. We can only pray that the Judge will accept it."

I was praying daily for Isabella. I asked God to keep her from killing someone. I asked God to help her. And it came as no surprise when I found out Isabella was back in jail, knowing she was not taking her meds. But the most disturbing thing now about Izzy being back behind bars was Izzy's depression.

Her bipolar high had now swung her so far past rock bottom that she was attempting suicide by not eating. The jailers didn't know what to do with her other than put her in the medical unit and feed her through an IV.

There was little chance that a Judge would grant her a stay at a halfway house with her not eating. Izzy couldn't even get in a wheelchair by herself. Let alone stand before a Judge in court.

Court to me is like the holding cell to the bowels of hell. I believe that is why I feel so drained after I go there. Its spiritual warfare on a level only my unconscious can conceive. It drains my brain and my strength.

Lord Jesus, please make this rollercoaster stop. Let us off this ride to hell. Give Isabella some kind of strength to see Your Light to make her well.

The Judge granted Isabella the option to go into Grace of Yahweh, but Izzy had to sign the papers releasing her from the state and into a psychologist's care. If Izzy refused to sign, the court would release her into downtown Houston's streets, where she would have to fend for herself. It was like the courts were washing their hands of all this nonsense.

I sat down and wrote her a letter telling her we will not help her if she does not say to the judge she wants to go to Grace of Yahweh. I mailed it with priority one-day delivery and decided to go down to the jail for one last visit.

"Izzy, you have to sign the papers. If you don't sign them, then it's the last straw. We will not help you. Period."

"Sans, I am not going to sign any papers. I won't go into a stupid halfway house. There is nothing wrong with me."

"Look, Izzy, if you do not sign the papers, the Judge will release you into the streets. You will die in the streets, Izzy. Is that what you want? You will die because we will not help you anymore."

"Don't be so dramatic! I will not die in the streets. I will die if I am left in this horrible jail. That's where I will die, Sans, not in the streets."

"Are you taking your meds, Izzy?"

"Ha! No way!" Gee, what a surprise!

"OK, Izzy, I mailed you a map of downtown and marked where you can take shelter at some charity houses. You can get food there too. I pray that you will use it."

The guard called time, and that was the end of that.

Lord, you have to help her. It is in your hands now.

Mom, Raymond, and I have done all we can to help her.

Two days later, Isabella pleaded with her caseworker in jail. She finally saw the light and agreed to sign the papers releasing herself into Grace of Yahweh. Mom and Raymond rushed to the jail to pick her up.

"Hurry, Raymond, I don't want her to be on the streets."

"I'm going as fast as I can, Janice. Be patient. Isabella's caseworker said it could be hours before they process her out. We have time. Did you pack some of her clothes up?"

"Yes, it's all in the suitcase. I just don't think Izzy will fit into any of it since she's lost so much weight."

"It'll be fine, Jan. Stop worrying."

Grace of Yahweh was a strict halfway house run by Christians. They would make sure she took her meds and talked with a psychologist regularly. They assured Mom and Raymond that they could come to visit twice a week.

"Once we drop her off at Grace of Yahweh, we will see her again, Jan, in just a few short days. And we can hug her and kiss her since she won't be behind bulletproof glass."

"I know that, Raymond. I still worry, though."

Isabella was released late in the evening as Raymond and Janice patiently waited for her. I went outside that evening, and there was a rainbow across the entire sky, not the usual partial rainbow that I see most times. Perhaps this was a sign from God that things will be ok for her from now on. I thank the Lord that she made it this far.

CHAPTER 23

"Sandy to Building Services," I called over the Forest Ranch Center radio.

"Go for Building Services," came the response.

"Hey guys, when you get a chance, can you please remove all the chairs and music stands that are on the stage from last night's orchestra concert? I also need the Orchestra walls removed as well."

"Sure, on the way!"

"Copy! Thank you!"

Last night's concert was the final show for the Forest Ranch ISD orchestra students. The school year would be over within a few short weeks. The only thing left that I had on the Theater's schedule was a local community dance group's recital to be held this Saturday night.

God had given me this job, and I am so very grateful for it. This job pays my bills and puts food on the table. The only thing that I couldn't figure out is why God put me here in the first place, with so much heartless evil lurking in the hallways.

Perhaps it was for times like these when there is a community show. With my skills and love for the theater, I can make lasting memories for the children who perform for their parents. I can create an experience that would last them a lifetime, and for that, I am grateful.

Pervis from Building Services interrupted my thoughts, "Miss Sandy, we're here to clear the stage."

"Great Pervis! You can start by dragging all the platforms off the stage and stacking the chairs over there. The music stand carts are in the cage stage left. Once the stage is clear, you can roll the orchestra walls over to the dock area."

"We'll get right on it, Miss Sandy!" Pervis turned to his crew and rattled off what I just told him in Spanish.

I watched them drag each chair across the stage and stack them neatly in piles near the stage door. Then they flipped the platforms over on their sides and folded them up, as two others were dragging the music stands off the stage to put back in their carts. It is the end of the school year, and I didn't care that they were scratching up the stage floor. I was sure Pervis would re-paint it during summer maintenance.

It took them about half an hour to clear the stage and leave the theater. I called my crew in to start working on the set up for tomorrow night's event.

"Sandy to Lisa and Aaron," I called over the radio.

"Go for Lisa and Aaron," was the reply.

"Please come to the theater. I am ready to set for tomorrow night's show."

"Copy!"

Aaron was my lighting guy. He is in charge of all things light-ing and lighting effects on stage. Lisa is my sound person. She is in charge of all music and all microphones that are on stage. It didn't take them long to make their way to the theater stage.

I greeted them as they entered the theater, "Hi guys! How's it going?"

"Pretty good. Where would you like for us to start?"

"Aaron, these are the dance numbers that they will be per-forming." I handed him the list. "The client has picked out colors for each dance. If you could please get started on pro-gramming the lights to match the dances, that would be great!"

I turned to Lisa. "Here are the tap mics they will be using. The client wants them taped down at the curtain line." I handed her three boxes of microphones that will amplify the tapping of the children's tap shoes. "If you guys want to get started, I will go get the flash drive that contains their dance music."

I watched Lisa move across the stage with the microphones in hand. She was seven months pregnant and still moved pretty gracefully. She placed the microphones on the stage floor and began taping them down so the children would not knock them over. Aaron made his way to the control room to start programming the lights. I turned and made my way to my office on the theater's loading dock to grab the flash drive that had the Little Feet Dance Studio music files.

It was going to be a cute dance recital. The Little Feet Dance Studio is located in the Forest Ranch community. They taught tap and ballet to children from 4 years old to 12 years old. I can remember being that young on a stage and performing *I'm a little teacup*! My Mom was so proud of me. I imagine it will be like that for most parents who come to see their children perform on a big stage. They're not going to care if their children don't perform perfectly because most parents send their toddlers to dance class to work on their coordination and social skills in a fun way. They also want to see their cute kids dressed up along with their classmates.

The theater was packed full of anxious parents eagerly waiting for the show to begin. Backstage, the Little Feet Dance Studio teachers were herding the toddlers into their positions on the stage. The main curtain opened, and the show began.

The first group on the stage was the four-year-old toddlers. They were so cute in their pink tutus with tiny little pink bows in their hair. There were eight toddlers in the group, and Susie was the littlest one on the stage.

As the music began, Susie plopped down and stuck her thumb in her mouth. She sat there staring out into the audience, occasionally smiling. Just as the music changed beats, Susie took her thumb out of her mouth and started to draw on the stage floor with her saliva. No one really cared. It's what all children do at that age. The parents were just happy to see her on a stage. The music changed beats again, and the thumb went back into Susie's mouth.

Finally, the eight toddlers took their bows, and the teachers herded them offstage. As the curtain closed for the final time, I have to say that it was a pretty cute show, all said and done. The Little Feet Dance Studio was pleased with all of it. But the crew and I still had to close up the theater.

Lisa got down on her hands and knees and started pulling up the tape she had put down around the microphones. I noticed that the tape had pulled up little slivers of paint. It didn't matter since the stage floor was extremely scratched up from all the tables and chairs that had been dragged across the stage floor over the last three years. I knew Pervis would be painting it soon. Edgar had sent me an email just this morning confirming that.

I was looking forward to the weekend, so I called my crew to the stage, thanking them for a job well done, then dismissing them. Whatever else needed to be done could wait until Monday morning.

Izzy had settled in at Grace of Yahweh. They woke her up at 6:00 a.m. for breakfast and prayers. Then in the afternoon, just after lunch, they had art classes she attended. In the evenings, she had the choice to watch TV or play in the recreation room. Then it was lights out by 10:00 p.m.

Mom and Raymond went to visit with her twice a week. Sometimes they stayed to have dinner with her. The counselors who ran the place assured us that Isabella was taking her medications and speaking to her psychologist regularly. It seemed like God had finally answered our prayers.

Isabella was getting back to normal. She always seemed happy. Izzy didn't talk about crazy things anymore. The years of pain she has caused this family was slowly fading into the background. I went to see Isabella that Sunday after church. She looked healthy! She looked like Normal Izzy! I gave her a big hug.

"Izzy, you look wonderful! How's life at Grace?"

"I like it here, Sans. Everybody is so nice. The food is great too!"

"Well, it shows! Have you gotten to talk to Preston any?"

I knew Preston still didn't believe that his mom had gotten better. I still had my doubts too, but I have not seen any signs that would send the red flag up the pole to this day.

"No, I haven't spoken to him. Mom said that he's still mad at me. I don't know anymore, but I wrote him a letter, and I apologized profusely. I just hope he reads it."

"He'll come around, sis. He just needs a little more time. He'll forgive you. I just know it."

"I hope you're right, Sans. I sure do miss him. Want to go play a game of ping pong?"

I laughed, "Sure! That sounds like fun!"

We played ping pong for hours and hours. We laughed. We hugged. We told childhood stories. It was amazing and wonderful seeing her like this! As I left Grace of Yahweh, I gave Isabella another hug. It sure is nice to see Normal Izzy again.

Thank you, Lord, this is all Your doing!

Monday morning came around way too fast. I took a long swig of my coffee and opened my email. At the top of the list was the email from Edgar. The same email that I saw but didn't open before the show started Saturday night.

Sandy,

I am assigning you the project to paint the stage. The paint that we used the year before you got here is in one of the theater cages. Please get with Pervis to get whatever you need to get this done. Also, do not paint the stage when Community Engagement is in the building because they breathe the same air as the theater.

What? I'm supposed to paint the stage? OK, I can do that, but why can't I paint when Community Engagement is in the building? Why do I have to paint the stage anyway? Pervis paints all the time when they are here. He paints the hallways, and he paints the offices. He paints everything, and paint doesn't smell all that bad. I don't get it.

The more I thought about it, the more curious I got. I shut my laptop and went looking for the paint. What was so bad about this paint that Community Engagement doesn't want to breathe it? Why do I have to breathe it?

I found six cans of one-gallon paint in the stage right cage where the staircase that leads to the catwalks is. Now that's a funny place to store paint. As I have gone up and down that staircase many times, I never noticed the paint cans.

I grabbed one of the cans and took it back to my desk. The name of the paint was SPW LUSTRAL Enamel F95B67. It seems harmless enough to me. I turned to my favorite search engine and looked up the paint's name. At the top of the list was the material safety data sheets for the paint. I clicked on the link, and it brought up an eighteen-page document that first identified the hazards of using this paint. I read the first page.

The SPW LUSTRAL Enamel F95B67 paint is considered hazardous by the OSHA Hazard Communication Standard. For Industrial Shop Application ONLY. Obtain special instructions before use. A specialist should be consulted before handling this product. Use explosion-proof ventilation equipment.

Oh no! What? Explosion-proof ventilation? For Industrial Shop Application only? This paint is not supposed to be on the stage floor. But just how bad was it? I read on.

Flammable liquid and vapor. May cause an allergic skin reaction. May cause cancer. Suspected of damaging the unborn child. May be fatal if swallowed and enters airways. May cause respiratory irritation. May cause drowsiness or dizziness. Causes damage to organs through prolonged or repeated exposure. Contains solvents that can cause permanent brain and nervous system damage.

Abrading or sanding of the dried film may release Crystalline

Silica, which has been shown to cause lung damage and cancer under long term exposure.

Oh, my God! The dried film may release Crystalline Silica? This stuff is toxic in its dried form? This document is listing eighteen pages of death! What is Crystalline Silica?

I turned to my favorite search engine, and it sent me to osha.gov, The Occupational Safety and Health Administration [OSHA] website. They explained crystalline silica this way.

> *"Dust sized silica particles, invisible to the naked eye, are generated during a variety of activities and can be breathed into the body where they reach deep into the lungs. Once in the lungs, these particles can be coughed up, or pass from the lungs to other organs in the body through the bloodstream or stay stuck in the lungs.*
>
> *"Breathing in very small ("respirable") crystalline silica particles causes multiple diseases, including silicosis, an incurable lung disease that leads to disability and death. Respirable crystalline silica also causes lung cancer, chronic obstructive pulmonary disease (COPD), and kidney disease. Exposure to respirable crystalline silica is related to the development of autoimmune disorders and cardiovascular impairment. These occupational diseases are life-altering and debilitating disorders."*

My heart sank, and my body got the chills. An incurable lung disease? Leads to disability and death? My head was spinning. What this means is everyone who danced on the stage floor came in contact with the crystalline silica substance. Everyone who tap-danced on the stage floor kicked up the crystalline silica dust. Everyone who pulled up the tape from the stage floor came in contact with crystalline silica.

Every UIL One Act Play student that was on their hands and knees pulling up spike tape after the contest was exposed to the crystalline silica. Every chair, every table, and every prop that was dragged across the stage contaminated the stage with crystalline silica. And I have been exposed to it for over three years.

And then I thought about the last show. That toddler. That

toddler that drew on the stage floor and then put her fingers in her mouth. How many children have done this in the past? And then I thought of Lisa. Pregnant Lisa. Oh no! This paint kills unborn children. Lisa pulled up the tape that which, in turn, scuffed the paint. She breathed in the crystalline silica—the poison.

Lord, please protect her child. I prayed.

How many shows have been held in this theater? How many children have been exposed? How many people in the community have been exposed? What about the audience? If this stuff, this silica, was invisible to the naked eye, wouldn't it have floated into the audience seats? Wouldn't the audience be in jeopardy too? The entire Forest Ranch Center staff and the surrounding community have been exposed to it for years.

The more I thought about it that list grew. It was endless.

The Good Lord said we'd have trouble in this dark world *(John 16:33)*, and its name is the Forest Ranch Center with Lady Satan at the helm.

But fear not, my friends, for God is still on the throne and in control. He is not dead!

Do not fear, for I am with you; do not be dismayed, for I am your God.
I will strengthen you and help you; I will uphold you with my righteous right hand. – Isaiah 41:10

God is GOOD!

ALL the time!

THE BLESSING

May the Lord bless you and keep you;
May the Lord make His face shine upon you,
  And be gracious to you;
May the Lord lift up His countenance upon you,
  And give you peace.

Numbers 6:24-26

THANK YOU!

I am so very grateful that you took the time to read my book. This novel has been weighing on my heart for over five years now. My hope is that it brought you closer to the truth and the Lord Jesus Christ!

If you would be so kind as to leave the book a review on Amazon.com, I would greatly appreciate it. I would love to read what you think of the story.

Feel free to send me an email at CotoTKing@CTKPublications.com and tell me how this story helped you! I would love to hear from you!

May God Bless You, and Thank You Again!

Coto T. King

CTKPublication.com

ABOUT THE AUTHOR

Coto T. King

Coto T. King is the writer of Christian Fiction and Non-Fiction books, short stories, and articles. She is an author at CTK Publications (CTKPublications.com)

She is a follower of Jesus. A Do It Yourself rock star, a lover of dogs, a computer nerd, an all-around fix-it queen, a carpenter, a mechanic, and a great cook.

When nothing needs fixing, on an average day, you will find Coto writing, cooking, walking the dogs, playing computer games, and gardening.